Damascus

Also by Richard Beard:

X20: A Novel of (Not) Smoking

Damascus
A NOVEL
Richard Beard

ARCADE PUBLISHING • NEW YORK

FIRST U.S. EDITION 1999

This is a work of fiction. Names, places, characters, and incidents are
either the products of the author's imagination or are used fictitiously.

ISBN 1-55970-460-8
Library of Congress Catalog Number 98-74755
Library of Congress Cataloging-in-Publication information is available.

Published in the United States by Arcade Publishing, Inc., New York
Distributed by Little, Brown and Company

10 9 8 7 6 5 4 3 2 1

BP
PRINTED IN THE UNITED STATES OF AMERICA

To Laurence Nagy

'A newspaper is a parcel containing many individual packets. Anybody who read them all would be mad.'

—*The Times*, 11/1/93

Damascus

0

It is the first of November 1993 and somewhere in the Kingdom, in Quarndon or Northampton or Newry or York, in
Kirkcaldy or Yeovil or Lincoln or Neath, a baby girl is born.
Her name is Hazel. Her father Mr Burns, a salesman, puts
the tip of his finger inside her tiny fist. He waves his head
from side to side and puts on a childish voice and says:

'Who's the most beautiful girl in the whole wide world
then?'

It is the first of November 1993 and somewhere in the
Kingdom, in Harlow or Widnes or Swansea or Ayr, in Read-
ing or Glentoran or Nantwich or Hull, a baby boy is born.
His name is Spencer. His father Mr Kelly, a warehouseman,
circles a tiny upper arm between his thumb and index finger.
He frowns and says:

'You're not as big as your brother was.'

1

All regions will have a mostly cloudy day
though some bright and sunny intervals
could develop.

THE TIMES 11/1/93

11/1/93 MONDAY 06:24

Hazel kissed Spencer's shoulder and then covered him with
the blanket.

'Amazing,' she said. 'Unbelievable.'

She re-positioned her cheek against his outstretched arm,
pressed her body up against his, and closed her eyes. 'Let's
spend the whole day in bed.'

An amber street-light hummed outside the curtainless
window. On one side of the bed, which was a single mattress
on a wooden floor, Hazel's discarded dress invented a
charcoal-coloured landscape. On the other side, over the

3

back of a chair, a silver space-suit flopped limply. A toppled stack of plastic-backed library books paved a trail towards the door.

Spencer, eyes wide and awake, wondered if this made him a changed man. Could a single event change everything? It had all happened so suddenly, and so definitively, but before he could make any sense of it her hand brushed up across his chest, reaching his cheek. That was nice, he couldn't deny it but then uninterrupted niceness had been part of the problem the first time around.

'The whole day,' she said, murmuring it into his skin, 'in bed. You and me.'

'All day?'

'I'll allow you to get up from time to time,' she said, 'to make me nice things to eat.'

Spencer stared up at the emerging whiteness of the ceiling, and pinned to the wall above his head, a single red-and-white-striped knitted glove. He tried to remember what it had been like being alive this time yesterday, before he'd ever woken up with someone he hardly knew, right now, in the present tense, her in the bed beside him with her breath curling up in his ear. He told himself not to panic. This type of thing happened to other people all the time.

The street-light in the window turned itself off, leaving behind the greyish yellow of dawn and the beginning of a London day. Spencer turned the back of his hand against Hazel's hip-bone, and waited for the warmth of her skin to spread through his fingers. It was true, then. Here he was in his own bed, her beside him, neither of them wearing any clothes. It therefore couldn't be long now before the light fattening in the window made her open her eyes and complain that this could never have happened. How could an apparently adult and fine-looking blonde woman with a job and a portable telephone possibly end up naked in bed with an unemployed warehouseman? Spencer ought, therefore, to be making the most of the fact that she was half-asleep and fully naked and wanted them to spend the whole day together. In bed.

'I can't,' he said, immediately wishing he hadn't. He stared past the flat red fingers of the woollen glove. 'I have a hundred and one things to do today.'

'Ignore them all, one to a hundred and one.'

'I have to show some Italians round the house. I have to make William his breakfast.'

'William?'

'He lives in the shed.'

'Well do that and then afterwards come back to bed.'

'It's my niece's birthday. She's coming for lunch. I have to go and fetch her.'

'Fine. I'll wait for you here.'

'And,' Spencer said, wisely resisting the real reason he had to get up and go out, 'my library books are due back.'

'Big day,' Hazel said, pulling herself a little closer. 'It's half-past six in the morning. Let's just stay in bed.'

'I'm usually up by now. I should get up.'

She stretched her leg possessively over his stomach, kissed his neck, and told him everything was going to be alright.

Then she pushed herself up onto an elbow. She touched a strand of pale hair away from her eye. She said:

'You look completely terrified.'

'It's all been very sudden,' Spencer said.

She licked the tip of a finger, and wiped it across his cheek-bone. 'I feel like I've known you for ages. It was amazing, wasn't it?'

'Yes,' Spencer said. 'It was amazing.'

She was right. It had been amazing. It had been a complete disaster, obviously, but it had still been pretty damn amazing. She looked from one of his brown eyes to the other, and asked him if he was frightened.

'No,' Spencer said. 'Sometimes.'

'Don't be frightened,' she said. 'We're not in any hurry. Let's just take it one day at a time.'

————

It is the first of November 1993 and somewhere in Britain, in Alloa or Arundel or Linfield or Dereham, in Manchester or Rotherham or Maesteg or Goole, Hazel Burns is ten years old and this is a sunny interval. Seagulls, sweeping in from the sea, along the coast, far and unexpectedly inland, swing vigilant and white in the high wind, the sky blue and wide behind them. Sometimes, as a sharp reminder that this is the here and now, the seagulls cry out, loud and fading in the wind.

Mr Burns, Hazel's father, has hired (for the afternoon)

the clubhouse terrace of the local golf course. A railway embankment shadows the eighteenth fairway and an occasional train rattles by, overlooking this small celebration of Mr Burns's Successful Selling '93 International European Award for Salesperson of the Year, sponsored by Queen's Moat House or W.H. Smith or the Co-operative Insurance Society. A dedicated, distinguished-looking man, Mr Burns likes travel, meeting people and making friends. He often wishes he could spend more time with his family.

He introduces a new secretary to his two young daughters:

'This is Hazel, who is ten, and Olive, short for Olivia, who is eight. My brilliant daughters. The most beautiful daughters any father ever had in the history of the whole wide world.'

Hazel grins and stands up. The breeze flutters the skirt of her best white dress and pushes at her brown hair, which she tries to keep in place with her hands. Olive, wearing an identical dress, sits at a table reading *The Secret Garden* or *The Wind in the Willows* or *The Water Babies*, her legs swinging happily beneath her. She sometimes picks grapes or cherries or orange segments from a bowl on the table. She wears glasses with clear frames and Hazel wishes she didn't.

'So,' says Daddy's secretary (cream blouse, dark shortish skirt, good with children), 'what does Hazel want to be when she grows up?'

Mr Burns has spied a colleague and he really must. He does, and his wife takes his place because she's naturally

7

suspicious of a new secretary, especially near her children.

'Hazel wants to be a lawyer,' Hazel's Mum says, and Daddy's secretary says, 'That's a nice ambition, isn't it?' and Hazel says: 'No, not really. I'd prefer to be an Olympic freestyle swimmer. Actually.'

Mummy puts a hand on Hazel's shoulder. 'Or a doctor,' she says. 'A lawyer or a doctor.'

'Can we go swimming now?'

'Olive's just the same. She has a reading age of fifteen. She wants to go to Oxford or Cambridge to train as a lawyer or a doctor.'

'I want to be a swimmer,' Hazel insists.

'Good for you,' says the secretary, and then notices the look on Mrs Burns's face. 'I mean if that's what you want.' She makes excuses and wanders away.

'Really, darling,' Hazel's mother says, 'it's about time you grew up a little.'

'I don't want to be a lawyer.'

'Of course you do. You have to start living in the real world like everyone else.'

'I could be a footballer then.'

'Please, Hazel, don't start.'

'Daddy says I'm good enough.'

Mrs Burns sighs. She looks round the terrace for her husband but he's nowhere to be seen. Then she looks for his new secretary in her white, flimsy, almost transparent blouse, because Hazel's mother has no doubt that anxiety is the right response to life. Her timidity is therefore very assured, almost aggressive.

'And besides,' she says to Hazel, 'swimming pools are full of other people's infections.'

She checks that both her daughters have taken their various health capsules and vitamin supplements. Then she advises Olive to chew her fruit more thoroughly, because she devoutly believes a mother can't be too careful. Hazel notices that when Olive eats, her glasses move up and down.

'I want to go swimming,' she says, 'it's not fair.'

'We're not going swimming. You should read more, like your sister, and then you might get a scholarship to big school.'

A short train makes an unscheduled stop on the embankment, and Hazel sees a small boy wearing a football shirt pressing his face against the window. She bets he can do whatever he wants, every day of the week, including eat handfuls of Bourbon biscuits or Jaffa cakes or Cadbury's chocolate. He probably goes swimming whenever he likes, all the time.

'If I can't go swimming,' Hazel says, 'I'm going to make funny faces and stupid noises until all Daddy's friends think I'm a nutcase.'

'Not today, darling.'

Hazel's Mum smoothes Hazel's hair. She finds it desperately sad that children in general, but her own daughters in particular, must one day find out how vulnerable they are. She reads her newspaper every morning and the growing number of hazards to be avoided constantly horrifies her. Left to itself on any normal day, like today for example, life can deliver meningitis or a mugging or murder, a car crash

9

or a cliff-top fall or kidnap. Every single day it seems as if there is someone mad and reckless and dangerous, out there somewhere, which is why Mrs Burns considers it her duty as a good parent to teach both her children, little by little, how easily things can go wrong.

11/1/93 MONDAY 06:48

William Welsby inched open the door of his shed. He peered carefully out at the vegetable garden. As far as he could tell the unrushed daylight was doing its usual job clearing up the grey mess of dawn. It was overcast and rain looked likely, but he couldn't be discouraged by that. In fact it seemed altogether an excellent day for changing his life.

He pushed the door wide open and filled his lungs with the morning. As of today, according to the newspaper he read, William Welsby was a new and changed man because overnight, through no great effort of his own, he'd become a citizen of the European Union. In honour of this occasion he'd searched out his special-occasion clothes, which were the same as his normal clothes, only cleaner: white shirt, black braces, black trousers. He checked the shine on his German army boots, and then pinched himself on the upper arm. Then he punched himself on the jaw, though not very hard.

'A pinch and a punch,' he said, 'first day of the month.'

He stepped down into the garden from the raised floor of the shed, lost his footing and nearly fell. As he steadied himself, it started to rain. He ignored it, just as he ignored the low-level noise of traffic from beyond the walls, and wondered whether moving to Europe would have made any overnight difference to Georgi Markov. William listened closely, recognised the song of a mistle thrush and then, exactly on schedule, the morning warble of Georgi Markov, a Siberian robin who should have been half-way to Asia. Instead, he'd decided to stop over in the garden's only mulberry tree, and William habitually made a point of wishing him good morning. He vowed to continue doing this no matter how dramatically, after today, his life might change for the better.

He stepped back into the shed, found a mirror, and tried to flatten his wiry grey hair. The rain should have helped but it didn't, and William's hair refused to be flattened. Giving up, he then manoeuvred himself past a shoulder-high stack of yellow plastic buckets, and leant to inspect a potted plant in its specially reserved place on an upturned box beside the bed. This flowerless shrub was William's ambitious attempt to cross a pimento plant with a tomato plant, supposed eventually to create a sweet though spicy fruit he would call a tomento. He crumbled one of the small leaves between his fingers. Once he'd developed it, perfected it, and found someone to buy it, the tomento was going to make him a fortune.

First of all though, he had to re-learn the under-rated skill

11

of going outside. This meant beyond the garden, beyond the house, and out into the London streets. Today was the day. He'd successfully turned into a European, overnight, and with a bit of luck maybe other changes could be made just as easily. Because despite being nearer sixty than fifty, William still refused to accept the jowly conclusion that he wasn't a lucky man. There was no obvious reason why unexpected but brilliant things shouldn't happen to him, like they did to his brother. No particular reason why, on this special day, he shouldn't rise to the challenge of going outside.

This would actually be the third time he'd tried it in the last month, on each occasion hoping there was still something of Britain left to be seen. With hindsight, he now blamed his earlier failures on errors of timing. For the first attempt he'd studied the newspaper in advance for a day of sufficient significance to inspire him, and eventually settled on the 96th anniversary of the poet Edmund Blunden's birth. When this didn't work he tried to be more spontaneous, and his second attempt was an impulse decision on the day *Mr Confusion* won the two-thirty at Newcastle. Now he was back to his original theory, believing that certain days were special, and marked out for special deeds like his. He'd therefore waited attentively for a day of greater significance than Edmund Blunden's birthday, and the newspaper had been in no doubt that the beginning of Europe was it.

William looked at his watch. Spencer would be making breakfast in the kitchen, the table already laid and *The Times* in its usual place between the knives. The teapot and the mugs would be arranged in a diagonal across the table, just as they always were, and Spencer might be wearing his apron which said *If you don't like it write to the Queen.* William hoped it was kippers. He closed his eyes and said a little prayer for kippers, and then pulling on his black jacket he peered into the top bucket of the yellow stack. It was half-full of water and three small goldfish turning slow circuits, one after the other. Another day and all still alive, and if there was one thing which could be said in favour of fish, William always thought, it was that at least they weren't horses.

Behind the buckets was the beginning of the disordered jumble which filled up the rest of the shed. William reached in and rustled around for a plastic bag. He rejected the first one he found because it had holes in the bottom to stop children from suffocating. He wanted one of the old-fashioned child-killer type bags, with no holes in it, and eventually he found a white one with a Union Jack printed on either side. He dipped his hand back in and this time came up with an orange plastic sandcastle mould, which he used to scoop a fish out of the bucket. He then emptied the fish into the plastic bag, along with a generous amount of water.

Checking the bag didn't leak, he took it with him as he stepped carefully down from the shed, this time without stumbling. It had stopped raining. He closed the shed door and set out along the wet and winding path towards the house. November and a gloss of rain had turned the last leaves on the chestnut trees a rich ochreous yellow. The hornbeams added a different tint, more like lemon. It was like living in a park, William thought, only better than that because no-one came to move you on or spray you with graffiti as you slept. As he scuffed across the damp grass of the lowest of the terraced lawns, William had his first view of the top half of the columns of the colonnaded dining room.

He hoped it was kippers.

It is the first of November 1993 and somewhere in Britain, in Bath or Hartlepool or Londonderry or Yarmouth, in Haverfordwest or Tunbridge Wells or Stirling or Grimsby, Mr Kelly, warehouseman, asks his son Spencer how much a footballer can make in a week.

Mr Kelly and two of his three children, Spencer (10) and Rachel (8), are standing in the goalmouth of a football pitch in the middle of a municipal sports field. Spencer is wearing a replica Coventry City, Manchester United, Blackburn Rovers, Queens Park Rangers, Southampton football shirt with the number 10 on the back, and Rachel is wearing the same, but with the number 8. Mr Kelly is wearing his work clothes.

Spencer clutches the white football high up on his chest and looks across at Rachel, who says:

'Average transfer fee, about 2.75 million, for a midfielder.'

Rachel's hair, which could be blonde if it was longer, is cut even shorter than Spencer's.

'The answer,' Mr Kelly says, as he paces out the boundaries of their pitch, 'is lots. Bucket-loads. But you have to be strong. You have to be robust. What do you have to be, Spencer?'

'He has to be robust,' Rachel says, grabbing the ball. She drops it and starts dribbling expertly across the six-yard box, and her legs look just right, slim and strong. She wears her football shirt outside her white, black, blue, green shorts. Spencer's legs are thin and very pale.

Mr Kelly finishes marking out the pitch, determined to prove that Spencer is made of sterner stuff than his brother Philip (13), who because God is cruel to men like Mr Kelly (Mr Kelly thinks), has turned out to be a great wet wimp. Philip likes to read books and newspapers, and always lets a frightening story frighten him. This is his morbid imagination, according to his mother, and Mr Kelly wouldn't mind knowing where it came from. Not from his mother, anyway. Philip is so old, nearly fourteen, that Spencer rarely thinks about him. Instead, he watches the way Rachel runs, is proud of the way her body-swerve bamboozles imaginary full-backs.

'Last to touch the posts is goalie,' says Spencer's Dad, and touches the post which is right beside him. From the middle of the penalty area Spencer runs as fast as he can, enjoying himself and trying hard but not, in fact, going very fast. Rachel calmly cruises past him. She touches both posts and then starts laughing, making champion fists beside her ears. Catching her breath, she leans her hands on her narrow knees, which are bent inwards slightly. She looks up at

Spencer and smiles brightly and in that moment Spencer sees clearly that everything, always, is going to be alright. There is no need to worry because it all turns out just fine.

'I'll be Argentina,' Rachel says, and dribbles the ball to the edge of the area, turns, flips the ball up for a volley, then flights a beautifully weighted cross to the far post. Mr Kelly meets it with a powerful header which leaves Spencer stranded. There is no net in the goal and the ball stops rolling somewhere half-way down the next pitch. Mr Kelly sighs and tells Spencer to leave it where it is. After a moment of hands-on-hips and significant head-shaking, he fetches a rugby ball and tosses it to Spencer, who drops it but then quickly picks it up again.

'I'm the Australian defence,' Mr Kelly says, bending his knees and leaning forward. 'You and Rachel have to get past me and score a try. But remember, no pansying about. This is rugby league, and there's good money to be earned.'

Spencer passes the ball to Rachel who shoots out of the blocks and beats Mr Kelly with an incisive left-right side-step. She dives and touches down, all smiles.

'Give Spencer a go.'

Spencer takes the ball, and shadowed by his father he runs in a long curve first one way and then the other, but without actually making any forward progress. Eventually he slips in a pool of mud and falls on his bum. He laughs, and Mr Kelly ponders, not for the first time, whether these days babies still get swapped at birth. Is it too late to take Spencer back?

'Rely on your natural talent,' Mr Kelly says. 'Get past me once and you'll never look back.'

Spencer stands up. Rachel flattens him with a tackle and steals the ball and scores another try.

Mr Kelly sighs and fetches a cricket bat and a tennis ball.

Rachel bats first, Mr Kelly bowls, Spencer fields. Rachel scores a brisk 37 off 35 balls. Then she retires and it's Spencer's turn to bat but he claims an injury sustained in the outfield: a damaged rib cartilage or a groin strain or severe concussion. It starts to rain. Mr Kelly looks up at the grey heavens, and follows the smooth flight of a seagull before squatting down to put his hands on Spencer's shoulders. He looks his second son directly in the eye.

'Do you *want* to grow up to be a warehouseman? Is that it?'

Spencer looks at his feet and kicks at the grass.

'Come on, son,' Mr Kelly says, 'there must be something you're good at.'

Rachel looks up at the gathering cloud, and holds out a hand to catch the early rain. She makes a suggestion, only trying to help:

'Swimming?'

————

11/1/93 MONDAY 07:12

Lying on her side, watching him dress, Hazel was hoping that at last her life had really begun. He wasn't as gorgeous as she'd sometimes imagined him, but then he wasn't as

17

ugly either. Instead, like most things, he was somewhere in between.

'You have nice legs,' she said.

He found some trousers underneath the space-suit, and while he pulled them on Hazel felt like touching his knees. He also had good muscles in his back, and she liked to see a man's ribs. He pushed his arms into a dark shirt, brown, with a tartan kind of design, fastened the lowest button and worked his way up. Sensitive hands. He reached for his jacket. His black hair was also nice, rufflable.

'What's so funny?'

'I never imagined you in a suit.'

'It's a Simpson suit.'

'It's cool. I like it. I think.'

It was double-breasted though he didn't button it. It hung loosely over the pockets of his trousers and it looked alright. It would look better with a tie, of course, and a proper shirt, but she didn't want to race ahead.

'I bought it in the sale,' Spencer said. 'I liked your dress last night.'

They both glanced at where it lay wantonly on the floor, empty and anybody's. 'Earlier this morning,' Hazel corrected him. 'It wasn't really last night.'

'I didn't realise it was so late.'

'I phoned after midnight. It was well into today.'

'Does it matter?'

'No. I don't suppose it does.'

Hazel rolled over onto her back and slipped a bare leg outside the blanket. Keeping it straight, she lifted it up like

18

a dancer, moving her foot slowly up and down from the ankle until the bones stood out. She tried to imagine a day in which everything went right, but Spencer kept glancing at her hair, trapped behind her ears by the pillow.

'I hadn't expected you to be so blonde,' he said.

She let her leg drop and pulled the blanket up over her nose. Did it always have to be like this? It wasn't as if they were complete strangers: they'd already slept together. She wished they could learn everything about each other instantly, or at least in a single day. That might be possible, if it was love, building on the feeling that she'd always known him anyway, which is what persuaded her into bed with him in the first place. She wished she *had* always known him. It would have made everything so much easier.

'Tell me about the house,' she said, pulling the blanket down to her chin. 'How many rooms?'

'I have to make William his breakfast,' Spencer said.

'I know, you already told me.'

'Then I have to get a present for my niece. It's her birthday.'

'And don't forget your library books,' Hazel said. She turned towards him and reached up her arm, hoping he'd take her hand. 'How about making some more babies?'

'William's breakfast,' Spencer said. He took Hazel's hand all the same, and she pulled until he gave in and sat himself down on the edge of the mattress.

'How many rooms?'

'I've never counted.'

'Try.'

At least eight bedrooms, Spencer tried. Three dining rooms. A gym. A jacuzzi. There was the swimming pool and several different types of marbled bathroom, four or maybe five of them. The main drawing room had wood-panelled walls and a ten-metre-high dome, the main dining room was flanked by columns, and suddenly Spencer seemed relieved just to be talking, as if he found it much easier than actual conversation. The house was eighteenth century, he said, Grade 2 listed, and the swimming pool, did he mention the swimming pool? It was granite-lined and had a glass roof. It connected the main part of the house with the garages and staff apartments, where they were now, and although Hazel was already impressed Spencer thought she'd like to know that Charles Kingsley once lived here. Charles Kingsley was a vicar who wrote *The Water Babies*, but even so Hazel put her hand on Spencer's knee, hoping to calm him down.

He told her the house had the second largest privately-owned garden in London. There were terraced lawns and semi-circular flowerbeds and a mulberry tree planted by Elizabeth the First. Relax, Hazel wanted to say, I feel I know you already so there's no need to be nervous. But he'd forgotten to mention the walled garden where William lived, as well as leaving out the house's valuation at twenty-five million pounds, and the billiard room which had once been painted by David Jones. David Jones was a painter.

'Stop,' Hazel said. 'Just stop a minute. Tell me what's wrong.'

'Nothing's wrong. I have to make William his breakfast.'

20

'Come on, Spencer. You can do better than that.'

Spencer reached under the chair for his shoes. He turned his back to Hazel as he put them on and laced them, very slowly.

'Let's not fool ourselves,' he said. 'We hardly know each other.'

'We've just spent the night together.'

'It was very late.'

'Didn't you want to?'

'Yes,' Spencer said, 'I wanted to.'

'And?'

He let himself fall back across the bed, as if it was all suddenly too much. Hazel's stomach became his pillow and he stared up at the ceiling, shading his eyes with his hands. Hazel stroked his hair.

'We ought at least give it a chance,' she said.

'I know.'

'This might be it. This might be the one moment which changes everything.'

'That's why it frightens me.'

'Let's give it a day. One day. Today. If it doesn't work out then no hard feelings. We can pick up where we left off yesterday, living very happily and very far apart.'

'Don't you have to go to work?'

'No.'

'How will we decide?'

'Decide what?'

'If this is it.'

'If we end up back in bed,' Hazel said. 'I don't know.

21

Look out for signs, omens, anything that says in the grand scheme of things we fit together. I mean other than the fact that I don't have a boyfriend, you don't have a girlfriend, we're both twenty-four years old, speak the same language, and have recently had totally amazing sex.'

'I really ought to be making William his breakfast.'

Spencer sat up, stood up, and Hazel grabbed hold of a turn-up on his suit trousers. 'So it's agreed then, we have the whole day?'

'I still don't see how we'll *know*,' Spencer said. 'We'll probably go back to bed anyway, just because we feel like it, or because it gets dark.'

'Alright then. Pretend we're vampires in reverse. We'll make the decision in daylight.'

'Okay,' Spencer said. 'Let's do that. Sex isn't everything.'

'Stay a bit longer.'

'I can't, really. I'm already late. William.'

'Your niece.'

'My library books.'

2

Real people are endlessly complex and
quite beyond the comprehension of
others.

THE TIMES 11/1/93

11/1/93 MONDAY 07:24

Henry Mitsui had run out of money, almost lost contact with
the woman he loved, and was about to be deported. He
turned up the collar on his white raincoat, even though it
was warm in the hotel room. Things could be worse. His
father could be awake.

Henry's long-fingered hands searched deftly across the
dark surface of the dressing table. He found his father's
Rolex and transferred it silently to his pocket. He'd been
hoping for the wallet. He took a step towards the window
and eased the curtains apart. Overcast sky, soft dawn light,

London. A songbird made itself known and Henry recognised it instantly: mistle thrush. At this time of year, with winter coming on, they were already defending their store of mistletoe berries (*An Introduction to British Birds and Trees*, Week 2).

In the light let in between the curtains he could make out the shape of his father in the further of the twin beds, lying on his back, his hands crossed over his chest. He was fatter than when Henry had last seen him, more than two years ago in Tokyo, and then Henry saw the wallet. He memorised its position on the table between the beds, let the curtain fall closed, stepped lightly to his own bed, rolled across it, plucked up the wallet, rolled back and returned to the window. He nudged the curtain open with his shoulder to see what he was doing.

He took out the cash first, folded it, and slipped it into the back pocket of his jeans. Then he flipped through the cards, noticing his father was much thinner on his identity card. His hair wasn't grey and he didn't have two chins and he wasn't balding. He didn't have that worried look in his eyes. He had it on his Toyoko Metropolitan corporate card, Vice-President (Design), but then that was much more recent. Henry selected American Express, Access, Visa, but ignored the frequent flyer cards from major airlines because he wasn't planning on going anywhere.

Right at the back of the wallet, behind all the plastic cards, he found a passport photograph of his mother. She was looking to the side, and upwards, as if planning an exit now that the photos were finished. Her blonde hair was about to sweep across her face. Her eyes were very blue and her thin

24

arm as it reached up to open the curtain had caught the flash, and was instantly pale and very white. Henry squeezed the photo between the credit cards in his pocket.

He put the emptied wallet on the dressing table, then checked the pocket of his raincoat for the reassuring plastic envelope of powder. It was still there, jammed underneath his telephone, and his long fingers were suddenly tempted by the phone's raised rubber buttons. It was far too early to phone the woman he loved because she'd still be asleep, or reading, but he took out the phone anyway and turned it on, hiding its green light by pulling the raincoat over his head. He keyed in the number he knew several times over by heart, not necessarily to speak to her but just to hear her voice and know that another day was worth living.

No connection. Henry rearranged the collar of his raincoat and moved soundlessly towards the door, which was when the bedside light snapped on. His father, wide awake, was sitting up in bed with his hands folded over his stomach. He smiled sympathetically. He leant his head to one side, paternally. He said something in Japanese, tolerantly, and Henry stared back at him as if he didn't understand a word.

His father leant his head the other way, smiled again, then spoke in English with a faint New Jersey accent.

'Henry,' he said, 'you're not well.'

'I was going outside to make a phone call.'

'In your coat?'

'On the portable. In the hotel garden.'

'With all my credit cards?'

Henry sat back on the dressing table, and his father told

25

him if he ever wanted money all he had to do was ask.

'All right then, Dad,' he said. 'I want some money.'

'You're not well, Henry. Tomorrow we'll be back in Tokyo and you'll soon be better.'

'I'm not going back.'

'The tickets are all paid for. I've made appointments with Dr Osawa.'

His father had always called Osawa a neurologist, never quite finding the right word. This might have been deliberate, but even so Henry added it to other evidence which proved his father consistently misunderstood the essential nature of his only son, the world about him, and everything. There was nothing wrong with Henry. He was in no need of rescue. He was twenty-three years old and could take care of himself.

'You've been studying too hard,' his father said.

'I've been furnishing my mind.'

His father stopped smiling and his round face suddenly looked pained, long-suffering, resigned. He said something in Japanese which Henry stubbornly ignored.

'We're leaving this evening.'

'You just said.'

'You're ill, Henry, but you mustn't be frightened. I've forgiven you for what happened in Tokyo.'

'I'm not frightened and I'm better now, I promise. Britain has made all the difference.'

———

It is the first of November 1993, and somewhere in Britain, just outside Penzance or Edinburgh or Hastings, close to Southampton or Newport or Torquay, it's the holiday season for the families Burns and Kelly.

Another bright and sunny interval but Philip Kelly (16), Spencer's elder brother, claims a weak chest and lingers in the town arcades playing car-racing games like *Hell of a Ride* or *Racing Demon* or *TOCA Shoot-Out Touring Cars*. Mr and Mrs Kelly play miniature golf (Mr Kelly has a three-shot lead but Mrs Kelly, a great lover of cinema, is playing well below her best because she is mourning the death of Fellini. She keeps saying 'Ciao Federico' under her breath until her husband tells her to stop mumbling. He then takes a four-shot lead and punches the air because if this was a real tournament, like the Madrid Open say, or any leg of the PGA tour, he'd be close to earning hundreds of thousands of pounds.).

Mr and Mrs Burns on the other hand, not very far from the miniature golf, have hired a fisherman to take them out for a day's crab-catching. Mrs Burns is not happy. If only her husband wasn't so busy they could take a holiday in the summer like everyone else, and then her children wouldn't have to miss school, damaging their prospects. Nor does she like the look of the weather, which the fishermen describe as changeable, nor the idea of boats generally and their obvious temptation of a terrible fate. Most of all she doesn't like to leave her children, even though her husband tells her that Hazel is twelve now and almost grown up and perfectly able to look after herself. Eventually Mrs Burns has no choice but to step onto the boat. Her husband might be having an affair and if she never spends time with him then who can blame him? As the boat slips away from the jetty Mrs Burns makes Hazel promise not to swim in the sea.

'And don't talk to any strangers!' she yells, the wind crumbling her words as they break across the water.

By now there's quite a breeze blowing across the low summit of the sand dune where Olive (10) lies on her front and absent-mindedly waves her feet as she reads *At the Back of the North Wind* or *Death in the Tunnel* or *Little Women*. Seagulls go very fast coming in from the sea, dipping towards land, turning figures of eight over the swell of waves in which Hazel stands waist-deep, steeling herself for the swim to a distant red buoy. She ducks her head under the cold salt water, shivers and shakes out her dark hair and turns to make a last check on Olive. A girl, about Olive's age, but with slim brown legs and short sun-bleached hair, sprints towards Olive, skids round her (Olive barely looks up from her book), and then sprints back inland disappearing behind the curve of a dune.

It's a diabolical liberty. Hazel leaves the water, strides up the beach, and reaches Olive just as she's about to be lapped a second time. Hazel sticks out her leg, says whoops sorry, and then helps the unknown girl to her feet. She asks her what she thinks she's doing.

'I'm training for the World Cup marathon.'

'Well you can't do it here,' Hazel says. 'This is *our* sand dune.'

But the girl says she has orders from her coach, and

she slides back down the slope, sprints away, disappears.

Hazel is outraged. She wraps a towel around her waist, picks up the bag her mother insists she carries at all times, and doggedly pursues the girl's footprints until she finds herself at the top of the enemy sand dune, where there is a boy of about her size with no head. This is because he is getting in a mess with a T-shirt which says I Follow The Town, The Rovers, United, The Rangers, City, and which he is hurriedly trying to put back on. Eventually his head pops out in the right place and he has a crop of black hair and sand stuck to his forehead.

'That's our hill,' Hazel says.

'Do you want to see my stop-watch?'

'I don't talk to strangers.'

He clicks the button and Rachel races off on another lap of Olive, whose waving feet are visible over the top of the dune. Rachel is a beautiful runner. Her legs are long and brown and she holds her head high and still. Mr Kelly says that if Rachel were a racehorse she'd be worth thousands, and unasked, Spencer shares this information with Hazel.

Rachel makes it back and Spencer clicks the stop-watch. He tells her it's a world-record time for this particular circuit and Rachel laughs as she catches her breath, her hands on her knees. Everything's going to turn out just fine. Hazel says:

'I bet I can run faster than that.'

'I'll time you,' Spencer says.

'If I wanted to.'

Rachel sets off again and as they watch her run both

29

Spencer and Hazel, without knowing why, are thinking in a vague way that this is better fun now, to be standing on top of a grassy sand dune with the other, than it was when they were doing whatever they were doing before, not standing together. They try each other out with some simple questions, starting with where do you live and what does your Dad do, quickly followed by are your parents married and who's your favourite famous person? And shouldn't you be at school?

'We're on holiday,' Spencer says.

'Why?'

'It's cheaper.'

'You're missing lessons.'

'Dad says it doesn't matter because we're going to be professional athletes.'

'Are you?'

'Rachel's going to be the Olympic champion of the world. She's my sister.'

Rachel runs some more laps while Spencer explains that his family moves around a lot, and Hazel says same here. Her father has just been voted Salesperson of the Year '93, whereas Spencer's Dad, in his job as a warehouseman, often stacks boxes full of furniture belonging to famous people.

Like who?

Like John Major.

They both laugh out loud.

Hazel's parents are married all the time, she says, even though her Mum thinks her Dad is having an affair.

'Is he?'

'Of course not,' Hazel says, 'he's married.'

Spencer says he isn't sure about his parents, because his Dad sometimes worries he was swapped in the hospital at birth, so maybe his real parents aren't married, no.

'River Phoenix,' Hazel says.

'What?'

'My favourite famous person.'

'The Queen,' Spencer says, which is funny enough to set them both off again. Rachel comes back. She asks for her time but Spencer's forgotten to set the watch so he makes something up. It's another world record.

'Spencer's my coach,' Rachel says. 'We're going all the way to the top.'

And because Hazel sees this as a challenge, she says:

'My Dad writes one hundred Christmas cards every year.'

Spencer tries to think of something better, but he can't, so he asks Hazel what she has in her bag just as Olive appears at the top of the slope, lies down on her front, carries on reading.

'My sister,' Hazel says. 'Her name's Olive. She reads a lot.'

Rachel lies on her back and does some bicycle kicks while Hazel empties her bag onto the sand. It contains a towel, three oranges, a bag of chopped walnuts, a bottle of vitamin supplements, a phonecard, a spare sweater, *A Fresh Wind in the Willows*, a pair of red-and-white knitted gloves (for cold November hands), and a white Conchita Martinez tennis skirt.

Spencer picks up the phonecard. Instead of being the normal green colour it has a fuzzy black and white photograph

31

of a pair of eyes staring up from it, and these eyes clearly belong to Charlie Chaplin.

Hazel stands up and brushes sand off her legs. She unwraps the towel from her waist, shakes it out and starts to dry the ends of her hair.

'It means we can ring up if anything goes wrong,' she says.

'What could go wrong?'

Hazel rolls her eyes and Rachel copies her, still upside down, her legs pointing straight at the sky.

'Something unexpected and very nasty,' Hazel says.

'Like what?'

'I don't know, it's unexpected.'

'Why not just money?' Spencer asks.

'Because then we could be robbed,' Hazel tells him. 'Or mugged.'

'Or raped,' Olive adds, without looking up from her book.

'Murdered,' Hazel says. 'So anyway, Mum decided we better have a phonecard. Last to touch the sea's a walrus.'

And Hazel is already sliding down the sand dune, waving her towel, and Rachel is right behind her followed by Spencer, desperately clicking his stop-watch. Rachel and Hazel reach the sea in a dead-heat. 'Spencer takes bronze,' Rachel says, and then Hazel starts slapping water at him, and Rachel tackles him into the shallows.

Later, they take turns to dry themselves with Hazel's towel. Spencer pinches Hazel, though not hard, and then punches her arm, but only playfully.

'Pinch and a punch,' he says, 'first day of the month,'

32

and lies down beside her, looking up at the sky, the clouds moving, the sky.

Hazel pinches him back, and then kicks him. 'A pinch and a kick for being so thick. What's better,' she asks, 'rich or famous?'

'Famous,' Spencer says.

'Wrong.'

———

11/1/93 MONDAY 07:48

'Not today,' Spencer said. 'Any other day. Maybe tomorrow.'

William stared hard across the breakfast table. Between him and Spencer there was a teapot, *The Times*, and an empty plate covered in a clear film of butter from William's kipper. William took a sip of tea from his mug – *Celebrating 100 Years of the Liverpool Victoria Friendly Society* – thinking that Spencer looked unusually haggard this morning, as if he hadn't slept very well. He was unshaven and his dark hair was unruly, although this was nothing new. He also had on his double-breasted suit, flapping open over a brownish shirt, which meant that at some stage today there were people coming to look at the house. For prospective buyers Spencer always made the concession of a suit, but never a tie, and this always annoyed William.

'I want to go out,' William said.

'Tomorrow.'

'Today.'

Spencer's mug said *Mal Pelo – The Southern Dogs Tour*, but his tea had gone cold while he watched William's goldfish exploring his new home, a glass fruit bowl further down the table. Spencer was definitely acting strangely this morning, and he'd already upset William by pretending not to have known it was the last day of Britain.

'I must have missed the build-up,' he said, enthralled by the slow circuits being made by the fish.

This was just about possible, William conceded, because even *The Times* could only spare half a column on page six: *European Union born in confusion*. As for the front page and the rest of the day's news, it was so long since William had been outside that he didn't know what to believe any more. According to the newspaper, outside was a choice between toddlers abducted by ten-year-old boys and Irish gunmen in large black hoods. Or it was a nation buoyant with pride because its Rugby League team could thump New Zealand into the back of beyond (twice in a row. Ha!). Fellini was dead and so was River Phoenix. Youth crime was up and it was National Library Week, but none of this greatly mattered to William unless he could see it for himself. He was determined to go outside, and Spencer was going to help him.

'It won't make any difference,' Spencer said, at last looking away from the fruit bowl. He balanced a knife across his finger and told William that Britain was unlikely to have

34

changed since yesterday. We could still be consoled by Buckingham Palace and teenage vandalism and Thomas More (Saint). We still had Norwich and disaffected Celts and the Princess Royal as Upper Warden of the Honourable Woolmen's Company.

'Don't be silly,' William said, wondering what could possibly be wrong with him.

'We still have fox hunting and the National Trust and a criminal stock exchange, and there's usually a Test match to be lost in your sport of choice to Australia. The NHS is never far away, slow but free, trundling up and down the M1. Policemen in tall hats care deeply about radio licences for drug offenders, so there's no need to worry, William. It all carries on, just the same as always.'

'I want to see it for myself.'

'There's nothing to be seen,' Spencer said. 'Nothing ever changes. Overnight nothing changes at all.'

'It might be different this time.'

'And I'm a walrus.'

'And anyway,' William said, 'don't you have to do what I say?'

'Not always, no.'

'I think you do.'

'Not today, William.'

'Today and every day. You have to do what I say. Those are the rules.'

With the end of his knife Spencer drew a stick-man in the film of butter setting on William's plate. This rebellion was very unlike him, William thought, unless he'd secretly been given one of the acting jobs he always said he wanted, was imminently about to be flown to LA, and therefore expected to fall in love with a dippy actress who'd provide him with a home of his own to go to. He should be more careful. Nothing lasted for ever, and William's brother was always trying to sell the house, so it was only today that there was this. Tomorrow there might be something else entirely.

'I want to go out,' William said. 'And I want you to come with me.'

'Why?'

'Just in case.'

'Just in case what?'

Just in case, in the absence of an overnight miracle, William stepped outside the front door and turned red in the face and found it hard to breathe and clutched his heart in his hands while he hyperventilated and his knees gave way, just like the last time and the time before that. Luckily, on both those occasions, Spencer had been there to save him, catch him, carry him back inside.

Spencer pushed back his chair. He stood up and went looking through cupboards, ignoring packet soups and corn-flakes and upended tins of beans, until he eventually found some loose teabags. He brought them back to the table. He dropped them into the pot.

'Look, William,' he said. 'I'm sorry, but today's not a good day. My niece Grace is coming for lunch. There are lots of things I have to do.'

'Let's do them together.'

'There's something urgent I have to do outside, by myself. I can't afford to waste any time.'

'So why are you making more tea then?'

William may have been more than twice Spencer's age but he wasn't born yesterday. In fact, Spencer was so absent this morning that he even went to fetch another mug down from the cupboard, the one with thick green and white bands which said *Glasgow Celtic Football Club – For Ever*.

'I have a guest,' Spencer said.

Busying himself with the extra mug, re-filling the teapot, Spencer suddenly looked less tired, more eager for the day. And then it began to dawn on William, quite slowly at first, hardly believable in fact, until gradually the awful and obvious truth became increasingly clear to him.

'It's a woman, isn't it?' he said, amazed. He rubbed his eyes. 'It's Jessica, isn't it? I knew this would happen.'

––––––––

It is the first of November 1993 and somewhere in Britain, just outside Penarth or Holyhead or Dover, close to Redruth or Havant or Tenby, it's the last day of the holidays and Spencer Kelly (12) wants to hold Hazel Burns (12) by the hand. This is the meaning of life. He wants to sit beside her on a sand dune and hold her hand and then kiss her. Just kissing, in a nice way, on her cheek perhaps and then a little bit at the top of her arms.

The thought of it makes his chest and the corners of his mouth hurt, and this is happening right now, with the seaside wind in his hair and the seagulls wheeling above. If he can kiss her this once then he'll always have kissed her, and everything which follows will be different. The sun will stay out and the wind will drop. His father won't mind when he doesn't practise his football, snooker, running, basketball for the end of century Olympics, because a kiss with Hazel Burns will be equally as good. It'll be like the winning goal or try or run in the last and deciding game of the Carling Premiership or the Heineken League or the Sharjah trophy. It's to be the one moment which instantly changes everything.

Spencer and Hazel are out walking on the dunes, alone. Nobody knows where Philip is, but Mr and Mrs Kelly are playing bowls on the front (Mr Kelly 44 Mrs Kelly 9). Mr Burns has hired a small yacht and is sailing. Mrs Burns, not knowing when her husband will next have time for a holiday, is sitting in the bow of the boat scanning the horizon for storms. Rachel is on the beach teaching basic boxing stances to Olive, who only stopped reading when Hazel told her she'd better walk somewhere before she lost the use of her legs.

'Mummy said you had to look after me.'

'Mummy says lots of things.'

'You're in big trouble.'

In return for keeping Olive busy, Spencer promises Rachel a timed game of Ironman triathlon. Later, when he and Hazel get back.

Now, Hazel steps over a tuft of sandy grass. She is wearing her swimming costume and her tennis skirt and no shoes. She's thinking it's no crime to leave Olive behind because I love you, I have always loved you, I will always love you. Love you for ever. A long flat cloud rolls across the sun, and the seagulls are suddenly closer, clearer, each movement of a wing like a rearrangement in a shrugging shoulder. Their yellow eyes see everything that moves but remember nothing, not Hazel and Spencer at the top of a dune, the way they stop, stand still, glance nervously at each other's fingertips.

They hear someone coming. They turn and shade their eyes and it's an older boy with walking boots and a rucksack. He wants to know where the coastal path is, but not the one which goes up to the cliffs. He says the cliffs are dangerous at this time of year. He wants the low-level path which follows the shore, and Hazel tells him they don't know.

'We're on holiday,' she says.

The older boy walks away with the big rucksack bouncing on his back and Spencer and Hazel lie down out of the wind, head to toe, looking up at the sky and the evenly-wheeling seagulls. In a blue gap between two white clouds, a bright interval, a tiny silver aeroplane pipes out a neat pair of vapour-trails.

Hazel moves her wrist so that the ends of her fingers touch the back of Spencer's hand, and this now, both of them think, this now is truly phenomenal, this is really happening right now and in real life, me and a girl, me and a boy, and this will last for ever. I shall never forget you. I shall love you always. This is love, and it's wonderful and frightening because there must be a right and a wrong way to move on from here. But in the meantime there is only me and a girl, me and a boy, and the slow progress of a jet plane to capture as it angles steadily across the pale blue sky.

'Aer Lingus,' Hazel says.

'Iberia.'

'British Airways.'

'SAS.'

'Lufthansa.'

There is a pause as the plane slips behind cloud, heading for the sun.

'You know your airlines,' Spencer says.

Hazel pinches his shoulder, but squeezes only softly. When he lifts his arm to protect himself she punches him in the side. He grabs her and they roll each other over, once, twice, until they end up side by side and breathless, absolutely equal no winners.

They break apart and sit up quickly, as if someone was coming. Hazel inspects a fingernail and some sand stuck behind it.

'I've got a scholarship to a new school,' she says. 'At lunch you always have to sit in the same seat.'

'I hate school,' Spencer says.

'If you were at my school you could sit next to me.'

And then when Spencer doesn't say anything Hazel says:

'You can kiss me if you like.'

It is the first of November 1993 and Hazel says:

'You can kiss me if you like,' and Spencer thinks someone might be watching. He doesn't want to smile but he smiles and with his little finger he draws a stick-man kicking a football in the sand.

'You can't kiss until you're married,' he says. He doesn't look up, not even when Hazel asks him when was the last time he watched a video? *Everyone* kisses before they're married. She starts rummaging through her bag, saying they should make a pact, and Spencer likes the idea even though he'd never have thought of it himself.

'Now?'

'Right now,' Hazel says. 'Before we kiss. Why not?'

She pushes right to the bottom of the bag and pulls out the woollen red-and-white gloves. She puts one of them on, the right hand one. She tells Spencer to put on the other one and then they hold hands, glove to glove, right hand to left hand.

'Why are we wearing gloves?' Spencer wants to know.

'It's a pact. You have to promise to love me for ever.'

'What do I do with the glove?'

'Afterwards you keep it. First you have to promise to love me.'

Spencer is thinking they ought to check on Rachel and Olive, and what will Hazel's mother do when she finds out that Hazel's made a pact? Why can't he stop thinking like this and just kiss her?

They hold on tight to each other's gloved hands.

41

'Promise,' Hazel says, shaking his hand up and down, looking straight into his eyes. 'Cross your heart and hope to die.'

11/1/93 MONDAY 08:12

At the bottom of the deep end of the empty swimming pool, Hazel mouthed a mouth breathing underwater bubbles. Then she made a face like a fish. She looked up brightly at Spencer and asked him if he knew what time it was.

'It's twelve minutes past eight,' Spencer said, but Hazel already knew what time it was. She meant, 'Have you seen how early it is?'

'I brought you some tea,' Spencer said.

He climbed down the short ladder into the shallow end, walked carefully past the full-size billiard table, and then carefully negotiated the steep slope to join her at the bottom of the deep end. The tiles in the pool were dark blue, and the dusty light falling from the glass roof felt thick like underwater. Hazel had her telephone with her and Spencer's library books, and she was already twenty pages into a crime novel called *Sir John Magill's Last Journey*. Something terrible was always about to happen.

Spencer slid his back down the side of the pool, his vertebrae clicking on the plaster lines between tiles.

'It's like being in a huge bathroom,' Hazel said, 'but without a bath in it.'

'Bow-wow,' Spencer said, showing her the echo.

'Boing,' Hazel said. 'Bing-bong.'

'Boom.'

Hazel's hair, parted in the middle, was darker than usual because it was still damp from the shower. She was wearing her long charcoal-coloured sweater dress, loose-necked with finger-skimming sleeves and obviously an evening outfit. It was all she had with her. She wore a gold chain and a little lipstick and a pair of Spencer's socks she'd borrowed to keep her feet warm. They were very big and woolly and a kind of oatmeal colour. She hoped he didn't mind.

'Great house,' Hazel said, taking the green-and-white striped mug which Spencer held out to her. 'Quiet.'

The tea wasn't very hot but she blew some steam off the top anyway, getting a good look at him without making it too obvious. Not bad. Could have been a lot worse.

Alas, he seemed to have brought a funny smell into the pool.

'Kippers,' Spencer said. 'William likes a kipper for his breakfast.'

'This is the man who lives in the shed?'

'In the vegetable garden. He doesn't go out much. His brother owns the house but they don't get on.'

'And what happens to William if someone buys the house? What happens to you?'

Hazel's telephone went off like an alarm. They both looked at it, black on top of the library books, its insistent electronic noise finding echoes in the sharpest angles of the swimming pool. Spencer said: 'That'll be the phone.'

'Does it bother you?'

'I don't know,' Spencer said. 'Depends who's ringing.'

The phone went quiet, and the broad silence which followed sank slowly to the bottom of the deep end. 'Nobody,' Hazel said. 'Not anymore anyway.'

Spencer stood up again, and Hazel wondered if he was always this restless. She followed him back up the slope to the billiard table and skidded the last metre or so in her socks.

'The billiard room's going to be re-painted,' Spencer explained. 'They had to put the table somewhere.'

'How did they get it down here?'

'I don't know. Act of God.'

'Pool table.'

'Heard it.'

Spencer looked at her as if he had something to say, and then he just looked at her. She touched her hair to check it hadn't gone funny. It was nearly dry. She crossed her arms over her breasts.

'Are you alright, Spencer? You look . . .'

'What?'

'More worried than I expected.'

He rolled a red billiard ball towards its spot at the end of the table. 'I'm just a worrier. I worry about what's going to happen.'

Hazel raised her eyebrows. 'We could always go back to bed.'

44

'I mean apart from that.'

He wasn't looking at her when he said it, a bad habit of his which was beginning to annoy her.

'I have to go out,' Spencer said. 'I won't be long.'

'It's not to take your library books back, is it?'

'Yes,' Spencer said, 'I have to take my library books back. You can check the date.'

'There's something else, isn't there?'

'I should get a present for my niece. It's her birthday.'

Hazel took a deep breath, suddenly distrusting her earlier feeling that she'd always known him. How could anybody know anyone else? She took another deep breath. Then she asked Spencer if he wanted her to leave.

'No,' he said, 'no, of course I don't,' but he was looking round the pool, licking his finger and drawing a football goal on a tile, and then, as an afterthought, a football inside it.

'Is it because of last night?' she asked, suddenly worried that sleeping with him had changed everything. 'I thought it was amazing. It was amazing, wasn't it?'

Spencer blinked and for a moment his eyes stayed closed. He opened them and turned the red ball a fraction with his finger, rolling it minutely one way and then another.

'What's *wrong*?'

'I don't know. I'm sorry. I think I'm in shock.'

'Why?'

'I never thought something like this could happen so quickly.'

'Well, it's happened. It's here we are.'

'Hazel, do you believe in Damascus?'

For the first time, across the billiard table, he looked at her directly. Clear brown eyes, most attractive. He should do that more often.

'I don't know what you mean.'

Spencer meant did she believe in the one moment which changed everything? But he wanted to explain it more clearly than that. Did she believe in lightning and bolts from the blue? Were there certain events which made everything look different, overnight? Could people be converted to different ways of thinking, without any warning, waking up as one type of person and then waking up as another? Was anyone singled out for enlightenment? Did miracles exist? Look. Basically. Were there signs from God, telling people what to do next?

'You want me to leave, don't you?'

'No,' Spencer said, 'no I don't.'

'You do.'

'I do not. I just have to go out. But I definitely want you to be here when I get back.'

Forcefully, using the bottom of his fist, Spencer started to erase the drawing he'd made on the tile. Hazel walked round the table, put her hands on his shoulders and kissed him on the ear.

'What was that for?'

'I've no idea,' Hazel said. 'It must be your birthday.'

3

History is, in a sense, the sum of our
transformations. In contemplating the
evidence, though, we are as likely to be
struck by ruin as creation.

THE TIMES 11/1/93

11/1/93 MONDAY 08:24

Just when you thought you were actually getting somewhere.
Bam, life could change, just like that. Spencer had to go and
get a woman involved.

William faced up squarely to the front door. He straightened his braces and checked his flies. He took a deep
breath. All he had to do was open the door and step outside. He would come to no harm. The last time and the
time before that the traffic had been unusually frenetic, or
in the street an unscrupulous contractor had been using

paint with a high solvent-content, poisoning William's nerves, increasing his heartbeat, deflating his resolve. High-solvent paints were everywhere. It was often in the paper.

He should pull himself together. Even though it was the last day of Britain he was still British, and people not unlike him had until very recently controlled a quarter of the earth. There was therefore no need to be frightened, and he could manage perfectly well without Spencer.

He failed to reach out for the latch and corrected himself: it was only good sense to be frightened. He checked his braces and his flies. He tried to flatten his hair. His knowledge of outside life came almost exclusively from the daily paper, and hidden away on the inside pages of *The Times* were most of the modern possibilities of a day, including stabbings, shootings, stranglings, muggings, stonings, and a single instance of murder by a poisoned pellet fired from a customised umbrella. He could be shot in the face at point-blank range, abducted, tortured, left for dead on forgotten wasteground where he wouldn't be discovered for more than a month. It never seemed to get any better. As of today, for example, someone out there had nearly two thousand pounds of stolen Czech Semtex, of which any one pound could turn up under a nearby car wrapped in an Irish or Algerian or Libyan flag. William would die instantly, or on the way to hospital, or in surgery, and all this was as true for the new Europe as it was for the old Britain. There were mad killer nutcases everywhere, and when not hiding behind black hoods they looked just like everyone else. It was only natural,

48

therefore, faced with the front door and these possibilities for outside life, that William should hesitate to reach for the latch.

He noticed the junk mail on the mat. Sighing, he supposed he should pick it all up, and by pushing aside two copies of the Yellow Pages he found space for it on the telephone table. He discovered, now that he was suddenly inclined to count them, that there were sixteen items, including an introductory offer for American Express Membership Miles Points, a subscription discount for *Antique Collector* magazine, a 2 for 1 coupon from Pizza Express, and a prize draw from the Leukaemia Research Fund. *Don't Delay!* this last envelope was franked, *It Could Be Your Lucky Day!*

Of course it could, and William was about to open the door and step outside and come to no harm when Spencer nearly gave him a heart attack. Or at least, Spencer was behind him and William didn't realise and then Spencer said something. He said:

'Already finished the paper?'

'God you gave me a shock,' William said, recovering himself.

'Going out on your own?'

'Maybe.'

'I thought you wanted an escort?'

'And maybe not.'

William stared hard at the empty Celtic mug in Spencer's hand, with its obvious rim-prints of lipstick like an extra design.

49

'Things change,' William said.

Spencer shook his head and turned towards the kitchen. William followed him. 'How *could* you?'

'We always knew this might happen.'

'But not like this. It should have been with Jessica.'

'I don't see what difference it makes.'

'If it's not Jessica you might be wrong. What colour hair does she have?'

'Who?'

'This other one.'

'Her name is Hazel.'

'What's she doing now?'

'She's busy.'

'What's she doing?'

'She's reading. I gave her one of my library books.'

Spencer stacked Hazel's mug in the sink with the rest of the washing-up, then looked William in the eye as he wiped his hands on a cloth. Definitely not at ease with himself, William judged, and not enough sleep either.

'What does she do as a job? I bet Jessica has a better job.'

'She's a teacher,' Spencer said.

'It's Monday. She'll be late for school.'

On his way out to the hall, controlling himself and his voice, Spencer patiently explained that she was a distance-learning teacher. This meant that she taught adults by correspondence and telephone, and surprisingly, because it was the first time he'd ever thought about distance-learning, William discovered that he didn't like the idea of it. At the same time he knew he ought to give Spencer a chance, because maybe this girl was the one. It was unlikely, because it was always unlikely, but it was also always possible. There was even the cautionary example of William at the same age, but history didn't have to repeat itself. Expecting it to do so was a sure sign of growing old.

Spencer unlooped his raincoat from a crucifix-shaped pole they used as a coat-stand. He shrugged himself inside it and picked up the plastic bag full of books which he'd left by the door.

'I have to take my library books back.'

'I thought you said she was reading one.'

'I'll take it back tomorrow. One day for one book won't make any difference.'

Just before Spencer opened the door, William put a restraining hand on his arm.

'But she's not Jessica, is she?' he said. 'That's my point.'

'I don't know,' Spencer said, reaching for the latch. 'She might be.'

———————

It is the first of November 1993 and somewhere in Britain, in Carrick or Kidderminster or Redditch or Holt Heath, in Howe of Fife or Egham or Marlborough or Herne Bay, Hazel's mother is taking charge. As often as she can, she drives back from the hospital in her husband's Ford Mondeo or Peugeot 405 or Vauxhall Cavalier. Mr Burns is away on

51

a sales trip to New York or Delhi or Moscow, but he telephones at least once every hour, either to the hospital or the house, where Hazel is thirteen years old and all alone. She knows that at her age she shouldn't mind so much, but today everything is different.

She stays mostly in the front room, where she sits on the beige sofa or on one of the matching chairs. She turns the television on or off. She plays the piano or she doesn't. She reads a paragraph in the newspaper or starts one of Olive's books. She makes chess moves on the board where the king of the black pieces is Napoleon or King Richard or Mao Tse-tung. She tries a crossword book or stacks dominoes or loiters by the window, waiting for the arrival in the drive of Mum in Dad's car.

Everything around her, which only yesterday seemed so familiar, is both all she can be sure of and instantly forgettable. A print of Vermeer's *Guitar Player* over the fireplace, that much she remembers, or it might be a Lowry or a Van Gogh. A shelf displaying card invitations to the New Paradigm Conference or *The Times* Dillons Church Debate or the Getty exhibition at the Royal Academy. The bookcase neatly filled with the complete works of Orwell or Kipling, Kenneth Grahame or Edward Lear, *Rebecca* or *Pride and Prejudice* or *Little Women* or *Kasparov vs Short 1993*. The glass corner cabinet with its collection of china animals: at last, something which never changes.

Hazel's Mum likes to collect them in pairs. She already has dogs, cats, rabbits, seagulls, goldfish and horses, and every time they move house Dad buys Mum some new ones. The latest addition is a pair of badgers, a good sign because they move house whenever Dad gets a better job, to somewhere slightly larger, quieter, and a little further from the town centre. This year Hazel's Dad has been voted Salesperson of the Year '93, and they've moved house again.

Hazel sees all these objects and herself and her family moving from house to house as if none of it has anything to do with her. For the first time she stands separate from her own life and watches it from the outside, actively trying to memorise this room, this moment, her mother's china animals, because who knows what else might be different before tomorrow?

Exactly now, the Ford Mondeo or the Peugeot 405 or the Vauxhall Cavalier pulls into the drive. Hazel picks up *The Times Book of Jumbo Crosswords*, suddenly embarrassed to be thinking thoughts which seem out of place, under the circumstances. Or it might have been *The Times Jumbo Concise Crosswords* or just *The Times Crosswords* or even the *Jubilee Puzzles*, but whatever it is, Hazel puts it down again as soon as her mother opens the door. She is carrying a plastic bag bulging with provisions from Tesco's or Sainsbury's or Waitrose or Safeway, and Hazel follows her through to the kitchen, asking if there's anything she can do to help.

Together, mother and daughter unpack and stack in cupboards muesli, soya beans, cod-liver oil, apples, oranges, milk, prunes, walnut-halves, lavender tea, instant chicken soup.

'She's still not well,' Mum says. 'I bought her a few things, in case she wakes up.'

She holds open the bag and Hazel looks inside. There is a box of Jaffa cakes, a packet of Bourbon biscuits, a bar of Cadbury's chocolate, a Mars bar.

'She likes Jaffa cakes,' Hazel says.

Mum says: 'We all have to be brave.'

Olive has been admitted to the Queen's Medical Centre, to the Royal Princess Margaret General Masonic St Mary's Hospital. She is still unconscious, and X-rays have revealed extensive head and back injuries. It is possible, it is a possibility, that she may not wake up at all, Mum says. The bag swings between Hazel and her Mum as they both remember, on the way to the swimming pool, sudden traffic cones and a hole in the road. The car spinning round and round and then hits something, a wall or the bottom of a bridge or something. In the front of the car, Hazel and her mother unhurt, then outside the car, watching firemen take twenty minutes to cut Olive from the wreckage of the back seat. Mrs Burns, now in her own kitchen (back at the wrecked car) now in her own kitchen, takes Hazel in her arms and rocks her softly, side to side, forwards and backwards, stroking her hair.

Yesterday, Hazel would have been too old for this. Today, her age and her expectations seem irrelevant. All that matters now is now, and she moves with her mother, side to side, forwards and backwards. Her mother's cheek turns and presses against the top of her head.

'It's alright,' Mum says. 'Everything's going to be just fine.'

Hazel remembers this morning, waking up excited: Monday, swimming after school. She pinches and punches Olive for the first day of the month, not as hard as she could have, but still pretty hard, meaning Olive you are as embarrassing as ever with your non-swimmer's glasses and your books and being only eleven all the time. Probably it's all Hazel's fault for pinching and punching harder than allowed because it's only supposed to be a game. And now Olive may be dying while everything else is alive and carries on, her mother's hand on her hair, her own hair against her skin, her skin her skull her bones.

'You have beautiful hair,' Mum says. 'You *both* have beautiful hair.'

She slowly pulls herself away and says she has to go now, back to the hospital, and Hazel finds she's old enough to understand that her mother is being brilliant. She has made herself useful at the hospital, contacted her husband, garaged the smashed car, made Hazel feel involved. At last, something terrible has happened and Mrs Burns can cope with life like this because knowing she has always been right makes her strong. Her fears have been realised, so she is no longer frightened, and she acts without panic because a child in the hospital comes as no surprise to her.

She carries the nearly empty carrier-bag along the corridor and opens the front door. She shivers as if it's cold, looks back at Hazel and smiles, says 'at least it's not raining,' and then closes the door behind her.

Almost immediately the phone rings and it's Dad sounding far away, saying everything twice via the echo of the satellite.

55

He is checking all the airlines trying to get a flight, but when Hazel tells him that Olive is still unconscious (in her most controlled voice, imitating her mother) he runs out of things to say. Hazel suddenly knows why, without knowing how she knows: it's because he can't find a positive angle which applies to this, he doesn't know how to sell it to her. Instead he starts calling Olive Olivia.

'Mum's car's a write-off,' Hazel tells him, and her Dad gives up, gives her a number to call if there's any news, says he'll ring later when he gets a flight, says he's thinking of her all the time, of her and her mother, and of course thinking of Olivia, Hazel's new and unknown sister.

Hazel stares at the telephone, back in its cradle. It is green and plastic and so clean it shines. It has been made by somebody and transported by somebody and stocked and sold by somebody, all so that it can be used by her. She has never really noticed the telephone before, and its history of living people, and she suddenly wishes the room were full of all the people she's ever known and all the people she's ever going to know. She wants to memorise each and every one of them, feeling for the life inside them.

One morning on a day like any other she wakes up. She pinches her sister too hard and punches her on the way to the bathroom and now her sister is in hospital. She is dead already, perhaps. And if this can be true, then she wants a family of thousands around her, and her Mum and Dad and sister, and all the friends she's ever had, and all the boys she's ever met on holiday, and the feeling she remembers from several seasides that there are other human beings as

56

well as herself who are truly alive, and the instinct she has that knowing this is love.

11/1/93 MONDAY 08:48

Spencer stepped back against the closed door to make room for a woman carrying a young child. Then he looked up at the overcast sky hoping for a solitary ray of sunlight or perhaps its opposite, an oncoming storm, some easy evidence of the gods. The sky, however, remained neutral, clouded like the outside of a light-bulb.

Nothing in the street looked obviously different, and William would have been disappointed by his first European day. Jepson's the music shop opposite was about to open, like any other Monday, as was the bank and the travel agent and the charity shop and DJM Games. Cars were jammed in the road, either waiting to park or waiting to pass the cars waiting to park. Several pedestrians bustled past and an impatient motorist sounded his horn.

Spencer turned up the collar of his raincoat, and with his books under one arm he dodged between the cars and across the road to the games shop. The window display had been all chess ever since Short started losing to Kasparov, which he seemed to have been doing for ages, and the various chess-boards in the window were hard on the eye like grids for an impossible crossword. A present for Grace, Spencer thought, and decided to look inside on his way back.

He passed the Rising Sun pub, which was still advertising its Hallowe'en fancy dress party, then had to side-step its open cellar-shaft which was surely a hazard to children. A woman with a pram overtook him and he followed her until she stopped to look in at the butcher's, after which the shops thinned out and Spencer was left with an uninterrupted walk, past the registry office and the fire station, all the way to the library.

Hazel had been so unexpectedly gorgeous that he'd completely forgotten about Jessica. In fact, Hazel was so very much there and in the flesh that he could hardly think coherently at all. He wondered if she'd noticed. Did she mind? And why had he babbled on about the house when all he really wanted to know was are you my Damascus? He wanted a sign, any sign, telling him that he and Hazel were right for each other and that therefore his life had changed direction overnight. He looked closely at faces in the street or in the traffic-jammed cars, as if in any one of these faces he might find the sign telling him what to do next. If only he knew what to look for, or if it was likely that all these people, including himself and Hazel, were moving around each other day after day and meeting or not meeting in accordance with a readable pattern. If only he knew how to read it.

Either that or there was no grand scheme. Then life would be like a newspaper, disconnected and arbitrary from beginning to end. Nothing could be known for certain in advance. You had to wait for accidents and events to take place, and then make the most of them. You had to take life as you found it.

A bus stop had been marked out between a pair of lime trees in front of the broad flight of steps leading up to the library, an impressive Victorian brick building with a sharp roof and a spire-clock permanently stopped at half-past four. On top of the spire there was a flagpole, and the breeze slapped at a blue flag with black writing which announced *NLW – Libraries are Magic*. Spencer hesitated. It wasn't impossible that Jessica was inside the library, so he double-checked the arrival time of Grace's bus. He noticed that on either side of him the lime trees were bleeding a black tar-like substance onto the pavement. Before he could even consider accepting this as the omen he was looking for (with black traditionally meaning bad in the otherwise incomprehensible scheme of things) he jumped up the steps and pushed open the swing-door to the library, only to be faced, opposite the CD and Video section, by a choir of middle-aged people all reading from different books as loudly as they possibly could. They stopped as soon as they saw him.

Spencer coughed and walked self-consciously to Issues and Returns where Miss Irene Haliday (breast-badge), a spinster who lived with her parents (spontaneous value-judgement) was waiting for him, tapping a pencil against her teeth. She smiled brightly and told Spencer that the library was closed.

'I wanted to return these books,' Spencer said, keeping his back turned to the book-readers just in case Jessica was among them. It was the first time he'd ever done that.

'We don't open until ten today,' Miss Haliday said. 'We're

rehearsing for our Most-Noise-Ever-Heard-In-A-Library event.'

'The books are due back today.'

'For National Library Week,' Miss Haliday went on, 'which started this morning. We have a series of events, starting with the Most-Noise-Ever-Heard-In-A-Library, as I think I've already said. At lunchtime we have Miss Havisham in a wedding dress abseiling from the clock-tower down the front of the building.'

'*The* Miss Havisham?'

'Someone dressed up in a wedding dress to look like Miss Havisham. There are leaflets which explain everything.'

'I just wanted to bring my books back.'

'After ten. Everyone's welcome.'

Spencer glanced over his shoulder and saw that the choir of readers had now dispersed into separate little groups. 'Actually there's something else,' he said, lowering his voice. 'I was hoping to have a look at the reference section.'

'Ten o'clock, like everyone else.'

'It's quite urgent,' Spencer said.

Miss Haliday frowned at him over her glasses, becoming less bright and helpful by the second. He leaned forward over the counter and spoke so softly she had to turn her head to hear him properly.

'I need to find out about a contraceptive pill,' he whispered. 'I mean it has to be today, by definition.'

Miss Haliday looked at him with a new and unmistakable coldness. 'I'm sorry,' she said, 'the library is closed until ten. As I think I've already said.'

Spencer didn't linger. Keeping his head down and his collar up, and still in possession of his library books, he left the building and jumped down the steps outside. The lime trees were still spewing their ominously black and unpleasant muck. The council shouldn't allow it. They should chop them down and replace them with nice straight tall green leafy trees for the children. Names came into Spencer's head: Joshua Lucas Georgina Rose Sophie Jane Edward Jonathon Sholto Thomas Ellison Adam Peter Richard, all the names he and Hazel could give to their very recently conceived baby.

Because in the absence left by meaningful signs there remained the bald fact that earlier today he'd had unprotected sex with a virtual stranger. He wondered what to do next, and where to turn, but on the way home he encountered no sudden or eloquent sign which immediately made everything clear to him.

———

It is the first of November 1993 and somewhere in Britain, in Doncaster or Ruislip or Pontypool or Larne, in East Grinstead or Dundee or Exeter or Redbridge, the television is on in the Kellys' lounge, sound up loud, blaring out every crash and bang of *Henry's Cat* or *Cat and Mousse* or *The Greedysaurus Gang*. Mr Kelly yells at Philip (17) to turn it off, right now. Then there is only silence, and the uncomfortable Kellys gathered vaguely about the room, vaguely

61

uncomfortably aware that this is the kind of time when families should gather together. This is what families are for.

Spencer is hiding behind the television, his knees pulled up to his chin. He is thirteen years old and he's not going to cry. His mother is crying. Spencer concentrates on the dark ventilation cuts and the bright screws behind the television as his mother tells him don't be sad. As his mother, crying, tells him don't cry.

'Think of a happy memory,' she says, meaning any happy memory with his sister Rachel in it. 'Think it all the way through, from the beginning to the end.'

She says if Spencer can remember it now he'll always be able to remember it. He should keep it handy and bring it out whenever he needs it. If he does this then Rachel will always be with us, one of life's little miracles, is what his Mum says.

Spencer isn't coming out from behind the television set, not in a million years, and his mother gives up. She goes over to the leather sofa and sits down, forgetting to take off her scarf. Nobody has a clue what to do except Mr Kelly, who is kneeling in front of a low table covered by a white lace cloth, pouring stiff measures of Macallan or E & J or Knockando into a coffee cup. He sips. He swallows, his jaw working minutely backwards and forwards. He narrows his eyes. He has a pencil in his hand and there is an Oxford pad, lined, open on the table. He writes: UNFAIR.

'We can do this tomorrow,' Mrs Kelly suggests, attempting a smile.

'We'll do it now,' Mr Kelly says. 'Before we forget.' He sips and swallows and Spencer makes himself watch. His neck hurts and so does his knee, but somehow he knows this without actually feeling any pain.

'Tell me how you remember her,' Mr Kelly says, pencil poised above the paper. 'Tell me the best thing about her. Anything about her.'

Mr Kelly wants to write down everything they remember about Rachel before it's too late, but nobody says anything because treating her as if she's dead is as bad as actually killing her. Spencer wonders how his father can fail to understand this.

Philip is sitting on the front of the desk where he keeps his computer, a Sun SPARCstation or an IBM or an Acorn. He rocks backwards and forwards, arms crossed. He is thin, very pale.

'When the car slides like that,' he says, 'it's called a fish-tail.'

Mr Kelly starts to write this down, and then stops.

'That's not what I meant.'

'I can't deal with this,' Philip says, and he turns to play a game of chess already set up on the screen behind him. He mutes the sound and chooses black. He defends.

'Rachel wanted her ashes scattered at Wembley,' Spencer says.

His father, pencil at the ready, looks hopefully at his second son.

'After she lived to be a hundred and one. No flowers.'

The car, the swerve, Spencer remembers, what Philip calls

a fish-tail, the crash and the bang. The rest of them came home in a police car. On the inside it was very clean, as if it wasn't used enough.

'Philip started the argument in the car,' Spencer says, pointing at his brother's back. This seems relevant, and important.

'Not now,' Mum says, but it was Philip who complained that three in the back seat was too dangerous, even though there was no other way they could all go swimming and take Philip into town at the same time, was there?

Dad refuses to write this down. He sips and swallows from his mug, looks at what he's written: UNFAIR.

Spencer wants to retreat: behind the television, upstairs to his room, under his bed with the bats and the balls and the disassembled snooker table. Rachel would have hated him for thinking of giving up like this. He therefore makes a determined effort to concentrate on the stiff white lace of the tablecloth, or Philip's shimmering computer screen, or the author names on the books next to the special shelf reserved for quality videos. Harold Robbins and John Le Carré and Jilly Cooper and George Orwell. It helps him not to cry. *Stand By Me* and *The Light That Failed* and *Ginger and Fred* and *The Lavender Hill Mob*. He knows it won't work for ever: there simply aren't enough things to read, nor enough random words to hold back his tears.

Nothing will ever be the same again. Up until now Spencer has always been the same person with the same idea of how life should be, but now he suddenly isn't any more. He doesn't feel old enough for this. He hasn't had enough

64

experience to prepare him for it, and no experience from before now can possibly be strong enough to survive it. He wants it to teach him something, but what? People die and disasters happen bam, suddenly and without warning, just like that. Does it mean, if he knows this, that he is now grown up? Is it an essential grown-up truth that suddenness only works one way, and that anything which happens this suddenly can only be bad? And what if his mother is wrong, and it's not any memory of Rachel which stays available to him, but only the memory of losing her? In which case he'll always be able to trace the day he grew up to this single moment and its particular books and videos, to the way Philip rocks on his chair, playing black, refusing to move his queen.

Time can stop now, if that's alright.

If it moves on from here then that isn't fair to Rachel.

But no matter how hard Spencer tries to freeze the moment (he fixes the names of the writers, the titles of the films, his mother's scarf, his father's word, Philip's French defence and his isolated queen), time insists, eventually, on moving.

'Tell me how you remember her,' Mr Kelly says.

Rachel pinches him, punches him, and beats him to the bathroom. At breakfast she wins the competition to get the most Bourbon biscuits in her mouth. She is the first into the car, wearing her tracksuit covered in badges meaning one day she'll be International European Champion of the World, and in the paper every other day. She'll be in the paper tomorrow anyway, and Spencer has to work his jaw like his Dad so as not to cry like his Mum. He hides his face in his hands and tries ever so hard to remember how Rachel used to catch her breath, her hands on her knees, knees bent inwards slightly, looking up and smiling brightly. Everything turns out just fine.

11/1/93 Monday 09:12

Henry Mitsui had eaten late breakfasts all over the country in a hundred hotels no better or worse than this one. The tables in the dining room were round and the choice of pictures discreet and uneventful, like the engraving of a frozen Battersea Park on the wall behind his father. The rest of the dining room was occupied by the breakfast silence of single managers looking forward to the morning session of the Institute of Sales and Marketing Management Successful Selling '93 Awards. They wore badges to say so, along with their names.

From the buffet, Henry's father had served himself a bowl of prunes and a glass of milk. Henry had a pot of tea and *The Times*, which he'd folded in half over his empty plate.

'I was hoping we could talk,' his father said.

'I *always* read *The Times* at breakfast.'

His father pursed his lips and chased a prune round his bowl as Henry searched for a particularly British idiom, of the type he'd been collecting, to emphasise the distance between them.

'It allows me to fire on all cylinders,' he said.

He turned his attention back to the paper and the intricate problem of turning a page, flattening the creases and refolding it in half. Not much news today. More people had been killed in Northern Ireland. The Maastricht Treaty came into effect. Nigel Mansell had crashed a sports car and a rare bird had been spotted in a field somewhere. It was a good bad day for celebrity deaths: River Phoenix and Federico Fellini. Otherwise *The Times* was packed with its usual measure of life, with people changing jobs, winning and losing at games, reading and liking and disliking books, hoping for something good on at the cinema, confident that the theatre wasn't what it used to be or maybe it was, and just as curious now as always to learn of the births, marriages and deaths of strangers. Henry had grown to like this part of the morning, but today he was finding it difficult to concentrate, even on the headlines. He felt that no matter what had gone wrong elsewhere in the world his own problems were more pressing, excluding perhaps those of Fellini and River Phoenix.

He glanced at the racing page and was relieved to see that the paper's private handicapper had failed to pick out *Mr Confusion* at Newcastle. Then he laid the paper aside and asked his father what he was looking at.

'I was wondering how you felt.'

'Why?'

'I'm your father.'

'I feel fine.'

'Just fine?'

'I seldom feel murderous, if that's what you mean.'

'That's not what I said.'

'I seldom feel like hurting people until they squeak. A joke. That's a joke, Dad.'

'It isn't very funny.'

'Perhaps not.'

It was true that before leaving Japan Henry hadn't always been entirely himself. But he still found it astonishing that his father and Dr Osawa should separately conclude that only by asking him lots of personal questions (and smiling sympathetically at the answers) could they save him from a grim future as a serial killer. They'd obviously been corrupted by too many crime novels and police films. Or they'd been taking the newspapers too seriously.

'I've changed,' Henry said. 'Ever since I came here. I've taken Dr Osawa's advice and remind myself all the time that everyone has a life.'

'And does it help?'

'I've not hurt anyone yet, if that's what you mean.'

'It's not just now, Henry. It's not just today. It's all the other days as well.'

'You said you'd already booked the flight. Apparently today is the only day I have left.'

Mr Mitsui asked testily, in Japanese, if they could speak Japanese now, but Henry replied in English that he preferred to speak his mother-tongue. He then fiddled with the fascinating controls of his telephone before eventually managing to ask how she was. In Japanese, his mother was fine, although recovering only slowly. She sometimes had nightmares.

'Does she want to see me?'

Henry's father said he didn't know, and Henry unexpectedly felt sorry for him. He was always trying to do the right thing which meant that he was usually unhappy. When Dr Osawa had suggested, more than two years ago, that Henry could profitably spend some time studying abroad, his father had immediately set about organising a place at Trinity College Oxford or Sidney Sussex Cambridge or somewhere sounding equally grand. But Henry had explored the edges of a major tantrum (nervous breakdown) until his father gave way and allowed him to follow a distance-learning course. This meant that he could always be someone and somewhere else, travelling tirelessly round the country making his telephone calls and sending in his essays on *British Culture and Society*, *The British Detective Novel*, *An Introduction to British Birds and Trees*, or *The Kings and Queens of Britain*. For nearly two years he'd phoned Miss Burns at least twice a week until she became the fixed point of his nomadic life. She calmly answered all his questions, sometimes praised his written work, and gradually convinced him there was nothing she didn't know.

'You realise you're not allowed to stay here?' his father asked. He repeated it, more quietly, to be sure that Henry understood. 'You do understand, don't you?'

'Mum's British.'

'She's Australian.'

'She told me a quarter Irish a quarter English a quarter Welsh a quarter Scots.'

'She has an Australian passport. Listen to me, Henry. You

69

were allowed to stay while you were a student, but now you have your diploma you're not a student any more and you're not allowed to stay. Do you understand?'

Henry blamed it on Europe. If Britain hadn't signed any treaties he was sure he'd be allowed to stay because his mother was practically English. He spoke the language perfectly. He'd even promise to work like a Trojan so they wouldn't close the door on him.

'Henry, I'm your father. I want what's best for you. I've come all the way from Tokyo. I'm a design consultant with a multinational company and I have experience. I can see that you're tense, like you were before, and we don't want anyone to get hurt, do we?'

'You mean you don't want me to get you into any more trouble.'

'I want what's best for you. We can spend the day at the Getty exhibition. Yes?'

Henry fingered the plastic envelope of powder which he'd transferred to his trouser pocket. It was about the size of a sugar sachet and he liked to have it on his person at all times, for reassurance. It gave him a sense of power. It was a key to sudden change, and therefore real life.

'It's at the Royal Academy,' his father added. 'Not that far from here.'

'I'm in love.'

Mr Mitsui stared past Henry's shoulder, finding it as difficult now as always to resign himself to how closely the son resembled the mother. He wondered if it could ever have been any different.

'We're going to be engaged,' Henry said.

'Congratulations, Henry. We're leaving this evening.'

'Then I'd best ask her today, hadn't I? I'll ring her up, right now.'

Henry picked up the phone and keyed in the digits. There was an answer, and Henry nodded sagely for the benefit of his father as a woman's voice in his ear said:

'Mr Mitsui?'

No matter how many times he'd asked her to call him Henry. Oh the unwavering Miss Burns and her unmistakable voice, strict and beautiful. He took a deep breath.

'Miss Burns,' he said. 'I would like to invite you to lunch.'

'We are not going to meet up. I've told you so before.'

'It's my last day.'

'Not today. Not tomorrow. Never.'

'I wanted to thank you. I went to your house.'

Wherever Miss Burns was, it went very quiet. He thought she might be looking at her watch. Then he thought she might have gone, so it was a great relief when at last she spoke.

'I'm not at home. There's no point you going there again.'

'Perhaps we could meet somewhere else.'

'I'm not getting through to you, am I, Henry? Maybe when you came to my house I was there, but I didn't open the door because I didn't want to see you. Have you thought about that?'

'I know you weren't there,' Henry said. 'If you were there you would have opened the door. It's our destiny to meet.'

'I'm going now, Henry. Enjoy the flight back to Tokyo.'

71

'One last question.'

'No more questions, Henry, I'm sorry. Goodbye.'

Very deliberately, Henry turned off his telephone and placed it back on his plate. She'd called him Henry. He looked up at his father and smiled a sudden and dazzling smile, developed over years of being surprised by excellent presents. One of his two front teeth, the one on the left, was completely brown, of so even and deep a colour it was like a choice made from a colour-chart in a paint catalogue.

'She said yes,' Henry said. 'She'd love to meet me for lunch.'

4

Attitude makes a tremendous difference.

THE TIMES 11/1/93

11/1/93 MONDAY 09:24

This was a perfect example of a time not to be frightened, and not to act like her mother. Henry Mitsui wasn't going to find her here, especially if she stopped answering her phone, and tomorrow he ought to be back in Japan. If he wasn't then she could call the police, so there was no good reason to be frightened.

Waiting for Spencer to get back from the library, Hazel had made a complete tour of the house. Many of the impressive rooms were mostly empty, with perhaps just the odd chair or table to suggest how they might be furnished given the will and the means, and the furniture. She looked closely at the scattered paintings: a Van Gogh reproduction, posters of a Lowry and a Vermeer, an original E. H. Shepherd *Wind in The Willows* illustration of Mole in a snow-storm. She also recognised a Rowlandson and a Vanessa Bell because she'd once offered a course in *British Painters and Painting*.

Eventually she'd decided to settle down with *Sir John Magill's Last Journey* in the ground floor dining room which overlooked the garden, and by the time Spencer found her she felt quite at home in the corner of an ancient and enveloping sofa. Spencer pulled a chair out from under the polished table. He sat on it backwards, and asked her if she'd seen William anywhere.

'If he's the oldish man who looks a bit like Fellini, then yes.'

'How like Fellini?'

'Tall, chubby cheeks, grey hair. Late middle-age and still growing.'

'He didn't say anything to upset you, did he?'

'He didn't see me. He was just standing there, staring at the front door. I didn't like to disturb him.'

'He's scared of going out because he thinks it's the end of Britain. I'd better go and check on him.'

'You didn't see him when you came in?'

'I came in the back way. I won't be a minute.'

'In that case,' Hazel said, 'you can do me a favour.'

She turned off her phone and threw it across to him. 'I've

just decided I'm taking a holiday,' she said. 'And it starts right now. Put the phone somewhere safe, where I don't even have to see it.'

Back in the entrance hall, William was still standing opposite the front door, staring at it. This time he must have heard Spencer coming.

'I'm going to go outside,' he said, 'if it's the last thing I do.'

Spencer put Hazel's phone on top of the junk mail on the telephone table, where he was fairly sure not to forget it. William immediately picked it up and tried out various buttons.

'She's a rich teacher then?'

'She has to be available.'

William pretended to make a call.

'Hello,' he said. 'Is there anybody out there?'

Hazel was right, he did look a bit like Fellini, but in altogether better health. He seemed in no hurry to go outside, so Spencer decided it was safe to leave him on his own for a while.

In the dining room, while she'd been waiting, Hazel had pushed away her book and shimmied the skirt of her sweater-dress above her knees. When Spencer came back she let her hand drift over the cushion beside her. Spencer preferred the chair.

'Fine,' she said. She crossed her hands in her lap, and was surprised by how much teacher now crept into her voice:

'Would you mind telling me what's going on?'

'How's Sir John?'

'Sorry?'

'In the book. *Sir John Magill's Last Journey.*'

'It's his last journey. Come on, Spencer, we ought to be doing better than this.'

He did that incredibly annoying thing where he looked away, as if something somewhere else had urgently caught his attention. Hazel told him to stop it. They were alone, she said, in the same place for a change and together at last. They could actually try to enjoy it.

'We have the whole day,' she said firmly. 'So stop worrying. Or at least tell me what you're worried about.'

'I'm sorry,' Spencer said, changing chairs. 'I can never relax when people are coming to look at the house.'

'If there's something wrong you should tell me. We shouldn't have any secrets.'

'It's not a secret. It's just. Look. Imagine the worst possible scenario.'

'Of what?'

'Of us.'

Hazel breathed in, closed her eyes, and imagined more than one Spencer Kelly. This one in the dining room, although he looked something like the Spencer Kelly she'd been expecting, was in fact a completely different Spencer Kelly. He actually owned this house and his father wasn't a warehouseman. Instead he was a senior politician who'd made his fortune preaching fundamentalist sermons against sex before marriage. When he found out about Hazel's familiarity with Spencer's bed, he would automatically suspect an evil connection with Hazel's father's sales trips to Iran or Pakistan or Israel. In a fit of rage the father of the fake Spencer Kelly would then exploit his masonic contacts in the military to initiate pre-emptive air-strikes against any of the above-named countries, who would all retaliate instantly with various weapons of mass destruction. Total nuclear war would follow, resulting in the destruction of everything and the death of the planet.

And then Hazel Burns would never meet the real Spencer Kelly, for whom she may well have been destined in love.

'Well it's not that bad,' Spencer said.

'How bad is it?'

Spencer stared intently at a loose thread behind a button on his suit jacket. Hazel snapped her fingers. He told her that when he'd been in the library he'd asked about the morning-after pill.

'Well hello romance,' Hazel said.

Spencer looked up at her, embarrassed but still hopeful, as if she was contemporary art. She wished he wouldn't do that. It was almost as bad as when he looked away, and not for the first time in her life Hazel wished she believed in a romantic love like Spencer's Damascus. After the certainty of a revelation, little things like these probably didn't matter so much. She said:

'Is pregnancy really the worst thing you can imagine?'

'Of course not.'

'Then it's not so bad, is it?'

'There's also disease.'

'We know everything about each other. I thought this was what you wanted?'

'It all seems very sudden. Very quick.'

'Everything changes, snap bang, instantly. That's what you were always waiting for. And anyway, what's so wrong with children if we love each other?'

Spencer: the dreadful unstoppable momentum of it all, a wedding probably, a honeymoon if they could afford it, the child, temper-tantrums, and no more watching television in the afternoon, consoled by the thought that he was hurting nobody by doing nothing because there was nothing to be done and life could always begin tomorrow.

Hazel: on any particular day, not a special day in time of war or social unrest, but just any normal any old newsday, children could be abducted, fall from cliffs, collide with fireworks, contract meningitis. They could be shot in the face from point-blank range or stabbed or stoned or poisoned by a pellet from a customised umbrella. And even if they survived all this, they'd probably still run away from home to star darkly in dubious films with titles like *Hellfire Corner* or *So You Want to Be a Surgeon?* or *Clarissa Explains It All*.

There was, however, nothing to be gained from being frightened.

'There is also joy,' Hazel said. 'Let's try and live life as if the world was going to stop at tea-time.'

'Why should it?'

'What?'

'Stop at tea-time.'

'A thousand reasons. Anything could happen. I'm just saying don't be so frightened.'

'It's not fear, it's thinking.'

'Then you think too much. Fear is easy,' Hazel said. 'It's like being sad. Anyone can be sad and afraid. Now come and sit over here.'

Spencer went and sat on the sofa. Hazel put her hand on his knee. She asked him if he ever wondered what Charles Kingsley was like in bed.

———

It is the first of November 1993 and somewhere in Britain, in Ealing or Gala or Aberavon or Newmarket, in Thornton Steward or Durham or Matlock or King's Lynn, Hazel Burns is fourteen years old and a prisoner in her own home. In the front room she and her mother stand opposite each other, locked in full combat.

'It's only a mini-skirt. All the girls are wearing them.'

'Stop being so adolescent.'

'I *am* adolescent.'

'Do I have to spell it out?'

'Yes.'

'What would Sam Carter think?'

'Spell it out, Mum.'

'Imagine you're walking home. It's dark. You hear footsteps behind you. You're terrified and all you're wearing is that handkerchief, which, if I may say so, makes you look

79

like a prostitute. The footsteps speed up, following you all the way home. Eventually you reach the front door, you turn round.'

'And then what?'

'Use your imagination.'

And there he is, River Phoenix in sunglasses, having faked his death to start a new life as Hazel's secret long-term lover. Destiny would be a fine thing. Or at least, Hazel corrects herself, a fine destiny would be a fine thing.

'What's wrong with Sam Carter?' her mother asks.

'He's fat.'

'What about one of those nice boys you always meet on holiday?'

'They all live miles away. And anyway, we keep on moving house.'

'How about your black trousers? You could put on some trousers.'

'I'm not changing.'

Her mother loses her temper and says well then in that case young lady you're not leaving the house and Hazel thinks fine, if I'm not allowed to leave the house then I won't even leave this room. She sits on the sofa with her knees clamped together, arms crossed, and vows never to speak nor move again until either her mother relents or she starves to death. Her mother leaves the room. So, starving to death it is, then.

She will be sorely missed. She has the leading role in the school's Christmas play, a musical version of *Cinderella* or *The Secret Garden* or *Sleeping Beauty*, and the cast will be lost without her, utterly devastated. She can think of several boys (including Sam Carter) who will miss her glossy brown hair and her flawless complexion. In fact, it's only because she's so attractive to boys that her mother cares what clothes she wears. It explains why she acts as if Hazel is forever ten years old, and holds her captive in this room, unloved among the never-changing beigeness of the three-piece suite, the endless supply of crossword books, today's predictable paper, and, spread across the coffee table, all the phonecards left over from the disasters which never happened. Hazel and Olive use them as betting slips when they play poker. Hazel wins at poker. Olive usually wins at chess.

Nothing ever changes, Hazel thinks, except the things which always change. This is a different front room, for example, but the only way of telling is by the new pair of moles in the corner cabinet. The chess set is now Romans v Spartans or Crusaders v Saracens, who Olive likes to call the Vanguard of the Jihad, especially when she's winning. The furniture is perhaps a little more carefully spaced, for Olive's benefit, but essentially it's all the same and therefore no better than school, where Hazel is still expected to sit next to the same person every lunchtime. Probably even after she dies from starvation.

Nobody understands her, and Hazel has come to the conclusion that the only place the right way up on this spherical earth is wherever she is. Everyone everywhere else is unstraight and off-balance and only her father sometimes steps into her right-way-up world and remains upright. He is, however, Salesperson of the Year '93 and usually away on business in Jerusalem or Islamabad or Cleveland, selling lifestyle ideas to strangers. Hazel looks at the phone but doesn't honestly expect him to ring, and she can't say she blames him. He must be glad to get away from Mum, even though Hazel sometimes suspects her parents actually love each other. Otherwise why would Dad do so many things he didn't want to do? And why would Mum be so paranoid he was having an affair? The usual candidates are his new secretary or an air hostess or some mysterious swan-necked foreigner.

The door slams open, interrupting Hazel's ongoing attempt to perfect the terms and conditions of her early-life crisis. It is Olive Burns, Hazel's twelve-year-old sister, who now prefers to be called Olly. She free-wheels gracefully into the middle of the room, and then swivels to face the sofa. Hazel stands up and walks round her. Olive pushes her clear-framed glasses back up her nose and smiles broadly. She pivots her chair and follows Hazel towards the window. She says:

'Who's a naughty girl then?'

'Go away.'

'Guess who won't be coming swimming with us later? Nice skirt.'

Hazel goes back to the sofa and sits down again and crosses her legs. Olive attracts her attention by waving something above her head. It is a red-and-white striped woollen glove meant for a child. Hazel jumps up to grab it but Olive speedily reverses towards the window.

'You can't hit me,' she says. 'I'm in a wheelchair.'

Hazel looks at her sister and then at the glove. She shrugs. She composes herself, sits down, smoothes her very short skirt. Olive rolls forward and claims she can read Hazel's fortune by using the supernatural powers latent in the love-glove.

Despite herself, Hazel looks up.

'The *what*?'

'The glove of love. With my intimate experience of the dark-side,' Olive tells her, 'I can now reveal the secrets of your future.'

Hazel is a little jealous of Olive. Something real has happened to her, and by nearly dying she has really lived, which is only one of the many dilemmas which complicate her intimate experience of adolescence. Olive puts on a funny, spooky voice to announce that today is All Saints' Day, particularly suited to divination in the areas of marriage, health and death.

'Let's do marriage,' Hazel says, and then remembers she's supposed to be starving to death. She studies the top of her knee, and then a fingernail.

Olive strokes the glove and closes her eyes and says *I see* ... she says *I see* ... she says it several more times than Hazel considers strictly necessary.

'I see fat Sam Carter.'

'He is not fat.'

'I see fat Sam Carter grinning. Fat Sammy is Hazel's boyfriend.'

Olive sniggers. Hazel tells her that she doesn't have a

boyfriend and she doesn't want one. And if she did want one it wouldn't be Samuel Carter, thank you very much.

'Saving yourself for someone special?'

Hazel is not saving herself and she loves no-one and nobody loves her right back. She doesn't care about Sam Carter or any stupid glove. The truth is that she yearns for something different and real to happen. Something dramatic and dangerous like the stories she reads in newspapers. In short, she wants life to start. She wants to meet boys more exciting than those glossed in from neighbouring private schools (including Sam Carter), who all look far too good to be true. But how is she supposed to meet anybody real and different when her mother tells her not to talk to strangers and not to give out her phone number, and never, under any circumstances, to tell anyone her address? She isn't even allowed to choose her own clothes. The simple truth is that life is unfair, and she doesn't care if she never sees another boy as long as she lives, which won't be long now because she's already close to starvation.

'So I can throw it away then?'

'What?'

'The glove.'

Olive's eyes are sharp, perceptive, mischievous. Since the accident she has changed almost beyond recognition. Hazel moves a chess piece, a bishop.

'Of course you can,' she says. 'It's only an old glove.'

'So I can throw it away?'

'It's not as if it's any use to anybody.'

'And burn it? Can I burn it first?'

84

'For all I care, Olive, you can eat it choke on it and die.'

———————

The Central London Institute of Learning was the country's premier distance-learning centre for British and Cultural History. It said so in the advert. *Also for drawing, opera, photography, cooking – and always for location.*

Henry had never been there, but he knew the address by heart because of all the punctual essays he'd sent. He knew that Miss Burns was also unlikely to be there, but he felt brightly optimistic that if he presented his most polite self in person, smile included, he could find out where she was without having to phone her up again and beg. On the whole, he'd prefer to surprise her.

'You're making a mistake,' his father said. 'Stay here with me.'

Henry reached for the money on the table and his father grabbed his wrist.

'You're not yourself,' he said, squeezing hard, holding on, but Henry knew exactly how he wanted to spend his last day in Britain, so he punched his father in the arm until he let go. He let go quickly. He was a coward, scared of scenes and hurting people and being disgraced in public dining rooms. Henry gathered up his telephone and his newspaper, walked away without looking back, and now found himself

85

outside on his own in London, strolling jauntily along, some-times slapping his rolled-up paper against his thigh.

He had, however, forgotten his raincoat. In his shirt-sleeves he was soon reminded that it was already November (eight degrees centigrade) and nearly winter. A single low cloud covered everything, even other clouds, and Henry expected rain. He therefore found a Marks & Spencer and bought himself an umbrella. It was easy. He gave the lady some of his father's money and a dazzling smile, and enjoyed the way she admired his tooth. Money was an excellent invention. It nearly always made an immediate difference. Along with the umbrella he bought a chunky powder-blue sweater, patterned in a kind of hybrid cross between Nor-wegian and Navajo Indian. He pulled it over his head, and delighted with his reflection in the mirror he started swinging his new umbrella, a bit like Fred Astaire. Then he put his *Times* and his telephone in the M & S plastic bag, and set out in search of a newsagent. In another simple exchange for pounds and pence he successfully obtained a map of London. This was great: nothing could stop him now.

Consulting his new map, he rejected the possibility of the Circle Line, and instead found a route which took him through a park, at which point he nearly collided with a nice-looking girl who was shouldering her way out of a telephone box. She flushed bright red as she tried to fit a greyish phonecard back into her wallet, and remembering Dr Osawa's insistence that everyone had a life, Henry decided that this girl was Gillian Thomas, phoning for a flatshare in Wimbledon Village. Her father, and why not, was Secretary to the Bank of England. Dr Osawa would have been proud.

When he arrived at the park, Henry amused himself by correctly identifying horse chestnut trees, aspens, hornbeams and hazels. He heard more snatches of mistle thrush song, a pair this time, and was surprised by a small brown bird flying up suddenly in front of him. As it swooped away he recognised the short piping call of a meadow pipit, and even though the park was generally in a state of some disrepair, Henry could hardly remember feeling happier.

He had plenty of reasons to be cheerful. He knew the names of birds and trees. He knew that this historic urban park was a glory of Victorian design. He had money in his pocket, and a strong horse he fancied in the two-thirty at Newcastle. He had a new sweater and a portable telephone and his little plastic envelope of powder. Most important of all, he had Miss Burns, although admittedly only one safe day left in which to find her. He looked on the bright side, he put on a brave face, he said to himself: mustn't grumble. After all, one day was better than none, and he understood people were generally commended for seizing the day. He was in pursuit of a miracle and the rapture of a happy ending, and he saw nothing wrong in that. It wasn't as if he had any plans to hurt anybody.

In front of him and to his left, for example, high heels tap-tapping sharply along the concrete path, let's say Mrs Katherine Powell, founding committee member of Absent Parents Asking for Reasonable Treatment, and her small darling dog Panther. Every passer-by had a life and a connection with other lives, each one with their own habits and their own story and their own special days. Dr Osawa was right, and as long as Henry kept this in mind he remained calm and in control, glad to be a part of it all.

He checked his watch, a Piaget, another fine present from his parents. He found a bench and sat down and turned his telephone off, because only his father would try to ring him. Then he put the phone with the umbrella and the M & S bag on the bench beside him. He contemplated an unkempt moon-shaped flowerbed, and then beyond this jogging left to right Mr Peter Macarthur, part-time technical supervisor at a Batchelor's packet soup factory.

Henry's mother had once told him that Britain had the best parks in the world, but from where he was sitting Henry could see one beheaded statue and another encased in plywood. Further on there was a boarded-up pavilion, growing graffiti like a bright lichen: *Gary 4 Laura, Elliot Sucks, Utd 0 QPR 1*, but it wasn't like this everywhere. In the last two years Henry had seen much of the Britain his mother had promised. He'd watched the end of a cricket match lounging beneath a willow in a village called Brampton Abbotts. In Biggar in Strathclyde he'd sat out a St Andrew's Day Ball, breakfast included in the price. Outside the White Hart in Spadeadam he'd seen the meeting of a hunt minutes before departure, with nervous men and women calming huge brown horses. These were not illusions, but he knew it went the other way as well. During his stay in Belfast twenty-three people had been killed in eight days. From a stalled train outside Wakefield he'd watched lines of silent police searching wasteland for the remains of a missing woman. At Aintree racetrack he'd heard the sirens of circled ambulances after ten children had been hit by fireworks, but none of this was to say that his mother was wrong. Britain was still better than anywhere else he'd lived, him and his mother, following his father from one foreign posting to the next. In Algiers their French neighbours were taken hostage by nationalist fundamentalists, while in Jerusalem Henry was perversely mistaken for an Arab and stoned outside a polling booth. Henry thought it safe to say that neither of these things could have happened in Britain.

Right to left, beyond the neglected flowerbed, Libby Gorman of Jackson-Stops and Staff, humming a recitative from *Figaro's Wedding*. Left to right James Irvine, leader of a United Nations team of weapon experts. And then Panther the small dog came rolling up to the bench, jumping up so that his front paws landed on the plastic bag. 'Hello, Panther,' Henry said, and he let the small dog smell his fingers. Then he pulled the packet of powder from his pocket. It was the colour of dirty sand, with a slight shade of green, and he let the dog sniff around it, even lick the plastic envelope, knowing that should he feed the powder to the dog, poor darling Panther would be dead within minutes. Just then Mrs Katherine Powell, absent parent asking for reasonable treatment and owner of Panther, called him away using a false name.

No matter. Henry still had the powder, never knowing when it might come in useful. And anyway, he didn't want to kill a dog. Knowing the difference between thinking a thing and doing it was the essential trick of behaving like everyone else.

As if he was still following one of her courses, Henry turned on his phone and keyed in the number. He had until Miss Burns picked up to think of something to say, but this time the phone rang on and on, long beyond the moment when he realised that for once she wasn't going to answer. And then, just as he was about to give up, it was answered. By a man.

Henry thought quickly. He asked the man where he was, because the telephone's reception wasn't very good.

'Sorry?'

The man sounded confused so Henry rushed him for an address, for a postcode, anything.

'What? What are you talking about?'

'Where in London are you?' Henry said. 'Tell me where you are.'

'I don't know,' the man's voice said. 'I haven't been out yet.'

It is the first of November 1993 and somewhere in Britain, in Falmouth or Hampton Hill or Llandudno or Oxford, in Devonport or Tranmere or East Stirling or Glenavon, every boy of Spencer's age is having non-stop all-action sex all of the time. They openly admit to it, even though they're only fourteen years old. Spencer doesn't have a girlfriend,

90

but he does have an evolving pattern of facial blemishes. He also has a father who doesn't understand him and a mother who probably takes drugs and an older brother who is about to be married.

The Kelly family has moved again because their last home was compulsory purchased and re-developed as a car park, or a superstore, or a relief road for the M1 or the M4 or the M23. In the new house the lounge is much the same, except that above the mantelpiece there is now an embroidered quotation from the bible:

Woe betite those who lie in bed planning evil and wicked deeds, and rise at daybreak to do them, knowing they have the power to do evil.   *Micah 2:1 (REB)*

Spencer's mother is responsible for this, even though Spencer often gets no further than lying in bed, evil and wicked deeds requiring far more energy than he can usually spare. He hardly ever goes out, mostly because he refuses to travel by car but also because walking is boring. Instead, he likes to stay in and watch television, looking out for men and women who might be doing it to each other on *House of Cards* or *Brookside* or *Terror on Highway 91*. He watches until his eyes blur and he has no idea what time it is or what he's watching any more.

Today, however, is not like other days because this is the day of his brother's wedding. Spencer is wearing his good jacket, so precious and underused that he hides important objects in the inside pocket. There is a child's red-and-white-striped glove in there, as well as a personalised Christmas card sent to the Kellys by Mr and Mrs Burns and family, who they once met on holiday. Inside the card there is an address and a phone number and a hand-written message which says *Do keep in touch.*

Spencer has never written back because Hazel has a scholarship to a private school. The possibility of phoning, though, sometimes presses in on him like a weight on the heart. The act of dialling is so quick and easy, so possible, that it almost hurts him. It could be finished within seconds, in the time it takes to say while I'm saying this I've already rung the number. There: already ringing.

Mrs Kelly says it's time to go. She has put on weight and a wide-brimmed hat, and even though Fellini has chosen this day (of all possible days) to die, she can always find a smile. Spencer therefore thinks she must be on drugs, probably ever since the thing with Rachel. Spencer is tolerant of his mother's good humour. He likes to show how he is the strongest in the family, and has been entirely unaffected by Rachel and all that. She would have acted the same if it had happened to him, even as the rest of the family falls to pieces, his Dad drinking too much, his mother finding the Lord, his brother taking a sensible job and getting married to a plump girl called Alison.

'I'm not going in the car,' Spencer says. He switches on the television.

'It's one of those big wedding cars,' his mother patiently explains. 'It's more like a boat.'

A car horn sounds from outside. 'Get in the fucking car, Spencer,' Mr Kelly says. He is already drunk in readiness for the wedding, and has been for several weeks. 'It's your brother's wedding for fuck's sake.'

Mr Kelly yanks Spencer up by the shoulder-pads of his jacket, tugs him out of the house, and pushes him into the back of the wedding car. It takes them eight minutes to drive to St Oswald's or the Church of the Ascension or The Star of the Sea or St John's. Rachel could have run it quicker.

Philip and his wife to be, Alison, are both eighteen years old. After today, Philip can have sex with her every day for the rest of his life, proving that in marriage there's at least one miracle which can happen to anybody. Not married/ married. Easy. During the ceremony Spencer watches his brother and Alison ring each other at the altar, and somehow doubts that marriage is the miracle for him. And anyway, marriage is stupid because everyone dies.

And afterwards, it says on the invitations, at the White Hart Hotel, Bailgate, at the Bencroft House Hotel or the Bransdale Lodge Hotel or the Forte Crest at Glasgow or Manchester Airport, at Bolehyde Manor Hotel or the Avon Gorge Hotel, Bristol.

At the reception, several of the guests remark that Spencer acts his age. He doesn't talk to anybody, but instead concentrates moodily on his developing awareness of different types of disappointment. He is, for example, a great sporting disappointment to his father. Alison's adult bridesmaids are also deeply disappointing, in the sense that neither of them show any obvious enthusiasm for instant sex with a fourteen-year-old boy. Perhaps they've already heard that he didn't get a part in the school play. A disappointing audition, said

93

the disappointed teacher, and no bridesmaid on earth is going to have sex with a schoolboy lighting technician.

Spencer wonders whether girls in general are sufficiently aware of how deeply damaged he is by what happened to Rachel. He would graciously allow any one of them to rescue him, but in the meantime he sits alone at the bar, guarding his most recent glass of champagne, watching the television news. There is a pay-phone on the bar-counter, and after another glass of champagne he takes Mr Burns's Christmas card from the inside pocket of his jacket. He sees on the news, even though the sound is down, that Europe is united and River Phoenix is dead. He decides that if there's no news he hasn't already read in the paper, or if in the next ten minutes he isn't rescued by one of the bridesmaids, he'll phone the number on Mr Burns's Christmas card and ask to speak to Hazel. Please.

The barman changes channels. It is snooker, and the player at the table lining up a red looks like Ebdon or Parrott or Davis or Hendry, one of those. They earn sixty thousand pounds a tournament, his Dad says, but snooker is something else that Spencer's no good at, and unless there's some kind of miracle he's going to end up a warehouseman just like his Dad, on a hundred and seventy pounds a week. If Ebdon pots this red, Spencer will phone the number on the Christmas card and ask to speak to Hazel. I'm her boyfriend, an old friend of hers. If it isn't any trouble.

The barman switches back to the news, which finishes. It seems unlikely that Spencer is about to be rescued by a bridesmaid, which is when a hand arrives on his shoulder,

94

too old, too fat, the flesh pushing over the wedding ring which looks painfully tight.

'What's up, cowboy?' his mother asks. She was always cheerful, like a religion, but now she also has religion. When she's being particularly upbeat she likes to quote from films. Spencer gulps some champagne. His mother has a bottle and she refills his glass.

'Aren't you happy for your brother?'

'Wild with joy. Can I have some money?'

'This is his big day.'

'Some change. Some ten pence pieces.' The champagne is light in Spencer's head. 'Some Bank of England ten pence pieces please, Mother.'

She squeezes his shoulder. 'I know why you're upset,' she says, 'but you mustn't think she's gone. She's here with us and her spirit is all around us.'

'Her spirit begs you to lend me some ten pence pieces.'

His mother fumbles in her purse and puts some coins on the counter. 'We are never alone,' she says. 'And everything turns out just fine.'

She bustles away and Spencer doesn't bother to call her back to tell her that actually he might have other plans. He drinks more champagne, pushes several coins into the phone (long distance) and dials the number on the Christmas card in the same time it takes him to say I am dialling the number on the Christmas card I am doing it right now. What the hell am I doing? I am dialling the number.

As he waits for someone to answer his heart performs some amateur acrobatics, an imperfect somersault or two in the tender vault of his chest. Her father, her mother, her sister will answer. Or she'll be out at the seaside, wearing a swimming costume and a tennis skirt, lying on a sand dune staring up at the sky, listing favourite airlines.

11/1/93 MONDAY 10:12

The phone call was a sign. William was sure of it. He'd been about to change his mind about going outside when the modern portable thing had gone off and a complete stranger had told him he ought to go out now. One last try then. It had to be worth a try because miracles were always possible.

He stood boldly in front of the door. He went to check his braces, flies, thought I've already done that, and instead straightened his jaw. He blinked hard, put his hand to the latch, pulled the door open and stepped outside into a light unexpected drizzle. He felt the rain only vaguely because unused to the random generosity of outside life he stood transfixed by JEPSON'S PIANO SALE NOT ON!!, With Prices Cheaper Than Others' Sale Prices Who Needs A Sale? By Jeremy Yates and Tony Fellner listening to Nigel Coren's opinion that Maradona was no spring chicken on the top deck of a big red bus marked Clapham driven by Clive Webb, volunteer RSPB Birdline recorded message operator

96

and planning to get engaged at Christmas. By Mr and Mrs Peter Pinkerton, conservation officers at the Garden History Society in their new Vauxhall Cavalier with low-solvent content Bayer paint, and the flying bicycle of Stuart Dangerfield, two-times Newlands Pass British Hill-Climb Champion, and the non-stop left-right, right-left tennis of traffic and the noise of cars, Toyotas, Vauxhalls, Peugeots, Fords alongside distant shouting from the library which is National Library Week and The-Most-Noise-Ever-Made-In-A-Library. Outside the newsagents *Ulster Talks* and *Children Find Body* and *Film Star River Phoenix (23) Dead.*

And this was only the beginning.

William knew there was more than this, much more of it out of sight and branching away from here through the countless towns of the nation. All of it was peopled, named, full of explicit purposes achieved or frustrated, with reasons before and consequences after, all converging on now so that it was hardly surprising if William found it difficult to breathe with the sheer quantity of significant things crammed into this and any one tiny moment, the collision of everything that had ever happened with everything that was still waiting to happen, second after second after second. His eyes left right left, past the parked cars and a stalled Ford Transit, and on the far pavement he tries to contain in his mind and fully understand the simultaneous possibility of REVISED INTEREST RATES 7.00 (6.50) % gross, and flying south this winter with Forte Grand, 2 nights Jet-Setting in Monte Carlo from £269 per person based on 2 adults sharing a standard twin/double room with private bathroom single room rates available on request and 7 nights of majesty Cairo and the Nile from £699 per person, Historic Malta, Fabulous Algarve, £229 and £279 respectively per person per person, like per second per second as a maximum velocity per person per person of things to be and places to go.

There is no end to it.

Here come Raymond Pangalos and Giles Nuttall in vampire outfits teeth crooked stumbling home in morning tail-suits from a wedding or an epic Hallowe'en party, past the window of DJM Games, black and white with chessboards harsh on the rambling eye. A shrieking yellow poster for a three-way rock concert featuring *Mal Pelo* and *Southern Dogs* and *Ignominious Defenestration*, doors open 20:30 – LATECOMERS WILL NOT BE ADMITTED TO AUDITORIUM. In the sky above an Iberian Airlines jet plane deporting a pair of Kurdish asylum seekers, and then what?

And then Spencer is slamming the door behind him and William is back on the inside, leaning heavily against the wall, nudging aside the improvised coat-stand, panting fiercely and having to hold his heart in his hands.

This had all happened before, so Spencer didn't immediately panic. He loosened another button on William's open-necked shirt. He positioned his shoulder under William's arm, noting objectively that William was breathing erratically and his face had gone very red. Spencer then manoeuvred him past the telephone table and through the entrance hall towards the dining room.

Although Spencer was managing very well on his own,

and this had happened to him at least twice or even three times before, William wasn't getting any lighter. Spencer could have managed on his own, and he wasn't panicking, but Hazel was only a few rooms away and all she was doing was reading an old potboiler of a crime novel. William was a big man and really quite heavy, and he certainly wasn't improving as far as breathing was concerned. Spencer tottered forward a little, called out to Hazel, then stumbled backwards, almost losing his balance.

'Hazel,' he called out, although he could have dealt with William's panic attack entirely on his own. 'Hazel!' he shouted, louder now, hoping she'd come very soon. Not because he needed her, it was important to understand, but only because he wanted to make her feel involved.

5

Two in five teenagers believe sex at 15 is acceptable, with little difference between boys and girls.

THE TIMES 11/1/93

11/1/93 MONDAY 10:24

Britain was awful, horrible, dangerous, exciting, frightening. It was so *busy*, and you never knew what was coming next. It was dirty and disorganised and not at all what he'd been expecting. It was a vicious mixture of red double-deckers and disguised IRA scouts and loud shops and vampires in disarray. He'd seen the last day of Britain and the first day of Europe and it wasn't pretty out there. All the same, lying on the sofa in the dining room, wrapped in a thick green blanket, William was faking it.

'What day is it?' he murmured weakly, trying to squint a good look at the girl.

'It's Monday all day,' she said.

'And who are you?'

'Spencer's friend. My name is Hazel.'

'Where's Spencer?'

'He's making tea.'

William pushed away the blanket, lifted up his head, and meant to swing his legs to the floor. He then pretended to feel a fainting fit coming on, and lay back down again.

'I'm sorry,' he said. 'I'm not always like this.'

This was a shamefaced lie. Here in the house, safe in the dining room, William was once more undeniably himself. No change had taken place, and this was a day no different from any other, unfit for miracles. He was still unable to go outside, and nothing would ever change for the better. He took another sly look at the girl. It was some time since he'd last experienced a woman in real life, but he recognised that even by the standards of television she was a decent roundly shape and she was very blonde. She was also wearing a curvely woollen dress, but this only briefly distracted William from contriving the quickest way to get rid of her.

'A standard phobic anxiety attack,' she said. 'A surge of panic followed by heart trouble and possible loss of consciousness. Often, these physical reactions combine with a sense of doom.'

'You're very knowledgeable,' William said, meaning oh yes, a very smart young woman.

'My sister's training to be a doctor,' Hazel said modestly, which was all very fascinating coming from a stranger, William thought, but let's stick to the essentials. I'm more than twice your age and this house belongs to my brother so you can't come waltzing in here upsetting the excellent arrangement I have with Spencer. How old was she? No older than Spencer, with the same short memory of a life so short she wouldn't know what it meant to forget. She probably still believed that all the information she needed to decipher herself was available to her, if only she put enough effort into remembering it. Just the kind of foolish idea which made young people so optimistic, and so idiotic.

Spencer came in carrying a mug of tea, *Celebrating 100 Years of the Liverpool Victoria Friendly Society.*

'Don't say it,' William said, taking the mug.

'Say what?'

'I told you so.'

'You think we've been invaded,' Spencer said. 'The aliens have landed and they're all European, and the first thing they did was ruin absolutely everything, instantly.'

But William thought no, that's not it. I wanted to go out because I still have a secret dream of selling the tomento. And because safety and familiarity, it's just about possible, can drain the life from things. And yes, it was also true, because he didn't want to miss the last days of Britain.

'It was very busy,' William said.

'You shouldn't get so involved,' Spencer told him. 'When you see people you don't know, why think they all have to have names?'

'They all do have names.'

'Yes, I know they do. But you don't have to name them all.'

103

Spencer and Hazel had chosen neighbouring chairs, though they kept a certain distance. William sensed there would never be a better time to break them up than now, the first morning after the first night before. Spencer was saying never mind, all's well that ends well. 'You just shouldn't go outside, that's all.'

And it was about time that William, too, accepted the truth of this. In anyone else, he would have thought it a good definition of madness, this not getting on well with the world and everything in it. For himself, he'd make it a minor inconvenience to be endured more gracefully. There was no point trying to go outside any more. The time had come to accept that no sudden and brilliant event was going to turn his life around. The tomento would never make his fortune in the supermarkets of the world and miracles were reserved for others. He should therefore resign himself to a life in retreat, with one day indistinguishable from the next. As for the world outside, he would live as if it didn't exist, an ambition which was unthinkable without Spencer to help him through the days. The girl would just have to go.

'I disagree,' Hazel said. She then shared her considered medical opinion, via her sister, that William's condition wasn't so very difficult to cure. There was no reason he shouldn't go outside. He just had to be better prepared in what to expect. Fear was ignorance, nothing more.

'And how would you suggest he prepares himself?' Spencer asked her.

'We tell him what it's like.'

'Where?'

'Outside.'

'And what about our problems?'

'What problems?'

'The you know what. We ought to get that sorted out before Grace gets here.'

'Oh, that,' Hazel said. 'I don't have a problem with that.'

Spencer stood up, was about to say something, walked to the door, was about to say something, opened the door and left the room. William spread his fingers over the blanket, and then covered one hand with the other.

'So then, Hazel,' he said. 'How did you meet Spencer? Are you a friend of Jessica's?'

It is the first of November 1993 and somewhere in Britain, in Glossop or Peebles or Stroud or Diss, in Spalding or Greysteel or Liverpool or Llanrhaeadr-ym-Mochnant, Spencer is fifteen years old and tonight's the night.

The school is hosting its Hallowe'en party a day late to accommodate the handful of European students who are the school's temporary guests as part of an EU exchange scheme. They could be Greek or French or Danish or German, but there are also some Russians involved because it's important to be kind, or to look ahead, or to play it safe. The Hallowe'en party is the second of several activities planned for their entertainment, and it's being staged in the gym, a building Spencer hasn't entered since he opted for metalwork. He is new to the area and new to the school, where Shakespeare Studies have been replaced by Business in the Community. Along with its class sizes, therefore, the school is doing all it can to ensure that Spencer remains an integral part of the emerging educational underclass.

In the meantime, in his ongoing quest for a modern girl who'll let him, Spencer is dressed as an astronaut. There is also a Batman and an IRA terrorist, and a convincing attempt at the corpse in *Stand By Me*, but unlike Spencer most of the boys are dressed as vampires, although without the plastic teeth which look stupid. The girls, with the exception of a shocking seventeenth-century witch, dress exclusively in black, with black eye-shadow and black lipstick, not as an attempt at fancy dress but in collective mourning for River Phoenix. One person has misunderstood completely and come as a seagull, but at least everyone has made some kind of effort, except the Russians. Spencer finds it in his heart to forgive them. It makes them seem more exotic somehow, pooled in a defensive cluster in white shirts and wide black trousers. One of the girls surprises Spencer by looking straight back at him. She wears the regulation blouse and trousers, but from this distance Spencer can't tell if it's visible bras. She has dyed blonde hair, a very wide mouth and lots of gold jewellery. Being foreign, she holds his eye, but it's not for someone like her that he's spent hours rehearsing his original chat-up lines in the mirror at home.

He surveys the room, coughs into his hand. The teachers have chosen a live Country and Western band and Spencer pretends to hum along with a tune he doesn't recognise, maybe an instrumental version of *Let the Sun Shine In* or *Oklahoma* or *Bim Bam Bom* or something by Buddy Holly. He locates the target. To save time, Spencer has made the strategic decision only to try it on with Louise or Marianne or Lynne, the three girls from his year who are known (hundred and one percent certain) already to have let someone.

'Excuse me,' he says bravely to Marianne or Lynne or Louise, who peels away from the other two and says well hello there if it isn't the new boy with a skin problem.

'My sister's been chosen for the Olympic swimming team,' Spencer hazards, provoking a languid full-body examination.

'And my brother's the Pope.'

She giggles away with the others and Spencer curses himself, thinking he should have picked someone from the year below. He blames his Dad, who wouldn't give him any money to buy milk or orange or prune juice or whatever it is they're allowed to drink in here. If he doesn't first offer them a drink like they do on the telly (*Cracker*, *House of Cards*, *Clarissa Explains It All*), then obviously it looks bad. His Dad though, drunk as usual, just reminds Spencer of all the money he'll never earn as a snooker player (£60,000 a tournament) or a show-jumper (£15,000 and a car) or even a boxer (Frank Bruno or Oliver Macall or Lennox Lewis – seven million dollars a fight. One fight! Each fight! Seven *million* dollars!).

Spencer glances across at the Russian who confounds him by looking back again, not exactly smiling but not not smiling. He grins, thinking her eyes are nice, before choosing

107

Lynne this time, or Louise or Marianne, and asking her with cool abandon whether she was aware of his tragic separation at birth from his twin sister? The honest truth. Stolen, abducted, cruelly kidnapped from the cradle.

'Go on,' she says, chewing her gum very slowly, 'try me.'

'I thought you might be her,' Spencer says suavely, hopefully, desperately, anyway sticking to the script.

'Fraid not. I think you'll find she's in the Olympic swimming team.'

Another fit of giggles and then what the hell, the girls *heave* with laughter, as if together they comprise a single organism which feeds off the embarrassment of fifteen-year-old boys. Despite being made acutely aware of his position in this particular food-chain, Spencer has the traditional resilience of his kind (boys). He can withstand a setback or two because surely if his brother can manage it then so can he, and Philip has now proved beyond any doubt that he has sex with his plump wife Alison by making her pregnant. It's going to be a girl and it's due any day now, but just then Spencer notices, a little uncomfortably, that his Russian friend is still watching him. He turns away and draws strength from all those flawless rehearsals to make another approach to a briefly separated third of Louise or Marianne or Lynne. He says hi there again it's only me, and did you know that when you die your whole life flashes before your eyes?

'Before or after?'

'No. I mean. Important moments from your life flash before your eyes just before you die.'

'So what?'

'Now, if I die, you will always flash before my eyes.'

He looks at her expectantly. She shakes her head. Is that good? She walks away. That's not so good.

Spencer is left stranded, alone, but the world keeps turning because his best line he's saved until last. Perhaps he should keep it for later. He could try to have a normal conversation with someone. He could talk about his mother, for example, who wants to be ordained as a priest in the Church of England. He could describe how she's already been to see, without any luck, the Bishop of Birmingham and the Bride Valley Team Rector and the Substitute Chaplain at Belmarsh Prison and even, in a rare crisis of desperate optimism, the non-stipendiary curate-in-charge at St Oswald's. But even if this is all true it'll never work as a chat-up line, exactly because it's true.

A boy from the year below asks Spencer if he wants his caricature done. But apart from having no money, Spencer assumes he'll be drawn as teenage lust, with his eyes popping out and his tongue lolling, so he says no. He is tapped on the shoulder and he wishes death to all caricaturists, but in fact it's the Russian girl, with big grass-green eyes and a truly enormous mouth, her lips bold and shiny with bright red lipstick. She smiles with or between or around her wide even teeth. She is holding a can of Heineken, presumably a special concession to Russians. She offers it to Spencer and he takes it and drinks. She says:

'My name is Tidora Zhivkov.'

Spencer nods, and it's visible bras. He strays from the script and asks her what star sign she is.

'My name is Tidora Zhivkov.'

'I'm Scorpio,' he says, and then thinks why not, for all the luck he's having he might as well try out his last and best line on Tidora Zhivkov. He touches her arm, and she doesn't hit him so he guides her towards a corner. He tells her, his voice resonant with melancholy, that he once had a sister. He tells her the whole sad story, the championship medals unwon, the wasted talent, his own incurable grief. He falls silent and waits to be rescued.

'My name is Tidora Zhivkov,' the Russian girl says. She finishes the Heineken in one go, and then holds the back of Spencer's head and kisses him with her huge mouth. Her tongue tastes of lipstick and beer. She takes his hand and leads him from the gym, along empty corridors, and Spencer is grinning foolishly, meaninglessly, happily, trying to remember every moment of this so that he can describe it accurately later to Hazel.

It is an interesting thing to tell her, and they have fallen into the habit of telling each other interesting things.

11/1/93 MONDAY 10:48

Definitely a man's voice. It could have been her father or the landlord or a friend of the family. It was the gasman, who had no business answering the personal phone of a customer. A likely story. It was almost certainly a boyfriend, and Henry immediately despised him and was glad, because jealousy was among the best of signs. It was a safe way of knowing you were truly in love.

He had now arrived at the Central London Institute of Learning, and he'd been expecting something more impressive than this. Grander or quainter or older. Or simply more British. In its advert the school offered itself as a location, and he'd therefore imagined a façade easily cast into a BBC classic serial, instantly convincing as a Jane Austen town house or Kipling's London home. In fact the school buildings were long, flat, and mostly made of plastic in different colours, all of them fading. It was as if a series of temporary cabins had gradually evolved around a playground, following no recognisable pattern. But what surprised Henry most of all was that it actually seemed to be a school, a real one, with children in it.

Behind the gates, right to left bouncing a basketball, Iain Pike who would grow to seven feet tall and earn more than sixty-six million American dollars playing centre for the Orlando Magic. Left to right Alison Wood in a mini-skirt, outraged at being under-cast as a dancing cat in the school's production of *Cinderella*.

It wasn't what Henry had been expecting. Children made him nervous. He changed his umbrella and his M & S bag from one hand to the other and watched Mr David Brock of the British Bankers' Association, undeniably an adult with the unreleased Oceana Consolidated interims in his briefcase, turn in to the school and stride confidently across the playground.

Henry didn't know what to do. For inspiration, he summoned up a vision of Miss Burns from the clues in her voice. She was a strict bespectacled English rose, several years older than him, her greying hair tight in a schoolmarmish librarian's bun. She had a liking for tweed skirts, and a small black cat called Henry, although the name wasn't that important. As part of the miracle he expected from falling in love, Henry assumed she must be somewhere close. He therefore resolved to follow the courageous example of Mr Brock, who looked plausibly like someone who would want to learn at a distance, due to business commitments. Mr Brock walked straight across the playground, ignoring an unmissable arrow to Headmaster. Henry, hoping to avoid contact with children, followed these signs until he came to a door in a yellow plastic box which was genuinely a temporary cabin. Inside, the walls of an office were covered with term-planners exotically pocked with coloured pins, and behind a long desk there sat a broad woman with huge spectacles and wiry hair which quivered at the ends like antennae.

Henry asked in his most polite voice if she was the receptionist.

'I have a full PA role with the headmaster. Are you here for the reunion?'

He flashed her his distinctive smile. 'I'm distance learning.'

'We have nothing to do with that here.'

His smile wasn't having the best of days. He was brusquely informed that the school's only connection with the distance-learning centre was to provide it with a postal address. She pointed peremptorily at a tray containing a padded envelope, just like the ones he'd addressed so many times himself.

'I saw a man in a suit.'

'Business in the Community.'

However hard he tried, Henry found he couldn't imagine this woman having any life other than this, sat suspiciously behind her long untidy desk, obstructing him. He made sure of the powder in his pocket. He couldn't even invent her a name.

'Would you know anything of the whereabouts of the teachers?'

'Of course I do,' she said. 'Otherwise how could I send on the envelopes?'

'I'm trying to get in touch with Miss Burns.'

She said never, never under any circumstances did she give out home addresses, and Henry thought what about if I feed you enough poison to make your insides bubble? Remember Dr Osawa, Henry told himself, but he could invent no other life for this woman except as a victim of his urgent need to locate Miss Burns. With no name, and no life, she was hardly worth wasting the poison on, so perhaps instead he'd slip off one of his chunky oatmeal socks from Brook Street and strangle her with it until she told him what he wanted to know. Remember Dr Osawa. Or if that doesn't work, remember the difference between thinking a thing and doing it. Henry therefore postponed the woman's torture, and said he already knew where Miss Burns lived.

'Well you shouldn't do.'

'I was wondering if you had any other addresses for her. Parents. Special friends?'

He smiled again, hoping for everyone's sake that none of the friends were as special as all that.

'Absolutely not,' the woman said. 'No, no, no.'

Henry fingered the plastic envelope in his pocket. This woman had a life. Everybody did. She was personally responsible for the props (guns, lethal umbrellas, booby-trapped telephones, knives, more guns) needed for the hold-ups, police chases, hostage situations, kidnaps and drug-dealings which plagued the school whenever it was used as a location in films like *Lock Up Your Children* or *Fathers in Fear* or *Cracker*. The school was sometimes even used for school scenes, but only in *Casualty*.

The school buildings had more life for Henry than the woman, and he didn't need Dr Osawa to tell him that this wasn't healthy.

'About Miss Burns,' he said.

'There is absolutely no chance of me telling you any-thing.'

'We're supposed to be meeting for lunch. It's nearly lunchtime.'

'You don't fool me, you know.'

She gave Henry the benefit of a long, intolerant, anony-mous stare through her enormous glasses which magnified her eyes. 'I know your sort.' She pointed at him with a short fat finger. 'I wouldn't give you a woman's address in a million years. I can see straight through you.'

114

'I just want to know where she is, to confirm our lunch-date.'

'I bet you do.'

'Some people are nice. Not everybody's nasty.'

'I know what I know.'

If I was nicer than I am, Henry thought, or if I hadn't been ill and you had the least quality which inspired me to give you a life, I would pity you. As it is, I shall very probably push the tip of my new umbrella against your forehead until you fall backwards off your chair, fatally cracking your skull. After locating Miss Burns's file, I shall quietly bury the body in wasteground where nobody will find it for several months. It happens all the time. It's always in the paper.

Henry took a more decisive grip on the handle of his umbrella, when unexpectedly it came to him: Janet Kennedy, *unacknowledged* collaborator on *Baroque Needle-point*.

He let his grip loosen, he remembered Dr Osawa and calmed himself, turned on his heel, walked out. It was a relief to have invented Janet Kennedy just in time, but it was also a tragedy to have lost his best chance of finding Miss Burns. He ignored several children and whacked the concrete of the playground with the point of his umbrella. He swore at himself in Japanese. Back in the street, one two three people passed him by with no lives of their own so what did it matter what happened to them? Stabbing, kidnapping, mugging, shooting, poisoning: quotidian events because they happened every day to somebody, so why not to these random people today, whose lives he couldn't begin to imagine and who therefore meant nothing to him? He walked left, right, left again, not knowing where he was going, the possibilities of his own life receding with each step.

It started to rain, stinging him back to his senses and the here and now. He stopped walking and found himself alone, in a street he didn't recognise, feeling a devastation so complete its cause could only be love. He put up the umbrella between himself and the rain, wondering what to do next. He could catch the Circle Line back to the hotel, agree that his father was right, pack his bags and his diploma and board an aeroplane destination Dr Osawa. He could resign himself to his father's money and surprising presents which for the rest of his otherwise unchanging life would make tiny changes in his daily moods. He could grow old, unchallenged by miracles, untouched by lightning.

He stepped into the road between two parked cars and decided to try Miss Burns one last time. In a desperate final appeal for luck he whispered the sacred words, 'I love you'. Small words which changed entire lives, all the time, every day of the year.

He tapped out her number and it was answered almost immediately. A man's voice. Younger this time. Unsure of itself.

'I didn't know it was turned on. I haven't really used. Sorry, I thought it was turned off.'

Henry said he was hoping to get in touch with Miss Burns.

'Are you alright? You sound a bit wobbly.'

'It was today. I'm one of her students. It's planned we have lunch.'

'Where?'

'She told me to meet her there, except I've forgotten where there is.'

'Where where is?'

'Where there is.'

'Which is where?

'Where she is.'

'You mean here.'

'Yes,' Henry said, 'if she's there. She arranged it herself. It's my last day. It's been planned for ages. Please.'

'And who exactly are you?'

'I'm a very very good friend of hers.'

There was a pause in which Henry held his breath until the voice at the other end said yes, of course, he understood, these things happened. Nobody remembered everything, not even Miss Burns. He gave Henry an address, and then offered him the library as a landmark. He would know it when he saw it because the clock was permanently stopped at half past four.

———————

It is the first of November 1993 and somewhere in Britain, in Hayes or Sevenoaks or Sutton Coldfield or Dunvant, in Taunton or Newark or Kirkwall or Leeds, Hazel and her friends have transformed their school's Assembly Hall into the Viper Room. Sheets dyed black billow from the ceiling. Black and white posters lurk in the shadows, of Val Kilmer or Harvey Keitel or Dirk Bogarde, but mostly the Viper Room is River. River Phoenix, as was, in *Stand By Me* or *My Own Private Idaho* or *Mosquito Coast* or even *Indiana Jones and the Last Crusade*. The girls have turned their annual Hallowe'en party into a wake. They all wear black.

The teachers, however, have hired a jazz band. They want their girls to be nice girls, whereas the girls themselves prefer to be nasty. They hate this music. It's ridiculous, plain wrong, and worst of all, inauthentic. It is harmless and upbeat when everyone knows from newspapers that real life can only be recognised by its lack of niceness, and the real news is that River Phoenix lay abandoned outside the Viper Room on a West Hollywood pavement, drowning in his own vomit.

Hazel goes out into the maths block corridor and squeezes up against the card-phone. She slides in her card, John Lennon's eyes, and stiff-fingered she punches in the number. If Spencer isn't at home, she'll have sex with Sam Carter. Spencer's father answers, his speech slurred, and Hazel makes up a name. She is Grace Zabriskie. She is Helen Sharman just back from the moon, she is Emma Thompson wondering if Spencer fancies a quick one. No, she has no message. Yes, yes she does. How can he have deserted her like this?

Back in the Viper Room the boys are mostly dressed as extras from horror films, from *Dead Planet* or *Savage*

Harvest or *Terror on Highway 91*. Tastelessly, one of them has left a dummy of River's corpse slumped against the fire-door, but Hazel ignores it and looks at trousers and wonders if it's true that having sex changes your life. Then she wishes there was more than one way of finding out. She has a condom in her black bag, all squashed up and patient in its sharp little packet, waiting for its special moment.

She dismisses various boys with indifference, familiar with their clumsy advances. She tries in vain to look like the other girls, in black shoes, black mini-skirt, boil-washed black sweater, all in honour of River Phoenix for whom, tragically, there is no tomorrow. Hazel, however, is not like the other girls. On her fifteenth birthday, just when she thought things couldn't get much worse, she turned blonde overnight.

Sam Carter stands in front of her. He reaches out to the edge of his conversational range and says:

'Hello, Hazel.'

He has a nice wonky smile and Hazel has to admit he looks very fine in his tail-suit, like a vampire next best thing. He asks her if she remembers when he was fat. Has she noticed how much leaner he is?

'It's a miracle.'

'I work out in the gym,' he says, but let's get down to basics Hazel thinks. You want to lie on top of me and put it in. He looks shocked and Hazel realises she must have said this out loud. Whoops sorry well pardon me.

'But you do, don't you? That's what you want to do.'

Pathetically, Sam Carter pleads with Hazel to be nice to

him. He seems to think the evening has been pre-arranged as their special date.

'Another time, Sam.'

'Really?'

'I mean fuck off. Stop being so absurdly smiley all the time.'

Predictably, Olive has managed to crash the party, as if school rules don't apply to girls whose legs are paralysed. Before the accident, if Hazel remembers correctly, Olive was nothing like the person she's become, the go-anywhere, do-anything-twice girl. She likes boys and dangerous sports, as if any sense of fear vanished in the moment she discovered that disasters happen anyway, whether you're frightened or not. She is now collecting an audience as she goes through her fortune telling routine on the palm of a Ewan McGregor lookalike. He's falling for it even though Olive will soon be telling him he's destined for disaster. She always predicts disaster because otherwise no-one believes her, and she's already predicted that Hazel's first-time sex with the man she marries will be utterly disastrous, in the most extreme.

'Alright then you're right,' Sam Carter says, 'I admit to it.' His whole head flushes red to the roots of his blond hair. 'I do want to have sex with you. I find you very completely. I find you sexy alluring.'

'Are you drunk?'

'So what?'

'I don't know,' Hazel says. 'I don't think it makes much of a difference.'

Maybe Hazel should also get drunk. It'll be easier like that even if afterwards she won't remember it so well. It will make it less important somehow, and it seems careless to be drunk when her life's about to change for ever. Was it even possible to change your life if you were drunk? Sadly, probably, yes. It happens all the time.

Hazel waves Sam Carter away. She tells him to come back later. She'll have a think about it.

And there it is, she thinks, as she watches him walk away, sex on a plate. She wonders if there's a special type of divine retribution for people like her who feel the melancholy of good luck, which only the lucky can understand. Her easy victories seem banal against the chance of being touched closely and changed by car crashes. She regrets always coming out unscathed. She longs to be pale and interesting, truthful even, not blonde and very completely sexy alluring and in control, like now, when whatever happens is entirely her own decision.

She wishes that life, as it has with Olive, would show her who to be. She feels that home has nothing more to teach her, because if the world were really as frightening as her mother thinks then how would anyone live, how would they carry on from day to day? With the assistance of pre-scription drugs, is the lesson to be learnt from her mother. As for her father, he's always away in foreign countries convincing strangers that a single purchase can make all the difference.

If only Spencer was at home, waiting for the phone to ring. Then Hazel could forget how easy it all was: check none of the teachers are watching, kiss Sam Carter on the lips, take him somewhere quiet. Why wait? Spencer lives miles away, and she hasn't seen him since he was a child with no head wearing a single stripey glove. She doesn't even know what he looks like any more. She suspects, however, that he is somehow more real than her because his family has less money, and because he doesn't have a scholarship to a private school. She imagines that bad things happen to him all the time, just like on the television and in the newspaper.

Or perhaps it has nothing to do with Spencer and she's saving herself for River, or for Val Kilmer or Harvey Keitel. But River's dead and anyway, she should have grown out of that by now. It's time she started living in the real world.

Hazel steps over the slack corpse of the dummy River Phoenix, and pushes through the fire-door into the corridor. She feeds John Lennon's eyes into the mouth of the telephone and as she does so she hears footsteps behind her. She glances round and it's Sam Carter. She turns back to the telephone and he breathes on her neck. She punches in Spencer's number while Sam Carter, bolder, kisses the pulse behind her ear (Jesus!) and Hazel, waiting for the phone to be answered, has to do something. A decision won't solve all her problems, she knows that, but at least it solves the problem of indecision. And anyway, right or wrong the most it amounts to is a popular song.

Spencer's Dad answers the phone, and he tells her Spencer isn't back yet, but if it's that slut Emma Thompson again doesn't she have anything better to do?

'No,' Hazel says quietly. 'It's not Emma Thompson. It's no-one special.'

She hangs up.

———————

11/1/93 MONDAY 11:12

'This isn't turning out how I expected,' Spencer said. 'I was hoping we could have the whole day to ourselves.'

Hazel had found him sulking in the office, a small room at the front of the house with two chairs on wheels and an IBM on the desk. Next to the computer there was a colourful row of game-boxes. *Asterix and the Great Rescue* and *Mephisto Chess* and *TOCA Shoot-Out Touring Cars* and *PGA European Tour Golf.* Spencer often hid himself in the office, spending long hours sitting at the computer like a working person.

'God knows why he had to choose today, of all days.'

'It's not his fault, Spencer. He's had a shock.'

William had gone upstairs (second floor, front) to watch television. At this time of the morning he had a four-channel choice between *Good Morning with Anne and Nick* or *Day-time on Two* or *This Morning* or *Time for Maths.* Hazel had checked the paper, in case William ended up watching something which made outside seem even worse. She reckoned he was safe enough.

'You shouldn't worry about him,' Spencer said. 'He's a tough old bird. He's fine as long as he stays indoors, or in the garden.'

'And in my opinion he'll be fine outside, as soon as he knows what to expect.'

'And in your opinion we can have a baby, no trouble.'

'It's got nothing to do with that.'

Both her opinions were stupid, in Spencer's opinion. She seemed to have forgotten that Britain was a huge place. There were four separate countries involved and every day it was different, so how could they tell William what it was like? Which town or time of day or region or event best represented the whole? If William was disappointed by Britain, then outside the front door it was only one street in London, and it wouldn't be accurate to suggest that this was all there was.

'We can't give him a history of the whole country,' Spencer said.

'You could start with the people.'

'What people? The only person I'm qualified to talk about is myself.'

'There you are then.'

Hazel irritably flicked a speck from the shoulder of her dress. Spencer said: 'This isn't about William, is it?'

'It was supposed to be our special day.'

In that case, Spencer could have asked, why did you arrange to have lunch with an old friend? Instead, he betrayed a complete ignorance of women by looking at his watch. In less than an hour he had to fetch his niece from the bus stop, and he still hadn't bought her a present. She was only ten, and he didn't want her walking into the middle of an argument, especially on her birthday. It was therefore about time he and Hazel sorted themselves out.

'About this baby,' he said. 'What are we going to do?'

Hazel looked away, like someone who needed to count very slowly to ten. She covered her front teeth with her tongue and put her hands on her hips. She actually tapped her foot. Then she turned back to face him, unblinking.

'Who's this Jessica woman?'

'Who?'

'I think you heard me the first time. Jessica.'

'Nobody. She's not anybody.'

'That's not what William seems to think.'

'I don't know anyone called Jessica.'

'Come on, Spencer.'

'I promise you. I don't.'

'The name means nothing to you?'

'For God's sake, Hazel,' Spencer said. 'Half a day and you're already possessive.'

He didn't mean it. Or he did mean it but he didn't mean to say it. Or he didn't mean to say it quite like that. Or he had no idea what he meant to say. They let it hang there between them. They circled round it, Hazel moving from the desk to the chair to the desk. She said:

'I never expected you to be like this.'

There was a brief moment in which they could have stepped back from here, and away from the many things it was always possible to say which were usually best left unsaid.

'In what way, exactly?'

Well, for a start, there was his annoying habit of looking elsewhere when he spoke to her. There was his sporadic sense of humour. She would also like to explain, very slowly

125

so he'd be sure to understand, that a little tenderness was due when they woke up naked together in the same bed. It wasn't generally considered good manners to rush straight out for a morning-after contraceptive pill.

'I expected you to be more worldly,' she said. 'I thought you'd know that it doesn't literally have to be taken the morning after. You didn't have to panic quite so much.'

'I knew that,' Spencer said. 'And I wasn't panicking. I was increasing our options.'

'You had to ask at the library. I couldn't believe it. And what would Jessica make of all this? I presume she'd have an opinion.'

'It's not what you think,' Spencer said, looking down, relieved to see Hazel's feet still in his best socks. All the same, he was absolutely certain that Jessica would never have put him in a position like this. He stared at the blank computer screen, remembering all the times he'd crashed and burned on the track.

'I have to go out,' he said.

'Don't run away, Spencer.'

'I have to get a present for my niece.'

'You'll know what she wants of course,' Hazel said, and because he still refused to look at her she couldn't help the meanness that crept into her voice. 'You the renowned expert on what girls want.'

'She wants a horse,' Spencer said, no surrender. 'I read it somewhere. All girls her age want a horse.'

'You're getting her a horse then?'

'Of course I'm not. What's the matter with you?'

'Why won't you tell me about Jessica?'

'When did you give me the chance?'

Ideally, Spencer would have liked to climb down from here, a rung at a time. He would step down from her carelessness in sex to her infuriating attitude of hands up I'm the scholarship girl. Back down again to the way she knew what was best for William after knowing him for at least forty minutes, and down once more to the way she borrowed his socks and library books without asking, an annoyance so close to rung zero it was almost solid ground.

There was, however, no climbing down.

'Presumably,' Spencer said, 'if we're destined to spend our lives together I can tell you whatever I want?'

'It doesn't work like that.'

Hazel's lips quivered at the edges. Her hair curled to the inside where it touched her shoulders, something Spencer hadn't noticed before. He said:

'If you want to leave I won't stop you.'

'I might be pregnant with your baby.'

'But probably you're not.'

'You're right. Probably I'm not. Nothing will change and our lives will go on exactly as they were, except without the possibility of you and me. Is that what you want?'

'I want to go out,' Spencer said.

'Who's Jessica?'

'Forget about Jessica. Who's Henry?'

'Henry who?'

'Your Henry. Henry who's coming here for lunch.'

6

It beats having beans, for instance (5).

THE TIMES 11/1/93

11/1/93 MONDAY11:24

To be alive was glorious! The way everything could change so quickly! This was much better than money, and there was positively no better time or place to be alive than here in London on the first day of November 1993, following the road towards the woman he loved. Henry had decided to walk, calculating that he'd arrive at the library at the latest by noon, or perhaps quarter past. It had even stopped raining.

He doffed an imaginary hat to Gerald Davies, Rugby Union legend and journalist for *The Times*, to Jessica Brown, a spokeswoman for the Consumers' Association, and to Martin Purves, a city surveyor who'd handled the sale of the former Billingsgate market. Ever since leaving the hotel Henry had sensed that Miss Burns was somewhere close, and it turned out that he was right. He took it as a sign, a good omen, and it occurred to him that luck was just a question of finding and following what was already destined. He definitely felt lucky. He looked for a betting shop and immediately found a William Hill. In the doorway lay Matthew Beeston, former director-general of the National Economic Development Office, dressed as a beggar in a bath-robe tied with string. Henry stepped daintily around him.

Inside the betting shop a row of televisions was jammed into the angle between wall and ceiling. Half of them were running a preview of tomorrow's Melbourne Cup, while the others listed the afternoon's runners at Newcastle and Plumpton and Southwell.

The only other person in the shop was John Maxey, more commonly known as Mad Dog. He was chewing on a very short pencil while watching the Irish St Leger runner-up, *Drum Taps*, prance for some Australians in the paddock at Flemington. The set of John Maxey's face, bored but hostile but indifferent, reminded Henry of the wasteground outside Wakefield and the fireworks at Aintree, but this was no time to falter. He was doing this for Miss Burns, because a man needed money of his own if he was going to get married, and with enough money he could live wherever he liked. This was an unwritten international law properly sanctioned by very rich people who wanted to live in Geneva. Henry therefore took a deep breath and tried to ignore John Maxey,

Mad Dog, son of the former Romford Raiders' coach, with a tattoo on his fore-arm saying *Oberhof*.

For last-minute luck Henry crossed his fingers and closed his eyes and recalled his vision of Miss Burns. Older, English rose, spectacles from reading so much, small affectionate cat and hair in a schoolmarmish bun. Greying hair, or brown hair, or she had black, blonde, red hair. She was rich, virtuous, fair, mild, noble, of good discourse, an excellent musician (woodwind), and her hair could be of whatever colour it pleased God. It didn't really matter, although it would be nice to be right about the cat.

He went over to the ticket-window where Clive Milnes, veteran bookie and former member of the Ulster Defence Regiment, waited to take his bet. Henry glanced back at the TV screens, but the display had changed again, switching to a promotion of some of the wilder bets always on offer to the reckless. You could bet on anything in Britain: the chances of sighting rare birds or the probable dates of the deaths of famous people. You could speculate on the date of an Irish ceasefire, or the length to the second of the Queen's Christmas speech, or the recent employment history and physical condition of Elvis. It was as if life was only a wager where nothing was ever certain. Some things were more possible or more plausible than others, obviously, but all these bets created the impression that nothing was ever impossible: you could probably put money on it.

At this point, Henry would have liked to stake all his father's money on the long-shot of getting engaged to Miss Burns by the end of the day. It would be a way of showing faith, as if he could make it happen just by having the courage to make the bet on it. Following the same principle he would make several side-bets, even at longish odds, that the first man to answer the phone had been an old and harmless friend of the family. As for the second man, the younger one, Henry would bet it was just a boy delivering a pizza, or maybe a younger brother. He would bet, anyway, that it was a voice of no importance.

The afternoon horses for Newcastle were back on the screen, and Henry pushed most of his father's bundle under the grille for the unfancied *Mr Confusion* in the High Society Rated Handicap at 2.30. Clive Milnes, bookie, former UDR man, father of five, said:

'That's a lot of money.'

'It's my lucky day.'

'Then it can't be mine.'

Clive Milnes, bookie, former UDR, father of five, often dreamt he was an astronaut. He licked his thumb and counted the notes. Conversationally, because the British people liked a bit of conversation, Henry asked him if he thought *Mr Confusion* had a chance.

'Everyone has a chance, my friend. However, if this horse comes home a winner I'd call it a miracle.'

'Miracles happen though, don't they?'

'It is not unknown. Unfortunately.'

Clive Milnes, bookie, UDR man, father of five, dreamer of outer space, coveter of the new Peugeot 405, wished he had this much money to put on a horse. He pushed Henry's ticket back under the partition.

Mad Dog John Maxey, son of the former Romford Raiders' coach, *Oberhof* tattoo (fore-arm), recently charged with Grievous Bodily Harm, looked up sharply and asked Henry how he planned to spend his winnings. At which point Matthew Beeston, former director-general of the NED, dressed as a beggar, pursued by the Child Support Agency, fell through the door and just about managed to stay on his feet. He swayed alarmingly, trying to focus on Henry, and the TV screens, and then both at the same time. John Maxey, Mad Dog, son of the Romford Raiders' coach, *Oberhof*, charged with GBH, set free by the Crown Prosecution Service, stood up and shoved him back out to the street. Then he focused his attention exclusively on Henry.

'Nice holiday maybe? The Algarve. Lovely. Malta's not bad at this time of year.'

Henry wanted to be outside again, away from the accumulating, distracting, demanding weight of the full lives of other people. He wanted to concentrate on the ideal future he planned to enjoy with Miss Burns, where holidays would be intimate affairs somewhere at the British seaside, involving a little inshore yachting and idle games of bowls and special trips at dawn to catch crabs from the local sandbanks.

'Well where then?' said John Maxey, Mad Dog, son of the former Raiders' coach, *Oberhof*, GBH, freed by the CPS, bound over to keep the peace, and casual nutcase. 'Back home is it?'

Henry remembered Belfast, and it suddenly seemed vitally important to avoid all the terrible avoidable things which

133

could happen to him before he met Miss Burns. Now was not the time to be the victim of an arbitrary stabbing, or to be run over or stoned or kidnapped or poisoned or fall from a high place, nor for that matter to be hit by fireworks or attacked by a lunatic racist.

He quickly backed out of the shop, and immediately collided with Matthew Beeston, former director-general of the NED, dressed as a beggar, pursued by the CSA, who only needed a handful of coppers to see himself right again. Henry peeled off most of what was left of the money and gave it to him, just in case there was a God watching. He couldn't afford to be picked out and punished by untimely lightning, not now that Miss Burns was so close.

After he met her it would all be different, of course. She was going to save him from all this.

It is the first of November 1993 and somewhere in Britain, in Ipswich or Harrow or Walsall or Llanelli, in Ilkeston or North Walsham or Motherwell or Leigh, Hazel Burns has given up boys. She is sixteen. To replace the excitement of the opposite sex she has embarked on a life of crime, and as often as once a week she takes a bus into the town centre where she steals money from kind old people and students. It couldn't be easier. She has her own collection box and depending on what's in the news she attaches a sticker for the *Leukaemia Research Fund* or *Mencap* or *Corda* or *Help*

134

the Aged or the *Webb Orphan's Fund.* The trick is to smile brightly and project the image of suffering children, who would all smile as brightly if only they could. Most eager to be robbed are casual acquaintances of the family who vaguely remember Hazel's disabled sister, and unhappy students who look at her breasts. Towards the end of the afternoon, Hazel empties her collection box and launders the loose change by taking it to the Post Office to buy phonecards.

'It's good to have a hobby,' her Dad says, too busy to see it's not a collection.

It is now early evening on an overcast Monday in November, and it seems a long time since Hazel's last adventure in crime. Sitting in a new and bigger (Dad is Salesperson of the Year '93: china cormorants) but otherwise familiar front room, Hazel watches her mother hunched over the desk scrutinising recent bank statements from Lloyds or Midland or Natwest or the TSB. Hazel stays well out of range, sorting phonecards in thematic order on the coffee table. She asks if anything shows up yet.

'I can't see anything.'

'If he was having an affair it would show up somewhere in his bank statements.'

Hazel's mother is in need of drugs, of tranquillisers or uppers or downers. She angrily swipes a stack of statements off the desk and yells at Hazel.

'You know a damn sight too much, young lady! Go to your room!'

And then just as suddenly her face creases and she rushes

135

over to the sofa to apologise. Hazel keeps on grouping the cards because these mood-swings are nothing new, inspired as they are by the pills in the bathroom in packets marked Valium or Mogadon or Methydrine or Amitryptolene. They can make her mother lose track of what she's supposed to be feeling. 'Marriage is a ritualised alliance,' she unexpectedly says. 'It's like a sports team.'

'Do sports teams make people happy?'

'I never expected to be happy.'

Hazel stands up. She says she's going for a walk.

'Why?'

'Fresh air. You know, the great outdoors.'

'Don't speak to me like that.'

'To play in traffic, talk to strangers, the usual.'

Her mother snatches up the newspaper and slaps it with the back of her hand. She hopes Hazel knows what she's doing, because no-one wants to see her end up as the next *Drug Coma Girl Dies* girl.

And with this familiar warning ringing in her ears Hazel pulls on her overcoat, stuffs a pocket full of miscellaneous phonecards, and steps out into a light drizzle which is always about to stop. She can take several different routes to a choice of phone-boxes, depending on whether she wants to walk through the new Wimpey or Barratt or McAlpine showhomes and out into the country, or past the MGM Warner UCI Odeon multiplex and from there into town. It doesn't matter much because she knows all the routes by heart, and time passes uneventfully as she thinks of other things, like perhaps her mother is right and her father has love affairs all the time, or even worse, one big love affair which never ends. It seems unlikely, considering all the time he spends selling instant chicken soup in Jerusalem or yarmulkas in bulk to New York mayoral campaigns. Perhaps he's having an affair abroad with someone who doesn't speak English, if that counts, but it's more likely that he's simply far too busy. And besides, nothing shows up on his bank statements.

She turns right at the multiplex showing *The Piano* and *Mr Wonderful* and *The Fugitive* and *Dragon: The Bruce Lee Story*. Decisions, decisions. Even though she's only sixteen, Hazel has all sorts of decisions to make, like should she change her A-levels and does she want to take a gap year before going to University? Does she love Sam Carter? She sometimes sleeps with him, but this is mainly statistics: most girls her age are doing it. She hasn't made the subsequent decision to turn it into love, which she believes is no more than a decision made or not made, depending on personal preference and the time of your life. No thunderbolts for her and Sam then, though Hazel often finds herself wishing for a more romantic type of romantic love, which would happen to her whether she liked it or not.

She is now waiting outside the phone-box (a fumbling, bent-backed, white-haired old lady is inside, of the type Hazel routinely robs of a Saturday). It's still raining but Hazel likes to wait in the rain. Being rained on is authentic, as is feeling a slight chill because this is November and winter's on its way. In mild discomfort she senses the residue of real life which concentrates itself in the sharper pains

137

reported every day of the week in newspapers. Real life is everything which isn't her undramatic and comfortable existence, and she finds crime authentic precisely because it feels out of character. She often thinks back to the car crash, if only to reassure herself that at least once she knew a moment of real life sensation, but the crash also reminds her of Olive as she is now, swimming in championships, exploring waterfalls, trying to get in contact with a disabled luge team. She stays out late overnight and rolls home drunk in the morning, sozzled on real life ever since she realised it made no difference whether she cared or not. In fact it makes a huge difference: not caring looks like a lot more fun.

Out comes the old lady ('All yours, my dear') and in goes Hazel, sheltering inside the glass box with its glass sides, the rain needling its way past the scratches of *Laura loves Gary 2* and *Elliot Dies Tonight* and *Utd 1 QPR 1*. The rain is in the trees and under the tyres of cars as Hazel arranges a selection of phonecards on top of the telephone. She likes to buy picture-cards showing minority sports (bowls, yachting, ice hockey, basketball), or famous British people no-one's ever heard of (Edmund Blunden, Helen Sharman, Spencer Perceval, Alfred Mynn) or illustrated domestic advice (Phone Home!) or sometimes even poetry (*wavering blue floor of a skiff in the field's river softens a gash of red down the slant wreck of brick*). Hazel always keeps the cards after they're used up. Each one is like a solid artefact left over from her rebellion against her mother, as she carelessly talks to a stranger for dangerous ages which she can later take home and measure in units. If it wasn't for her mother's paranoia, Hazel could have made these calls from home. But her mother tends to listen in on the extension, convinced Hazel only ever speaks to drug-dealers or young men who mend motorcycles.

She selects a card with a seagull on it advertising a holiday in Malta and feeds it into the machine. Spencer answers the phone himself and there are no introductions, no hums and has, just him talking and her talking, his words and hers spinning each other to ground. They talk about yesterday, today, tomorrow, they play games, they gravely and not so gravely discuss the meaning of life. Hazel wants to know if Spencer thinks she should take a gap year, and then has to explain what it is.

'Is this before or after we meet up?' Spencer wants to know.

But Hazel isn't going to risk ruining it all by actually meeting him. Spencer will take one look at her body and her blonde hair and he'll want to put it in, just like all the others. Instead she tells him that the real meaning of destiny, the way they both keep moving round the country, would be a chance meeting in a place neither of them had ever been before. 'We probably wouldn't even recognise each other.'

'Of course we would.'

'Why would we?'

'We just would.'

'You know why I like talking to you, Spencer?'

'Because I ravish you with my voice.'

'Because we don't have to worry about sex. We can just

be friends, really just friends, and nothing gets in the way of that.'

Sometimes, although rarely, silences come between them.

———————

11/1/93 MONDAY 11:48

Time for Maths, financial special. There was a mathematical difference between the interest calculations made for gilts, bonds, and German bunds. There was a way to calculate yields by using consensus forecasts of expected inflation. Using the ex-MIPS measure, real yields on long gilts could be calculated by subtracting current inflation from nominal yields.

'Are you following any of this?'

'Not a word.'

Hazel stood up and turned it off.

'What we need is a good film,' William said. 'The skipper of a merchant vessel vows revenge when his ship is sunk by a U-boat in a neutral port.'

'Sorry?'

'You know the kind of thing.'

Along with the television, the room's token furniture included a single bed, a chair, and the Rowlandson Hazel had noticed earlier. William had closed the curtains, but otherwise he'd recovered from the more obvious effects of his panic attack.

140

'I was hoping we could have a chat,' Hazel said.

'About Jessica?'

Hazel rolled her eyes at the name, but yes, it was Jessica she wanted to chat about. She wanted to know where she really stood with Spencer. If he was in love with someone else then she was only fooling herself by staying. It also made sense, now that she knew he was coming, to leave before Henry Mitsui arrived. Or Mad Henry, as she used to think of him when he was still her student.

She went to the curtains and parted them slightly to look down at the road.

'Well go on then,' William said. 'Open them if you want to.'

She hesitated and William came over and opened them himself. He looked grimly down at the grey street.

'I was expecting another panic attack,' Hazel said.

'Not through a window. It's the same as watching television.'

'Tell me what you see.'

'Some parked cars. Some cars moving. People. Shops. Jepson's Piano Sale Not On.'

Hazel interrupted him, realising he'd just found a way to cure himself. All he had to do was step outside and pretend that everything was television.

'Tried it,' William said.

'And?'

'JEPSON'S PIANO SALE NOT ON!! There turned out to be a difference between real life and television.'

Hazel pointed out her car, and thought of home and a

change into more comfortable clothes. It was supposed to be easier than this, more certain. One of the main advantages of Spencer's Damascus, if it ever happened, was that afterwards there couldn't be a great deal of doubt involved.

'You know what you were saying earlier?' William asked, hoping she remembered. When she didn't reply he sniffed and wiped at his nose. 'About me going outside. You said it wasn't such a big problem.'

'That's what I said.'

'Did you mean it?'

'Tell me about Spencer and Jessica.'

'I couldn't,' William said. 'I can't. I don't know what to say.'

'Tell me what she's like.'

'Honestly?'

'Honestly.'

'She's just about perfect.'

'Really?'

'Really.'

'Well that would explain a lot of things,' Hazel said, not really knowing what it explained.

'He gets on your nerves, doesn't he?' William said.

Hazel watched two women having a chat in front of the music shop. 'I wanted him to be nicer.'

'He didn't tell you about Jessica, did he?'

'I thought if we got through today we might be alright.'

'I know the feeling,' William said. 'It looks like we both picked the same special day.'

'I was certain we could make a go of it.'

'Nothing's certain. People get hit by lightning.'

'Maybe I should go home,' Hazel said, and then: 'Why is everyone so *frightened* all the time?'

The end of the century was turning everyone into her mother, and it made Hazel furious. If Spencer wasn't so frightened he wouldn't be so pathetic and ineffectual, refusing to commit himself to the other side of the road for fear of being run over. Chicken.

'About Jessica,' Hazel started again, but this time William interrupted her.

'You really think I could go outside? Nobody else seems to think so.'

'Who's nobody else?'

'My brother. Spencer. They say I can't get to grips with the present tense. They say it's all changed since my day.'

'Not that much.'

'But it *is* more difficult now, isn't it?' William said. 'It's more violent out there, more unpredictable.'

'It is in films.'

'No, in real life.'

'You mean in newspapers.'

'I mean in real life.'

Hazel knew what William meant, but she didn't agree with him. Unsavoury things happened, of course they did. They were in the news every day and they were invincible, but the light they shed was unequal to their prominence. At least she hoped this was true, because otherwise how would people get anywhere? Where would they find the courage to move on?

'Could you really help me go outside?' William said. 'Do you really believe I could do it?'

'I don't know,' Hazel said. 'I haven't got time. I think I'd better go home now.'

'Don't.'

'There's not much point staying.'

'About Jessica,' William said. 'This is important. When I said she was perfect, that isn't exactly what I meant.' He stopped and winced, as if the words he wanted to use were all nastily mis-shaped. 'Not that she isn't perfect, of course.' He put both hands on top of his head and walked to the other end of the room and back again.

'William, are you feeling alright?'

'The thing is, I mean the true thing is, she doesn't exist.'

'Sorry?'

'We made her up. She's a figment of our imagination. That's why she's perfect. She has every colour hair and any kind of eyes. She's tall, short, a super-brain, thick as can be. It's because she's anything we like that's she's always perfect. See?'

'You mean there is no Jessica.'

'Well there is a Jessica, yes, but she's not real.'

'Which is exactly what Spencer told me.'

'It's my fault. It was me who kept bringing her up. I wanted to put you off.'

'Why?'

'I was frightened of you. I didn't want you to take Spencer away.'

'And what changed your mind?'

144

'You said you could help me.'

'Come over here,' Hazel said. 'Take a look at this.'

There was no Jessica. This didn't mean she forgave Spencer everything, but at least it was a start. She went over to the Rowlandson and waited until William was standing behind her, looking at it over her shoulder. It was a simple drawing of an eighteenth-century highwayman robbing a carriage, but for some time the two of them looked at it attentively and without saying anything, as if, like abstract painting, it had something important to tell them which they could never hope to find out for themselves.

Hazel told William to describe it.

'What?'

'What you see.'

It's once upon a time, he reckons, a century or so ago. A mounted masked highwayman with a pistol leans into the window of a two-seater horse-drawn carriage. He threatens a fat prosperous man whose hysterical wife offers up a gold necklace and begs for mercy. The coachman, or it might be another thief, sits on one of the two horses harnessed to the carriage, holding them still with a whip. There are some clouds in the background and some bushes in the foreground.

'That's it,' William said. 'Why?'

'Who made the carriage?' Hazel asked him. William shrugged, and then she asked him what was the name of the highwayman and how much did a horse cost and what was the name of the horse? Was the painting an original? When was it painted and how much was it worth and who painted it? How old was he and was he married and did he have any children? What were their names then?

'I have no idea,' William said. 'It's just a picture on a wall.'

'The point is,' Hazel said, 'you don't have to know everything about it to know what's going on.'

Sometimes it was better not to know, she said, and to block off large sections of life. It wasn't a case of pretending they didn't exist, just of realising they weren't always immediately relevant.

'Isn't that a bit sad?'

'Some things you just have to ignore,' Hazel said.

'And you think this could work for me, when I go outside?'

'You mustn't let real life overwhelm you.'

'You're right,' William said. 'And I'm sorry. But sometimes I find it overwhelming.'

It is the first of November 1993 and somewhere in Britain, in Kettering or Glasgow or Worksop or Porthmadog, in Goring-by-Sea or Andover or Rochdale or Ely, Spencer Kelly is testing his final assessed project from his favourite GCSE. He has perfected it over the summer in remote phone-boxes, a different one each time, and to cover his movements he sometimes cycles miles into the countryside.

He waits until he's inside the phone-box before taking it

out of his Adidas or Umbro or Diadora sports bag. The device has two connected steel pincers which he fits round the side of the phone. Where the pincers hinge there is a hole into which Spencer screws a steel bar. He aligns this with the lock in the middle of the cashbox and begins to tighten it using a jack-handle. As he waits for the lock to give way under pressure, he reassures himself that these days nobody uses public phones except old poor people and teenage lovers. He therefore isn't hurting anybody and it's hardly even a crime. Originally it wasn't even his idea. He was inspired by an Act of God, and that's the honest truth.

The first time: he is using a phone-box in a lay-by beside a wide expanse of agricultural land. It is cold, Novemberish weather and in the recently ploughed fields seagulls flock and caw over the turned earth. Spencer runs out of money. Hazel is disconnected, and like every other time there's something very important Spencer still has to say to her. He curses and thumps the phone, and suddenly coins start pouring out of the return slot, faster and faster, bouncing off the concrete floor like a jackpot. He collects all these coins which belong to no-one and phones Hazel back again. He talks to her for ages. He still doesn't tell her whatever it was which was so important, but that's not the point, is it?

Hazel asks him what will happen when he runs out of money for good, and the next time Spencer visits a phone-box he takes along a hand drill. Eventually, but mostly during metalwork class, he develops this much more efficient tool of his own design. He gives the steel bar another turn, increasing the pressure on the lock, not hurrying because

147

he's miles from anywhere with no reason to rush home. Since his mother left, he and his father live on a simple diet of packet-soup and beans, which his Dad supplements with Macallan and cans of Stones or Heineken or Boddingtons.

'And another thing!' his father shouts as his mother leaves the house for the last time (throwing a full can of beer at the already closed door and then another at the embroidery above the fireplace), 'The meek shall *not* inherit the earth!'

Spencer's mother, rejected for ordination, proves she still believes in miracles by telling Spencer he's destined for great things. She says that a belief in miracles is at the centre of Christianity and therefore Western civilisation, which is why she spends most of her time now in airports, in Manchester or Glasgow or Heathrow, trying to save Kurds or Iraqis or Pakistanis from deportation to godless places like Turkey or Iraq or Pakistan. This, she tells Spencer, is the role she has been chosen to play in the great connected scheme of things, and she invites him to join her.

'You don't want to end up like your father, do you?'

Pop. A sigh almost, as if the lock of the cash compartment gives way willingly. It swings open and Spencer carefully builds columns of large denomination coins on top of the telephone, for immediate use. It is Hazel's mother who answers, so Spencer says it's Sam Carter for Hazel. (He once put on an Irish accent, just to scare her, but she cut him off.) Whenever Hazel's younger sister picks up he tells her it's the Pope or the Home Secretary or someone else scary like Anthony Hopkins. This is their code, and he and Olive like a little joke together. Hazel's father never answers.

Spencer pushes in more coins, waiting for Hazel to come to the phone. Today he wants to tell her about his brother Philip, whose wife Alison gave birth only this morning to a baby girl. They have decided to call her Rachel, and Spencer is still trying to recover from the shock of his brother's stupidity. He is safely married. He has a dull but secure job at Computeach International or the Clydesdale Bank or the Equal Opportunities Commission, so why go and ruin it all by openly flaunting the gods and calling his daughter Rachel? Spencer intends to call her by some other name, although he could have discussed this in greater detail with Hazel if Hazel knew that Rachel was dead. Rachel his sister he means. Whenever Hazel asks about his family Spencer says they're fine fine and his sporting sister she's fine too, and then they move on to something else. Now he doesn't know how to explain it to her without making it sound like a chat-up line.

And here is Hazel saying 'Hi Sam' and sharing some nice-sounding problems about how to amuse herself with her Dad's money before University qualifies her to prosper as a doctor or lawyer or business person. Even her problems reinforce Spencer's idea that wherever Hazel is and whatever she's doing is better than being where he is, doing nothing much except rob phone-boxes. His own life seems so banal to him that he hopefully attributes significance to other people's lives in general, and to Hazel's in particular. She has a scholarship to a private school. She's going to University, and now he's desperate to meet her before it's too late, before success takes her up and away from him and into outer space.

She always puts him off. She says maybe next year, when they can both drive. In the meantime she suggests sending a photograph, and Spencer fingers an incipient boil on his nose.

'We could do that,' he says, and changes the subject by suggesting they play one of Hazel's games. Apart from Geography Endings, which can go on for ever, they tend to make up rules and games as they go along. One of their favourites is Right Now, where the person in the phone-box has to describe exactly what they can see through the phone-box window, right now exactly as they're describing it. Today, however, they end up playing If Countries Were People Who Wouldn't You Marry? Ireland, definitely not, Russia, Iraq, Israel. England. This leads on to Greatest Living Briton, and while Hazel compares the achievements of Helen Sharman and Frank Bruno, Spencer finds himself wondering why he can't just meet her, settle down, and live happily ever after. He loves her, of course, and she's beautiful even if he doesn't know what she looks like, just as he knows she's rich without knowing how much money she has.

In fact, Spencer is already taking steps to make himself worthy of her. At the library he now heads straight for Fiction A–Z, and Jane Austen or Jack London or Henry Miller. He never knew there was so much in it. He always keeps some of the phone-box money to buy a daily newspaper of the improving kind, and is constantly fed visions of public glory in writing, acting, politics, and even sport (he'd please his father yet). On the whole he tends towards a preference for Spencer Kelly: actor. This is probably because he still likes watching television more than reading books, but also because Hazel might reasonably be expected to love a successful actor. He'll then be able to tell her about his sister Rachel, and if it still sounds like a chat-up line he imagines he'll manage to live with it. After the falling in love there comes the happily ever after in Suffolk or Sussex or Shropshire, with a surprisingly large town house off the King's Road in London. They wouldn't actually do very much. They'd live like retired rockstars or top chefs between restaurants.

Spencer also decides, if he's serious about becoming an actor (and he seriously wants to impress Hazel), that he'll have to go to London. He knows how it goes. You arrive an unknown, usually by coach or train, then hang around for a while waiting for your lucky break. Probably you take on a colourful but menial part-time job, for biographical reasons. Then you get sighted in a public place by Polanski or Minghella or Jane Campion, and the next day you wake up a somebody. It's London and you're an overnight success and it happens all the time. It's a miracle. It's Damascus.

'So Helen Sharman then,' Hazel says. 'How much money have you got left?'

Spencer looks at his columns of coins and says he has a little while. He asks her open-ended questions and presses the phone hard against his ear until her voice seems to be coming from inside his head. He wills her to keep on talking, suddenly frightened for the frailty of his connection to a wider world.

———

11/1/93 MONDAY 12:12

Outside in the street again, disappointed by the pearl-grey cover of unmoving cloud, Spencer despaired of ever seeing any meaningful weather. A convoy of circus trucks was jammed in the road. Bright paint on the sides of the vans announced *Billy Smart's Strongman* and *Aladdin's Lamp* and *The Charlie Chaplin Clowns* and *Il Mago the Magician*. The convoy crawled forward and stopped again. Now, with the prospect of a family to support, Spencer wouldn't be running away with the circus. Nor would he be looking out for a Jessica to invite back to lunch. He would have to resist buying a plane ticket to somewhere romantic, with romance in mind, or impulsively ordering a horse for his niece, because such fanciful notions were only possible yesterday, back in the good old days.

Hazel wanted him to make the decision to move on to tomorrow, and Spencer wandered along the high street still praying for signs and a sudden revelation, in which everything instantly connected and it all made sense and he would *know* what to do next. And then he thought that to have the road to Damascus experience you probably had to be on the

152

road. He should go travelling, to Malta, the Algarve, even Syria, anywhere it was common knowledge that even the ugly women were beautiful and many of them were Russian, or the equivalent. It wasn't because he didn't like Hazel. In fact she was as good-looking as any girl he'd ever met. She was also kind and funny and clever. It was just that he still wanted to flirt with the infinitely tantalising possibility of all the girls and off-duty nurses he *hadn't* yet met. He didn't understand how she could make a decision before a) seeing a sign, or b) knowing everything about his past, especially if they were going to have a baby and make a life together. But the question, put simply, remained: was he ready to step into the future with Hazel?

He didn't know.

He wanted the eight-year-old Rachel hands-on-knees feeling. He wanted the what will be will be, thinking that with big decisions like these there really oughtn't to be so much choice. That, in short, big decisions should present themselves as no decision at all.

At the bus stop Spencer was unsurprised to see the lime trees still bleeding their sticky black unlucky stuff. Bad luck. Bad omens: Hazel had been acting very strangely just before he came out. It was as if she didn't want to be left alone in the house, even though William was always around somewhere.

'It's Henry Mitsui,' she said. 'The man you talked to on the phone.'

'What about him?'

'Nothing.'

'What?'

'Nothing. Forget about it.'

Out loud, she told herself it was wrong to be ruled by fear, and picked out another of Spencer's library books, *The Woman in the Car with Glasses and a Gun.* She started it at the beginning, even though she still had a long way to go on *Sir John Magill's Last Journey.*

At the library, the steps had been overrun by people in climbing helmets squinting up at the stopped clock. Spencer heard the words rain and Miss Havisham but saw neither, remembering that the abseil wasn't scheduled until lunchtime. Grace's coach wasn't due to arrive for another few minutes, so he crossed the road towards a phone-box. He was considering calling the hospital, because if the morning-after pill only worked the morning after then time was running short. But the cash-box of the phone had been smashed beyond repair, and who would choose to bring children into a world like this?

Grace's coach pulled in at the bus stop. Spencer jogged back across the road, and by the time he made it round to the far side of the coach she was already on the pavement waiting for him. She was wearing a green Spartan tracksuit and a rucksack which said European Space Mission. She had her hands on her hips.

'You're late,' she said, pretending to look at a watch which she didn't have. 'Well done.'

She had growing brown hair and dark intelligent eyes, and it quickly became clear that on her tenth birthday, as well as a full set of River Phoenix videos and a rucksack, she'd picked up the gift of sarcasm. 'I see you've re-membered my present.'

'Happy Birthday, Grace.'

'Great start.'

'We could go and look at the chess sets.'

'I want a horse. And a cake. How am I doing?'

'Sorry?'

'At being assertive. Mum said being assertive was the best way to avoid dangerous situations. Am I any good?'

Spencer laughed. 'You're a natural.' He did a playful pinch and punch first-day-of-the-month thing and then they held hands. Grace skipped every other step to keep up with him, at the same time asking whether he'd heard the news about River Phoenix. 'He's dead,' Grace said, 'it was drugs and you know what? Only this morning when I woke up he was in my dream. He was just hovering there and I knew he had something important to say, like an oracle or something.'

Past the registry office, past the fire station and no obvious signs.

'Alright then, Grace, tell me what River Phoenix had to say.'

'First he tried to focus his lazy eye. He has a lazy eye, you know. Had one.'

'What did he say?'

'He did the thing with his eye and then he opened his mouth.'

'And he said what?'

'He said: Hey Wow Man, Cool.'

'Is that it?'

155

'And today he's *dead*. I can't believe it. He was supposed to be a vegetarian.'

Grace shook her head in disbelief and Spencer took a firmer grip on her small hand. He felt sorry for River Phoenix because of all the things he'd never managed to do, just like Spencer would now never set up his own pirate radio station, hardly a job for a married man one child. And it seemed unwise to settle down before he'd taken his epic year-long walking holiday. It was also possible that any day now he might feel obliged, for the sake of his moral well-being, to leave in a food-filled truck for Central Bosnia. Not to mention the pilgrimage he'd always intended to make to Fellini's Cinecitta, and his ambition to wade fully-clothed into the Trevisi fountain in Rome, with or without Anita Ekberg. And he'd be losing his freedom to do all this in exchange for what? Nice things.

They crossed the road between the slowly rumbling circus trucks, and Spencer wondered why he'd never gone abroad. Why on earth had he never stolen a motorbike and whacked down to Milan with Grace Zabriskie on the back? Why had he never made a night of it at the Viper Room in LA or explored tropical waterfalls or joined a luge team? Why hadn't he hung around trainee secretaries complimenting them on their 80 words a minute or their mother-tongue German or their very special organisational skills, just to get them into bed? I mean at least once he should have made a proper effort to contact Emma Thompson. Now he'd never know.

To make up for lost time therefore, and taking into

account, like crimes, all the many other things he'd never done, Spencer decided there and then to abandon his ten-year-old niece and join the circus. As for Hazel, he never set eyes on her again.

7

So what do we do about all of this? The
answer is simple.

THE TIMES 11/1/93

11/1/93 MONDAY 12:14

Loitering in the lounge of the hotel, Mr Mitsui felt like a
loiterer, even though he'd changed into a blazer and RAF
club tie. Several young men in morning-suits, wearing card-
board badges saying Philip and Alison, were discussing the
rearrangement of the furniture. Mr Mitsui went back to his
room, locked himself in and sat on the bed. He should go
and find Henry and bring him back.

Or he should leave him, wait for him, trust him. He was
twenty-three years old and he couldn't be fathered all his life.

Mr Mitsui's arm hurt where Henry had punched him. With
the remote control he flipped on the television, and a text

screen announced the next feature on the hotel's movie channel. 12:30 The Kitchen (1993 b/w) *A cook tells his fellow workers to dream of a better life.* He flipped it off again and focused on his dull reflection in the blackening screen, remembering how Henry's birth had changed everything. It had been an accident, a surprise, an Act of God. And if only they'd been better prepared, it could all have been so different. Mr Mitsui tried to identify the one single moment when everything had gone wrong. He flipped on the television and flipped it off again. Which present was it, or which kindness or which particular tolerance that had made the difference between love and spoiling? At which exact point did it become inevitable that one day enough home-made poison would be found in Henry's Tokyo flat to incapacitate most of the city's self-defence force? It had been a poison called ricin, so Dr Osawa said, which Henry claimed to have extracted from castor-oil seeds. A small amount of it was later found inside a Jaffa cake intended for his mother's regular afternoon teatime. But nobody had actually been hurt, and it was Henry himself who'd warned them about the Jaffa cake. How far then could he be said to be dangerous?

Dr Osawa had probably overestimated the importance of certain diagrams discovered at the same time in Henry's bedroom, filed neatly in coloured folders. They represented a series of ingenious machines and ideas for committing murder in sealed rooms, including a gun mechanism concealed in a telephone receiver and a poison gas which made its victims strangle themselves with their own hands. There

160

was a system for pulling a pistol trigger using a length of string and the expansion of water as it froze. There was a long-case clock with a chime so hideous it rewarded any attempt to silence it by releasing a slashing stomach-high blade. Another pistol remained hidden in a piano until it was triggered by the opening chords of Rachmaninov's Prelude in C Sharp, and there were several intriguing variations on the theme of the untraceable dagger or bullet sculpted from ice. From a design point of view, Mr Mitsui had been impressed. From a neurological point of view, Dr Osawa suggested an immediate change of environment.

Whenever Mr Mitsui tried to see his son's life as a story with formative moments, he always came back to his own marriage, and Henry's mother. Everyone had warned him not to marry her. They all said she was mad, but being in love with her made it seem less important to actually understand her. Instead, to show his love, he tried to please her. After the accident of Henry's birth he therefore agreed, for example, that Henry should be called Henry after her father and her grandfather and so on. Her great-great-grandfather had been properly British, but the truth was (and this came out when he later tried to please her with an expensive genealogical search) that he'd been transported to Australia for robbery on the highways, and for shooting a woman in the face.

Maybe even this was important, and the single determining factor in Henry's inability to adapt to the world. Like any spoilt child, he expected the world to adapt to him. It was also from his mother that he'd inherited the Western

161

habit of investing hope in sudden changes, or quantum leaps forward, or polar reversals. He wanted to take a chance and be lucky, all because his mother used to gather him up in her arms and tell him he could be anything he wanted to be. He could be a film star or an astronaut or a concert pianist or a British gentleman, as if the simple act of listing the options made each one of them possible. Then they always had to be buying things for him, and doing things, because whatever they gave him next could be the one thing to influence him forever. They bought him a horse called Benjamin. Then to interest him in horses they took him to the Melbourne Cup, where Henry spent the whole day counting seagulls. There followed a trip to Europe, to see Seija Osawa (no relation to the neurologist) conduct *The Miraculous Mandarin* with the Vienna Philharmonic. They flew him to Rome and Berlin to hear Bach and Messiaen and Schubert. They took holidays into the present tense to witness unique historical events like Dinkins vs Guiliani in New York, or Yuko Sato against Nancy Kerrigan in Norway. Each event, history as it happened, should have been a kind of enlightenment which changed Henry for the better, even if all he obviously learnt was the dazzling smile which he sometimes used to say thank you, and always to say sorry.

It wasn't until Mr Mitsui was first posted abroad that the real strangeness began. The previous low-point had been in Jerusalem, where for several months Henry had insisted on dressing up as an Israeli, just to attract his mother's attention. He only stopped when he fell in love with the niece of the editor of the Arabic daily *an-Nahar*. It was perhaps then that he'd adopted the idea that women existed to save him, and like most boys his age he gave himself several chances at redemption. In Islamabad it was the daughter of the American ambassador, and back in Japan he was briefly engaged to a very beautiful lieutenant in the Asaka self-defence force. On parade her mouth slanted down at the corners, always, as if it was a prescribed military expression, like attention. But something had happened and she'd broken it off, although it was unlikely Henry had ever actually hurt her.

Maybe this time, in London, it would be different and the moment to turn him round. He could have been lucky. He may really have been blessed by the miracle of true love, which would excuse Mr Mitsui the strain of having to find the courage to say no, he'd been wrong all along, and his only son couldn't have everything he wanted.

Mr Mitsui slowly climbed off the bed, nursing his injured arm. He would phone the Distance Learning School. He would ask them where in London he might hope to find his errant and misguided son.

———

It is the first of November 1993 and somewhere in Britain, in Lancing or Great Wakering or Gretna or Ascot, in Toller Porcorum or Merthyr or Richmond or Derby, Hazel Burns is eighteen years old and these are the best days of her life. Her father has given her an allowance and told her so. He has also bought her a car, a small Ford or Vauxhall or

163

Peugeot, so that she can come home whenever she needs a break from her first year, first term, at the University of Warwick or Strathclyde or Oxford or Hull. She is studying English or Medicine or Natural Science or Greats, and therefore is convinced, along with most of the other students, that before long there will be almost nothing she does not know.

Already she misses home, or an idea of home which contains her mother, her sister, and a new pair of china vixens in the corner cabinet. She wishes she was there to see Olly win selection for the disabled luge team or compete in the qualifying heats for the BT-BSAD paralympic swimming championships. This is before she learns that Olive is going out with Sam Carter, which provokes her into driving her car at 60 mph through built-up areas until she remembers it's dangerous. Her mother often telephones (it's either her or Spencer), usually full of drugs and occasionally with such a confused sense of time that she treats Hazel like a child. Is she being careful? Does she lock her door at night? Is she avoiding alcohol, soft drugs, ecstasy, heroin? And she wishes she didn't have to say this, but someone has to, does Hazel know what to do with a condom?

'Which flavour?' Hazel asks.

Her mother, ignoring the lessons of her own experience, suggests marriage and announces grandly that marriage is a place safe for diversity. Oh yes, Hazel thinks, it can be so diverse that in some forms you never actually get to see your husband. Her father, Hazel begins to realise, has sold her an idea of a happy childhood which has reached its

164

sell-by date. He needs to make a fresh sale but he wouldn't know this because he's never there. As well as his frequent trips abroad he belongs to a thousand clubs, for the sales contacts, to the Detection Club and the Woolmen's Company and the League Against Cruel Sports and the 300 Group and the trade association Beama and the TocH movement and possibly also the Freemasons. It's as if his family was just another type of club, with its own tie, and her father only subscribes as a country member.

He is in fact directly responsible for Hazel's discomfort at University. She lives on a corridor with three other girls, Lynne, Marianne, and Louise, who spend their week-ends demonstrating against Serbian aggression or neo-Thatcherism or Gerry Adams or the persecution of the Kurds in Turkey. It doesn't really matter. Hazel's mistake is to have let it slip that her father is Salesperson of the Year '93, and in the global evil of a capitalist conspiracy there can be little doubt of his implicit guilt.

There is also the disadvantage of Hazel's unfortunate private education and her crisp RP accent. She is also blonde and unmistakably sexy, if a little on the short side, and even though by degrees she is dropping her accent she feels friendless. She therefore has no choice but to work hard and attend extra-curricular lectures, *Leeches and Lancets: Surgical Stories From the Past*, or *What Maastricht Means* or *Intensive Therapy in the 1990s – the Cost of a Life*. In such desperate circumstances it's hardly surprising that she breaks up with her first University boyfriend, and then her second and third, all of whom she meets at lectures looking

165

for girls exactly like her. It's at times like these that she likes to phone her only true friend in the world.

'Did you love *all* of them?' Spencer asks.

'This is University,' Hazel tells him. 'I was seizing the day.'

'So that's what they call it.'

None of these brief relationships turn out to be much fun, and although it would have been nice to know this a little earlier, Hazel still repeats the mistake several more times just to make sure. In fact, University is comprehensively failing to provide her with the best days of her life until one afternoon she comes back to the corridor and Marianne says, or Louise or Lynne says:

'Hazel, there's a gorgeous policeman waiting to see you.'

He is sitting at the table in the communal kitchen, shifting his uniform cap about the table-top. He introduces himself as a sergeant from the Northumbria or Manchester or Metropolitan police force. He is tall and thin, with short black hair and an aristocratic nose. He has forgiving brown eyes and his pressed uniform is very clean and black. His face is very kind and he smiles nicely and Hazel is terrified. Before she can confess to the fraudulent charity boxes and the phone-cards, he suggests she sit down while he explains quietly that in a series of marked public callboxes, all of which have recently been attacked, several calls have been made both to her parents' number and to the card-phone in the corridor outside.

Hazel suddenly discovers that she's unable to help this

gentle policeman with his enquiries. She draws on all her schoolgirl acting experience and says:

'I get lots of calls from phone-boxes.'

'From the same person?'

Hazel coughs into her hand. 'I was at private school. It could be anyone from anywhere in the country.'

'They certainly do come from anywhere.'

The policeman lists, without referring to the notebook he's supposed to carry, all the phone-boxes which have been broken into and the amount of money taken. Stolen, he corrects himself.

By the end of the list Hazel feels quietly flattered by Spencer's obvious devotion.

'I have lots of friends,' she says, and the policeman looks at her in a way she's learning to recognise and says,

'Yes, I imagine you do.'

He carefully studies the cloth on top of his cap. He picks off a thread of red cotton. He tells her that if anything else occurs to her she should contact him. He looks her directly in the eye.

'You do realise this is a serious matter?'

'Yes,' she says, 'yes I do.'

And after this visit Hazel's credibility soars. Rumours abound. Hazel works for MI6, she's a drug dealer, she's a violent feminist out on parole bound over to keep the peace. Her secret lover is a copper. Anyway, once the police are involved there can be no doubt that this is real life, and Hazel is in it. She's not just stuck up and blonde, and Hazel thanks heaven for Spencer, her own secret designated Act

167

of God. As a peace-offering Louise and Lynne and Marianne make a collection to buy her a poster of a seagull smoking a joint. Hazel puts this in the space previously occupied by a Van Gogh print, or a Vermeer or Lowry or David Jones, anyway by something so boring and staid that all the girls agree it should be replaced *immediately*. She is allowed to keep her poster of River Phoenix in the arms of Grace Zabriskie from *My Own Private Idaho*. River is a cult from the moment he died, today, forever.

The girls now take Hazel out to parties, and together they all discover that at University every student has a problem. Fortunately, these are usually the kind of problems they'd always hoped to have, mostly boys and girls (love comes into it) or philosophic discourse or the politics of conscience. Hazel finds it strange that here they are among ten thousand students, all free and equal in a godless world, most of whom spend their days praying for the glamour of Acts of God. These will come in the form of an amazing boy or a fabulous girl, or a fantastic exam result on zero revision. Everyone is hoping for a miracle, for a direct painless hit from a metaphorical thunderbolt, a kind of supernatural smart bomb to explode the start of their lives in the right direction.

Hazel is no different, and she goes out and waits, waiting on a conspicuous miracle. She comes home. She pulls a chair up to the card-phone and calls Spencer. She doesn't tell him about her visit from the police because maybe they're listening in. As a more subtle way of showing how much she appreciates him, and the risks he's prepared to take, she finds herself asking what happens if he ever runs out of money, and she also means what happens when I run out of phonecards? She's stolen nothing since she left home.

'Easy,' Spencer says. 'We move in together, settle down and have children. Think of all the money we'll save.'

'I mean really.'

'I don't know. What do you think?'

Get a job, Hazel thinks, get a phone of my own. It seems a long way away. 'I don't know,' she says, and then Lynne or Marianne or Louise is tapping her on the shoulder, silently with grand hand gestures inviting her out to sabotage a fox hunt or to smoke some drugs or to put through a hoax call to the bursar about explosive statues.

Hazel tells Spencer she has to dash. This is now, after all, and she only gets the one go at it.

11/1/93 MONDAY 12:18

'So Grace,' Hazel said, hands on knees, good with children. 'Why aren't you at school?'

They were in the kitchen, where Hazel had been hoping to speak to Spencer alone. She wanted to know exactly what Henry Mitsui had said on the phone, as well as what Spencer really felt for her. Instead, she'd been introduced to his ten-year-old niece, Grace.

'You have a choice,' Grace said. 'It's either because

169

there's school fireworks this evening and Dad thinks it's too risky, or I get a day off for my birthday, or I'm not allowed into school today because yesterday I dressed up as a vampire and tried to bite the neighbour.'

'It's an annual school holiday,' Spencer said. 'In honour of the Duke of Wellington's brother, an old boy.'

'This year it's also for the beginning of Europe,' Grace said. 'I'm only here until tea-time, but I want to stay longer because I hate my Mum and Dad.'

'Of course you don't. You shouldn't say that.'

'I like Uncle Spencer and William much better.'

'Only sometimes,' Spencer said.

'All the time. I can always tell you proper things, like what happened to my friend Nadine.'

'I'm sure you could tell your mother.'

'She'd go berserk. You don't know what happened to Nadine.'

Spencer lifted Grace up and sat her on the table. He pulled out a chair for himself and Hazel leant against the wall. When Grace was sure they were both ready, she let them know that one day her friend Nadine had been followed home from school by a man. She was absolutely terrified. She heard footsteps behind her and they followed her all the way home. Eventually, when she reached her front door, Nadine turned round, determined not to let him in and probably to scream. The man stopped by the front gate and stared at her.

Grace did some life-like staring.

'Then what?'

'You promise not to tell Dad?'

'Promise. What did the man do?'

'He asked her if she was alright.'

'And?'

'And then he said if she was so frightened she should have told him.'

'And then what?'

'He said sorry and went away. Nadine went inside and had her tea.'

Grace pushed herself off the table and landed solidly on both feet. 'Can I go and see William now?'

'I don't know where he is,' Spencer said.

'I bet he's in his shed.'

Grace simply couldn't believe that Hazel had never seen William's shed. She grabbed her hand and said she just had to see it, because it was brilliant.

Spencer leant on the table, closed his eyes, and prepared himself for some time-travel. He was going to go forward in time and consider his predicament like an adult, imagining every tomorrow as if it included Hazel, accepting the fact that this moment marked the end of his ambitious construction of a chequered past. He could still become a hundred different people, of course, but once he was committed to Hazel then the only person he could never be again was the person he was now.

Time-travel was hot and difficult work, so he took off his suit-jacket and shaped it over the back of the chair. He rolled up the sleeves of his shirt and then, fully prepared, sat down at the table and opened William's newspaper at the employment page. He stroked the paper from centre to edge, flattening it out, thinking that in any realistic vision he had of tomorrow, including Hazel, including their child (and if not tomorrow, then the next day, or the day after that), he would have to hold down a proper job.

As of today, or so he learned from the newspaper, he could apply for a Senior Research Fellowship in Law and Education at Manchester University. Failing that, he could suggest himself as the next Principal of Lady Margaret Hall, Oxford, or try out for the Chair in Law at Bristol. Dizzy from travelling so far and so fast, Spencer quickly demoted himself to assistant bursar of a private school, realised he still didn't have the qualifications, so fixed eventually on a more settled career as an enthusiastic and efficient secretary at a reputable/progressive company. All he needed to pick up before the interview was a bit of shorthand or mother-tongue German or his own transport or, as a basic minimum for most of these secretarial posts, some basic secretarial skills. If, on the other hand, he preferred to sell his services abroad, there was currently an opening for an Academic Director at the Indira Ghandi National Centre of the Arts, New Delhi.

Spencer failed to encounter a single offer he couldn't refuse. The idea of a tomorrow with Hazel seemed to drift away, no easier to imagine as an adult than as a twenty-four-year-old child. Perhaps she was right, and they should just go back to bed. At least that way they'd eventually fall asleep and at some stage wake up to find it was tomorrow anyway, whether they liked it or not. No special effort was required to get there, no previous experience or extraordinary enthusiasm or mother-tongue German.

It seemed obvious to him now that he should have listened to his father, and apprenticed as an overpaid sportsman. Or he should have rebelled more efficiently and become a man of business, a captain of industry, the director general of Ofgas or the BSI chief executive or chairman of the TSB group and president of the British Bankers' Association. Thinking like this was close to panic. It reminded him of his childhood, with everything still possible and nothing decided yet, when the need to make a decision was even more distant than the various triumphs imagined to follow it. But he wasn't a child anymore, and not everything was an option.

Spencer gave up on jobs. On the way to Sport he saw a small advert in the Personal Column for a birthdate copy of *The Times*, which would have been a good present for Grace if only he'd thought of it earlier. It was a bit like astrology, he supposed, believing that events reported on the day you were born somehow had a particular significance. Spencer, however, needed guidance of a less speculative kind.

He tried something which had worked for him before whenever a decision was needed. He made a conscious effort to remember his sister Rachel, and passed back through the crash, beyond Rachel running at the seaside, all the way back to Rachel very young and somewhere on a large playing field, wearing a number 8 shirt, kicking a football through the mud. Spencer was hoping that the past had something to teach him, and that certain memories would offer him signs and guidance if only he knew how to look. He therefore tried to fix down as many details as possible, but they remained elusive around the central event. Rachel was wearing a football shirt, for example, but Spencer couldn't remember what team they used to support at exactly that time. It was the same colour shirt as his, but he still couldn't remember. Was it important? Perhaps the details were what mattered most, and anything of importance to be discovered in memory lay hidden exclusively in the detail. So what were the games they used to play, and what were the scores?

Or the detail was irrelevant. Any guidance to be had was to be found in the events themselves. These were the defining moments of the past, the peaks in the hazy range of his memory, the significant events to be singled out, but still it wasn't clear what was there to be learnt.

He must have learnt something, surely. That's what mistakes were supposed to be for.

————

It is the first of November 1993 and somewhere in Britain, in Morecambe or Ebbw Vale or Epsom or Musselburgh, in Hounslow or West Bowling or Gloucester or Rugby, eighteen-year-old Spencer Kelly throws himself into another game of Right Now.

'Right Now,' he says to Hazel, 'looking out of this telephone box I can see some friends of mine. In fact a whole crowd of them. Many of them are potential international standard models and girlfriends. They want me to come out and play guitar for them. They want me to do one of my special funky dances. They're making faces *pleading* with me to join them, right now.'

'What are they saying, exactly?'

'I can't hear a word, it's too windy. It's so windy even the seagulls are walking.'

Outside the phone-box it is dark. A single spotlight across the road glares between a stranded post-box and a swinging pub sign for the White Hart or the Rising Sun. There is no-one out there, though it's true about the wind. Two seagulls walk ludicrously along the road. It's cold and Spencer is wearing his work jacket, the warmest one he has.

Hazel laughs. 'Alright then, *inside* the box. What's it like, right now, on the inside.'

'Lovely and warm,' Spencer says, 'in my brand new RAF leather bomber jacket.'

'What about right now, *inside your head*?'

Easy. Spencer plans to tame the future by training as an Oral and Maxillofacial Surgeon so that he'll never have to worry about money again. In his spare time he'll become an invaluable Private Secretary to a member of the aristocracy, to the Countess of Minto or the Duke of Kent or Viscount Goschen, all of whom tolerate his frequent trips to London because he's also a world-famous actor working the London stages opposite Emma Thompson or Alice Krige or Fiona Shaw. That, right now, is what occupies his head.

175

Hazel is still laughing out loud. 'Spencer, you're absolutely brilliant and I love you to bits.'

Right now, however, she has to dash, and not displeased with the effect he's had Spencer smiles and puts down the phone.

It rings again almost immediately. It has to be Hazel so he snatches it up, and a man's voice says hello there you terrorist enemy of law and order. Spencer puts it down. It rings again. He stares at it and lets it ring. This is new. He bites his lip. The cash-box, refilled after his conversation with Hazel, swings open. He closes it gently. The phone continues to ring so he picks it up. 'Hello?'

'Hello there. This is Operation Clean Hands.'

'Hello?'

'Hello hello hello. I'm Robert Walker and I'm a British Telecom undercover agent. No joke. This is Operation Clean Hands and you have recently broken into the cash-box of this public telephone. True or false?'

'I don't know,' Spencer says, 'did I?'

'All boxes at risk are now connected to a central system. The moment you rob one an alarm goes off. We know where you are and I can phone you up, see?'

'I didn't know they could do that,' Spencer says.

'We've had complaints from the Director of Property himself.'

'Thank you,' Spencer says, and then adds: 'I haven't hurt anybody.'

He puts the phone down. He gets out of the phone-box fast and tumbles his bicycle upright and pedals home like a maniac, helped madly on his way by the wind. Weirder things have happened, he decides, but not often to him.

At home he finds his Dad, the one parent in his new one-parent family, sitting on the sofa drinking beer and watching *Eurogoals* or *Trucks 'n' Tractor Power* or *Ringside Superbouts*. The divorce is now official, and Spencer knew it was finished when his Dad said:

'That chapter of our life is over.'

He was wrong. In fact Mr Kelly spends most evenings re-living episodes from the past and cursing the injustice of it all. He now suspects that Spencer's real talent was for something to do with horses. He's an untried champion jockey or a potential Gold Cup showjumper, but how is some-one on Mr Kelly's salary ever supposed to afford a horse? His son's talent will therefore remain latent simply because it's for a sport outside his father's social bracket. Because if it isn't horses then it's probably world championship bridge, or windsurfing, or chess. To alleviate his despair, and with any money left over after buying beer, Mr Kelly takes up gam-bling. He tells Spencer that apart from sporting success a big win on a game of chance is the only other way out of the ghetto.

'We're not in a ghetto, Dad. We never were.'

'Always were, always will be.'

Spencer still considers himself the only sane member of the family, but in real life, right now, he isn't the surgeon or private secretary or actor he wants to be. He works in the warehouse with his father. Each day is taken up with the barely sane activity of shifting boxes of furniture which belong to famous people.

His Dad asks what's for tea, then settles back in his arm-chair while Spencer goes to look in the kitchen cupboard. As usual all they have is packet soups. He asks his father anyway what he wants.

'What flavours are there?'

'Chicken.'

'What flavours?'

So Spencer tells him they have Crosse and Blackwell or Heinz or Batchelors or Knorr, and his father says fine, I'll have one of those then.

Spencer boils the kettle and empties powder into a mug, thinking about his surprise phone call and wondering whether he's done anything seriously wrong. He'd like to say that he always puts the money he steals back into the phone-boxes, using it to call Hazel. But in the early days he kept some of it to lose on fruit machines or to conquer arcade games like *Aladdin's Lamp* or *TOCA Shoot-Out Touring Cars* or *Racing Demon*. He spent some of it through turnstiles (Merthyr 5 Northwich 0 or Yeovil 0 Gateshead 2 or Workington 74 Wigan St Patrick's 6), and he half-remembered renting some videos (*Much Ado About Nothing* or *Mr Wonderful* or *My Own Private Idaho*). But apart from these occasional lapses and his daily quality newspaper, it's true that he puts most of the money back into phone-boxes, even if he doesn't repair the locks. He does it to speak to Hazel, which is a way of bettering himself. She used to go to private school. She's a good and improving influence, and Spencer's life undoubtedly has significant room for improvement.

Because Right Now, if Hazel's asking, his life is all about making an instant chicken soup for his drunken father while worrying about Operation Clean Hands and what they'll do to him if they catch up with him. He decides to ask Hazel for an immediate opinion, and creeps to the phone in the hall with the idea of phoning her. His Dad, however, lurches out from the lounge and gives him a cuff round the ear, though not very hard, not like a professional boxer ($7 million a fight).

'The likes of us can't afford to chit-chat,' he says, and without arguing Spencer walks out on his father and the instant chicken soup, slamming the door behind him.

Then he has to go back inside and upstairs to get his sports bag, before he can walk out all over again (slamming the door), climb onto his bike, head it into the wind and ride out of town like a hero. At the first suitable public phone, in the middle of nowhere, he swiftly applies the special tool.

Pop.

The phone rings. Spencer picks it up.

'You hurt all sorts of people,' Robert Walker says. He sounds at the younger end of middle-aged, and Spencer guesses that at college he enjoyed a contact sport to a decent level, Courage League 5 or the first round of the Regal trophy or the Neville Ovenden Combination League. He likes his job.

'Especially poor people who need to make urgent calls because they've been attacked, stabbed, shot, stoned. We'll catch you in the end. Public phones are everybody's miracle, and they don't only exist to get robbed by idiot criminals like you.'

Spencer drops the phone and lets it swing on its wire. He

sits down on his sports bag. He rests his chin in his hands and listens to the tinny voice-sound coming from the telephone, wishing devoutly that he was living another life in which he'd never stolen from a phone-box. His Dad sells the television. Father and son spend the evenings browsing respectable newspapers like *The Times* or the *Telegraph* or the *Independent*, while amiably discussing classic novels by George Orwell or Jane Austen or Jack London. Ah for such a soft sweet life, for the dolce vita. Spencer then easily passes the audition to drama school and in London is quickly identified as one of the greats of his generation, standing-room only at the Adelphi or the Old Vic or the Shaftesbury. The critics say he has a *compelling gaze and a good RP accent* or *the skill to handle sharp individual swings of mood* or refer to him as *a particular success* or *a refreshing change* or *truly rounded*.

Robert Walker is still talking, and Spencer flicks the handset to keep him swinging. He stays where he is, sitting, watching his breath condense, thinking that life owes him a miracle to make up for Rachel. He is calling it in now. His time without miracles is up.

———

11/1/93 Monday 12:22

Back in the shed, William could look round in some comfort without having to ignore anything. Maybe Hazel was right

180

when she said you had to block things out, simply to go on living, but that was outside. Here in the shed William could take his time, and he realised it wasn't a question of quantity because he could deal with any number of things, as long as they all conformed to a system.

As well as the stack of yellow buckets, the top one containing water and the two remaining fish, there was a wire bird-cage stuffed with yesterday's newspaper, and three televisions of decreasing size balanced one on top of the other. There were several colourful plastic sandcastle moulds, and a split carrier-bag full of bargain-basement videos: *Il Balcone, Hellfire Corner, Hell of a Ride, So You Want to Be a Surgeon?* Somewhere there was a box of Manoplax, the discontinued heart drug, and a miniature Statue of Liberty, and a chess set, and a folding ladder, and a collection of completed *Times* crossword books (*The Times Book of Jumbo Crosswords, The Times Jumbo Concise Crosswords Book* and *The Times Jubilee Puzzles 1932–1987*). He thought he could remember some cancelled novels from the Bern British Council Library, and a pair of real leather PVC Charles and Di oven gloves. And somewhere not too far back there was a booklet of caricatures of people in the news, including John Major, Federico Fellini, Barbara Mills, River Phoenix, Malcolm Reilly, Maradona, Emma Thompson and the Queen.

William never threw anything away: that was his system. And as well as the buckets and the caricatures, the videos and books and things, there were as many objects again which he couldn't remember or couldn't recognise or

181

couldn't name. The shed was full, so what was the point in going outside when he didn't have the room to bring anything back?

He got down on his knees and looked under the bed and then behind the television sets until he found his black rabbit, who was nibbling at the rind of a kiwi fruit. Animals were good chaps. You knew where you stood with them. He picked up the rabbit and showed him the tomento beside the bed, which seemed to have perked up during the day. The leaves seemed shinier, more likely to partner the best-selling tomento fruit which would make William his fortune. All he needed was the one lucky break, and everything would be different. He would catch up with his brother, who thought that all luck was good. It was his brother who'd inherited well, been outrageously lucky with his investments, gone on to buy a knighthood, eventually meeting the Queen to accept the honour of his changed name. From a common Welsby to Lord O'Brien Welsby, changed overnight. He speculated in the property market and secretly sold arms to the Irish, and his luck never ran out. He openly invested in films without losing money. He'd gradually turned himself into a standard, acceptable, end-of-the-century capitalist. He was a charming, cultivated, well-mannered villain.

William put down the rabbit. Believing he was a better man than his brother, he wished he hadn't been so unfair to Hazel. He shouldn't have gone on so much about Jessica, even when his future with Spencer felt threatened. It was, anyway, a poor retreat to live every day untested by the reality of women and outside life. Hazel had offered a

182

glimpse of another possibility, where William stepped out-side and discovered what was restricted but true. She'd taken him seriously. She thought he could be cured.

And she did look lovely in that dress.

Grace, looking very small, gave William, who seemed to have grown, an enormous hug. He wished her a Happy Birthday while at the same time beckoning Hazel into the shed. Hazel's feet were freezing. She'd taken off Spencer's socks to walk barefoot across the damp grass, and now she gratefully stepped inside, shivered, leant against a folding ladder and pulled the socks back on again. Straightening up, she had her first good look at the inside of William's shed.

'My,' she said, 'you have a lot of stuff.'

Her eyes came to rest on the tomento beside the bed and she was puzzled at seeing a plant she didn't recognise.

'It's a tomento,' William said. 'I invented it myself.'

'It doesn't look very happy,' Hazel said.

'Neither do you.'

As a place to sit, William was offering the shed's raised doorway, where there was just about room for the two of them. Behind them, apparently as usual, Grace was busy exploring. She'd already squeezed behind the televisions and the buckets, and only one of her legs was still visible. Hazel sat next to William, looked out into the garden, hugged her knees to her chest. Her feet were warming up nicely. She heard a truck braking somewhere, but it seemed a long way away.

'It's like a parallel universe out here,' she said. 'It's hard to believe what's just over the wall.'

'It's out there,' William said.

'I know. I saw what happened when you went to take a look.'

'I had to give it a go,' William said. 'It's not every day that's the end of Britain.'

'It's not the end of Britain.'

'You know what I mean. The Maastricht thing.'

From somewhere behind them Grace shouted: 'Treaty of Maastricht European Union! Everything changes today!' Her head popped out from behind the wire bird-cage. 'We learnt that in school.'

Hazel looked back over her shoulder. 'You really think everything changes today?'

'Of course it does. I'm *ten*.'

Grace disappeared behind the buckets and then immediately re-surfaced. She wanted to know the date of Hazel's birthday.

'Soon,' Hazel said. 'Or maybe it's just been, I'm not sure.'

'Tell me the date. You must know the date. Everyone knows their own birthday.'

'Not after twenty-one, they don't. It's not polite to talk about it. You shouldn't even mention it.'

'When's your birthday, though?'

'I'm not going to mention it.'

It was only then, looking round to smile and reassure her, that Hazel noticed Grace was holding a black rabbit. She sat cross-legged on the floor of the shed and stroked him

184

nicely, making Hazel suddenly nostalgic for how contented contentment could be made to look.

'I want to stay here for ever,' Grace said.

'You can't,' William said.

'Why not?'

'You know why not.'

'I could run away.'

And send your parents mad with worry, William reminded her, thinking their only daughter had been dragged into fields and left for dead, not to be found for years and years until she was completely rotten except for her teeth. Was that what she wanted?

'Does that type of thing really happen?'

'Yes it does, but probably not to any of us.'

'Why not?'

'Because we're lucky.'

'How are we lucky?'

'We get to have birthdays which are special days with presents and cakes. And you're lucky because you have good parents who worry about you.'

'Then why do they make me learn German?'

Grace let the black rabbit hop back into his warren beneath all the junk, and then she wriggled in behind him. William put his hand on Hazel's shoulder, and gave it a little squeeze.

'Don't give up on him yet.'

'I'm running out of patience,' Hazel said. 'He won't make up his mind about anything.'

'Doubt is the strongest fear, and therefore the most eloquent emotion.'

'Says who? Either he likes me or he doesn't.'

Grace suddenly popped up behind them.

'Europe is like marriage,' she said. 'My teacher says so. Everyone gets together for the good of everyone else. What she really means is that in the Easter term we all have to pay for a German exchange scheme. Hazel?'

'That's my name.'

'Are you going to marry Spencer?'

'I don't know,' Hazel said. 'What do *you* think?'

Grace found Hazel odd sometimes. 'It's not really up to me, is it?'

And then she wanted to know where William had hidden her present, because she couldn't find it anywhere among his stuff in the shed. William said it was a secret, and she had to be patient. Grace's eyes lit up.

'It's a horse, isn't it?'

8

At this time of year, I should be on the
qui vive (watch, guard, look out, patrol,
stand to, *cave*) for saints and souls and
things that go bump in the night.

THE TIMES 11/1/93

11/1/93 MONDAY 12:24

Fact: Lime trees were originally popular in London in the
nineteenth century as one of the few species of tree robust
enough to resist the horticultural rigours of the great pea-
souper smogs. In these clearer days, aphids and greenfly
have become partial to the tree's sweet flower-buds, and
these insects exude a colourless but sticky 'honey', which
drops on plants or the pavement. This, in its turn, nourishes
an unattractive black fungus. The lime trees themselves are
therefore largely innocent of the black muck they seem to

bleed, even though every year many are mistakenly destroyed, the unwitting victims of a misunderstood chain of events. The correct remedy involves judicious pruning, or spraying the guilty insects with a good strong sprayer.

British Birds and Trees, as taught by Miss Burns.

The area where she was staying was full of lime trees, planted at intervals along the pavement and ceremonially either side of the library steps. Facts, like those she'd taught him about trees, helped to keep Henry calm. They were like a drug, subduing whatever he was really feeling or thinking beneath something clearer and more certain. Knowledge became control, which at this moment was just what Henry needed because Miss Burns turned out not to be alone. Watching the house, he'd already seen a young man, black hair, in a flapping suit. And a small energetic girl with a rucksack, who he nearly missed completely because people kept getting in his way.

Left to right, could that be her? No, left to right Miss Anne Howard, the pre-eminent authority on ecclesiastical embroidery. Right to left Mr Michael Lloyd of the Worshipful Company of Chartered Surveyors, and left to right his unmarried daughter Helen, who had a double room in Wimbledon Village to rent to a non-smoking female for £85 a week. People, the first wave of workers out on their lunch break, seemed constantly to be putting themselves between Henry and Miss Burns, as if *on purpose*. Left to right Alison Thomas, a marine biologist from the Institute of Estuarine and Coastal Studies at Hull University.

Henry found shelter in a phone-box, and breathed deeply

188

on the unpeopled air. He dried his palms on the front of his patterned sweater and tried to focus through the scratches of *Gary marries Laura* and *Elliot is Dead* and *Final score: Man U 2 QPR 1*. From the phone-box he could still see the house, and he'd already familiarised himself with the street. Behind him there was a bank, a travel agent, a music shop, and a charity shop where British people learned to dress like beggars. There was a pub, the Rising Sun, and there were people everywhere, any one of whom could have been her or a friend of hers. In fact, there were altogether too many people, all blurring into each other, so that instead of having lives of their own they could only be explained as part of a group, as belonging to the 6000 employees of the Crown Prosecution Service or the 33% of children who owned a goldfish. How was Henry supposed to get the attention of Miss Burns among so many people?

He wondered if he should phone her, but just then a young woman tapped on the glass with the edge of a brightly-coloured phonecard. Henry's heart reeled. It could have been her, but actually it was Rachel Yates, a classically-trained dancer planning to get engaged at Christmas. Henry bowed (stop *doing* that) and even as he was leaving the phone-box Rachel Yates was pushing past him, breathless, already looking at the telephone and saying, 'Thanks you just saved my life.'

Henry decided not to phone. He wanted to surprise her, if only he knew how, if only all these people would stop getting in the way all the time. There seemed to be most of the 80% of young people who claimed boredom was the cause of juvenile crime, and a good number of the 290 next of kin to policemen murdered in Ireland. He escaped into Jepson's music shop. It was thankfully empty apart from Mrs Jepson, for seven years a Roman Catholic nun, who asked him if she could be of assistance. Henry left his umbrella and his plastic bag on the counter. He rolled up the sleeves of his sweater.

'Yes,' he said. 'I'd like to try out a piano.'

He chose the Forte Grand in the window, from where he had a good though often obstructed view of the house. Mrs Jepson, ex-Catholic nun, whose only child died of pneumonia aged fifteen days in 1973, showed him how to adjust the stool.

'That will be all,' Henry said, and with a flourish, not looking at the keys but outside at the street, he launched into the fearsome opening chords of Rachmaninov's Prelude in C Sharp. And then he kept going. He played loudly and he played all the notes, because his parents had given him lessons in Tokyo with an ex-pat veteran of the Festival Hall, yet another present which failed to make all the difference.

Henry distractedly ran through his repertoire of keyboard skills. Mrs Jepson, ex-nun, her poor lost child, let the music flood over her thinking it was never too late. The music also had its effect on Henry, making him more confident of recognising Miss Burns immediately, instinctively, as part of the miracle he expected from being in love. He looked out of the window and saw only people between him and the house. He stopped playing. Mrs Jepson, ex-nun, her poor lost baby, who sometimes thought it was never too late, thought now that perhaps, after all, it was. She asked Henry if anything was wrong.

He was staring out of the window. The door to the house was opening, was it? It was hard to say because people walking left right left kept getting in the way, like left to right Jessica Ashworth an articled clerk at Jauralde and Philips, like right to left Gerald Norcross a former captain in the Derbyshire Yeomanry, like standing still Sidney Keating, non-stipendiary curate in charge of St Oswald's, and if very soon he didn't get out of the way Henry would have to move him along, give him a shove, push him into passing traffic, just get out of the way please now Reverend.

Henry grabbed his bag and fled the shop, colliding with Norman Hopkins, a British Telecom agent working under-cover on Operation Clean Hands, stab him shoot him stone him to death and really, it would make no difference. By the time he'd untangled himself the door across the road had closed again. It was even possible he'd been imagining things. He bit his lip and wandered towards the pub, keeping one eye on the door, trying not to be distracted by the 70 business mentors who spend an hour a month in schools, or any of the 3000 birdwatchers on their way to a car park in Kent to see a golden-winged warbler. This was his big chance, and all these people were going to ruin it by getting in the way. He had the poison, of course, but it wasn't nearly enough. What he really needed was an automatic weapon. He would start with the anonymous drinkers in the Rising Sun, provoking instant and utter mayhem, the smell of fresh blood, cartridges and spent bullet cases careering off the

191

floor, off-duty nurses picking their way through the carnage using bar-towels and tablecloths as bandages.

Because obviously, what with the level of noise produced by a multiple massacre, Miss Burns would come out of that house over there and take a look. This was the moment he'd wait for, positioning himself somewhere unmissable between her and the pub. He'd give her the perfect opportunity to fall in love with him at first sight.

No, no, no. It was only in the beautiful countryside of Northern Ireland that you could spray bullets round a public house and get away with it. In London one of the victims would probably turn out to be someone important, an aristo-crat related to Lord Walton via the Honourable Lady Ogilvy, by marriage to Viscount Goschen or the Duke of Gloucester and onwards and upwards to Her Royal Highness Princess Alexandra and eventually the Prince of Wales. A foreigner would never get away with it. The Crown Prosecution Service would press for a jail sentence equivalent to all the years he would otherwise be spending in wedlock with Miss Burns, raising many children, holidaying at the tran-quil seaside. Everybody had a life (remember Dr Osawa), and some people even had a life which led to Prince Charles.

Persuaded against random massacre, Henry turned back towards the house, just in time to see the front door swing open again. A young blonde woman stepped out, balancing carefully on high-heeled shoes. Her feet seemed to be slightly green. She was carrying a small purse and wearing a long-sleeved grey dress and no coat, as if she was expecting a night out. She looked left and then right, shook out her hair, then stood on the very edge of the pavement peering across at the shops opposite. She folded her arms and stepped out into the road.

What kind of indiscriminate hostel was this? And why had they trapped Miss Burns inside?

Seize the day, Henry. Burn those bridges.

It is the first of November 1993 and somewhere in Britain, on a train between Pickering and Godalming or Gillingham and Maidstone, between Eskdalemuir and Raith or Hurstpierpoint and Treorchy, William Welsby is twenty-four years old and travelling with his back to the engine, a Class 91 locomotive. A boy further down the carriage wearing a Wimbledon or Manchester or Southampton football shirt eats a Bourbon biscuit or a Jaffa cake or some Cadbury's chocolate. Sometimes the boy pushes his grubby face up against the window, and William wonders if they share the same pride in the passing countryside, like a favoured personal possession. He sees a girl running on sand dunes, a warehouse, some playing fields and a cricket pitch with its summer scoreboard rusting at 199 for 7. They rattle past fields, lakes, buildings, parks, all of which have names, Prince's Park or Sefton Park or Penn Inn or the People's Park. Or Bitton Park or Leazes Park. Stop it, William tells himself, you don't want to start that nonsense again.

Obviously it's all his fiancée's fault.

She is sitting in the seat opposite, smiling and sympathising, unaware that William never experienced such crises of listing before his official engagement. To Miss K. L. M. Llewellen-Palmer or Ms S. M. Hurley or Miss C. R. B. Maitland Hume, daughter of the late Colonel O. Gibbon of Wivelsfield, Sussex or Mrs Valda Hope of Carinya, Cobbitty, New South Wales, Australia. She says:

'You have to put it all behind you.'

Because unfortunately, despite his engagement, William has just been rescued from an untimely affair with Louise or Marianne or Lynne or even Jessica, all of whom he truly loves. William stares over his fiancée's head, back in the direction he's travelled, thinking only divine intervention can save him now. Before the actual wedding she could always die of food poisoning. It happens. Or become another random victim of a hopeful bombing by the terrifying Irish or Libyans or Algerians. He wonders how many cliff-top walks he can justify between now and the marriage. How unlucky did she have to be, exactly, to catch meningitis or sclerosis or smallpox, or to crash her car, or unwittingly swallow a lethal cocktail of drugs in a celebrity nightclub toilet?

William understands that such thoughts are not the ideal preparation for marriage. She leans forward and takes his hand. 'This is all connected with what happened to your parents, isn't it?'

'No.'

'It must have come as a great shock.'

194

The best way to forget about his parents, and sometimes even his brother, is to think about four things when usually one would do.

'And anyway,' she asks, not expecting an answer, 'how would you survive without me?'

By busking on street-corners with a flute or a violin or a guitar or a recorder, William thinks, or by trawling for glory as a film director in the style of Robert Bresson or Antonioni or Ingmar Bergman, so filling the vacancy for an inter-nationally indulgent art director created by the death of Fellini. He would wear a brown cloak or a silk tunic or a scarlet blazer with black collar and gold buttons. Why ever not? He is twenty-four years old, and avoiding any consider-ation of the sudden and violent death of his parents he sees all possibilities with an 'or' between them. Nothing can be excluded, and he refuses to experience only a fraction of what is out there to be experienced. He senses that in later life, or in real life, the reduction of possibility will be the difference of greatest regret.

She says: 'We love each other. It's only your indecision which keeps us apart.'

Not true, William thinks, that's simply not true. Meaning it's true that he loves her but he isn't indecisive. In fact he loves decisions, and makes them all the time. He decides to get engaged. He decides to leave with Marianne, he decides to come back, he decides to leave with Louise. He makes any number of decisions while all she does is try her best to restrict him to one place at one time wearing the one set of clothes. She hates it when he moves sideways, in among

195

the teeming crowd of people he could still become. He understands this, and loves her for wanting to rescue him, but that doesn't stop him imagining her funeral.

'Come on, William, what are you afraid of?'

In Fellini's film *La Dolce Vita* the hero played by Marcello Mastroianni isn't married. Nor is Mr Darcy in *Pride and Prejudice* nor is the butler in *The Remains of the Day*. They're entitled to be fictional heroes because an important option remains open to them. It may well be that there are longer lists of married men in real life providing a better model by which to live, but to William it already seems a kind of defeat to take your examples from real life.

The train stops in the middle of nowhere. Further down the carriage the boy presses his face up against the window, and he and William look down at the long fairway of a golf course.

'I won't come back for you again.'

'I thought we were meant for each other.'

'There are limits.'

On the terrace of the club-house a drinks party is under way, and in a neighbouring estate a man relaxes in his garden, putting his feet up. The whole world becomes imperfectly silent and a flight of gulls crosses the sky, first one gull leading, then another, and William can't think of any place in Britain he'd rather be.

She says: 'If you carry on like this I'll leave you.'

'That's another possibility.'

'Sorry?'

'You could marry someone else, anyone else, a European or an Australian or a rich Japanese.'

'Is that what you want?'

'I'm just saying anything's possible.'

'Grow up, William. Not everything's possible.'

William knows there are significant moments, entirely unexpected, which change entire lives. It has happened to his brother, after it happened to their parents. His brother has taken the inheritance, all of it, and made a lucky investment at just the right time in gilts or bonds or German bunds. Now he eats salad in brasseries with Christian Dior or Helmut Lang or Vivienne Westwood, while giving generously to the campaign funds of the Liberal Democrats or the Ulster Unionists or the Tory party. If William allows himself one exception to his rule that everything is possible, he swears never to ask his brother for help, not that it should ever come to that. There's no reason he shouldn't be equally as lucky as long as he stays on the right road, even if he's taking the long way round. He's waiting for something extraordinary to happen, waiting to be singled out, wanting to be special.

She says: 'You're not thinking straight. You love me. I love you. We belong with each other.'

William wishes he knew. Either marriage is an ill-judged junction off the road, or it's exactly the instant difference he's looking for. Either/or, but how is he supposed to tell? If this is his Damascus, then shouldn't it be a bit more obvious?

'One day you'll regret this,' she says.

'Only if I remember it.'

There ought to be a sign telling him what to do. Because after today, if he makes the wrong decision, every option will remain open to him except this one. The world will overflow with all sorts of everything except this. His whole life, if he gets it wrong, will change at this exact point, until gradually his only sense of time becomes then and now, now and then.

———————

11/1/93 MONDAY 12:48

'I don't believe you,' Spencer said. 'She wouldn't have left without telling me. We agreed we had until the end of the day.'

'You don't know her as well as you think you do,' William said. 'You can't make up your mind. She went to fetch her shoes.'

Grace said: 'Can I have my present now?'

The three of them were in the kitchen gathered round the table, where William had draped a British Lions Rugby League tea towel over the fruit bowl with the fish in it. Like a magician, he made himself ready to whip the cloth away.

'Not yet,' Spencer said. 'We should wait for Hazel.'

'She's gone,' William said.

'Gone where?'

'I don't know. Home, I suppose.'

'She hasn't gone,' Spencer said. 'She would have told me first.'

'Can I have my present now?'

'What about waiting for Hazel?'

'She can see it when she comes back down.'

William shook his head meaningfully, meaning Spencer didn't have a clue. Then he concentrated on the matter in hand. With a flourish he snapped away the cloth, and both he and Spencer looked expectantly from the goldfish (still alive) to Grace. Her face was slow to light in a smile. In fact she didn't smile at all. William said:

'You *love* animals.'

'It's a fish,' Grace said.

'What's wrong with a fish?'

'It isn't going to win any showjumping contests.'

'Well no. No, it's not. In fact it's very difficult to argue with that.'

'What's his name?'

'Trigger. Don't you like him?'

Grace leant over the table and turned her head to stare through the side of the bowl. She made a face. Trigger flicked over to take a look and she giggled. 'Not bad,' she said. 'It looks a bit glum, though. Why does it keep going round in circles?'

'He has a very short memory.'

'I think it's a very nice fish,' Grace said. 'I mean considering it's a fish. Is it a boy fish or a girl fish?'

Spencer and William looked at each other. 'We don't really know.'

'I think it's a German boy fish,' Grace said. 'Because then his full name would be Herr Trigger. Get it?'

'What a lovely girl,' William said.

Grace had taken Trigger to learn some computer games, hoping to put a smile on his face.

'She is,' Spencer agreed.

'I meant Hazel.'

'It was you who upset her,' Spencer said. 'She'd never have left if you hadn't brought up the whole Jessica thing.'

'That was before I became a convert,' William said. 'Come on, I want to show you something.'

William made Spencer follow him out into the hall and along to the front door, even though Spencer would have preferred to go looking for Hazel.

'I am about to go outside,' William said, hitching up his trousers. 'Hazel showed me how.'

With little regard for his own well-being he opened the front door. He stepped outside and Spencer moved up quickly beside him, ready to catch him and carry him back in. The wind was stronger now, but not cold, and overhead the single cloud remained unbroken. William swayed a bit but he didn't retreat. He stood to attention and clenched his hands in tight fists at his sides. His face began to turn a deep cherry colour, but that was because he was holding his breath. He also had his eyes closed.

He opened his eyes, stared straight ahead, breathed out and then in again, held his breath, kept his eyes open. He looked like a man playing woodwind, but without any instrument.

'What's it like?' Spencer said. 'What can you see?' He had his arms out to catch William when he fell.

'A music shop,' William whispered. He breathed out and in again. 'I can see a music shop.'

'What else?'

'A Japanese man.'

'What else?'

'Nothing.'

'What about the bus going by?'

'No. Nothing else.'

'There's a bus. It's going by us now.'

'I see no bus.'

'People? You see the people on the other side of the street, looking into the shop windows? Some of them are looking over here.'

'I see a Japanese man. I see a music shop.'

He took a step backwards into the house, and Spencer quickly closed the door behind him. He started breathing raggedly as if he'd just stopped running. He grinned broadly as he caught his breath, bent over to hold his knees as he coughed a couple of times.

'There,' he said. 'Easy. Hazel taught me that.'

'What about the bus? And the other people? What about the travel agents and all that?'

'She said I had to block some things out. You have to stop thinking that everything might be important, even though it probably always is to somebody, somewhere. You can't try to see it all. You can't check everybody out, one by one. You just can't.'

'Isn't that a bit sad?'

'Otherwise you'd never move on from one day to the next. You have to believe it's going to be OK. That's what Hazel said, and she's right.'

'Well she's been to College, hasn't she?'

Hazel was brilliant, William said, and he wouldn't hear a word said against her. He was a total convert.

'Allah be praised,' Spencer said. 'But a pity she's gone home, then.'

'Maybe she hasn't.'

'She should make up her mind.'

At last William managed to straighten up without coughing. He spluttered a bit and clapped Spencer on the back.

'You two are made for each other,' he said.

'How do you know? How does anyone ever know?'

'Don't fuck it up, Spencer.'

It wasn't the kind of language Spencer expected from William. He thought he probably resented it. He had the same right to make a bad decision as anyone else.

'Something similar happened to me at your age,' William said. 'I talked myself out of it and look what happened to me.'

'It's not as if I have to decide today, is it? I can decide tomorrow, or the day after that, or next week. There's no need to rush into it, is there?'

'She might already have left. You'll only get her back if you decide today.'

'Tomorrow. I'll decide tomorrow.'

'Tomorrow never comes, Spencer. Everyone knows that.'

———————

It is the first of November 1993 and somewhere in Britain, in Staines or Swindon or Narberth or Horsham, in Melksham or Melrose or Erewash or Huddersfield, everything is stylishly patterned in Paisley. Sprightly white-haired old ladies sit and drink tea and knit one or pearl one or drop one, spooling out cardigans in angora or chenille or alpaca for their children or grandchildren or victims of natural disaster. The poor eat cake and shortbread biscuits. The blind have *The Archers* or *Book at Bedtime*. The mad and the bad and the jealous angry have successfully learnt, in the patient manner of the British, to suppress their emotions. Gruesome murders are no more than amusements, exquisitely investigated in grand houses like Heveningham Hall or Herstmonceux Castle by H. R. F. Keating or Philip Dickson Carr or Dame Ngaio Marsh. Children discover first love beneath blue skies on sand dunes. The schools instil a profound respect for Shakespeare and everyone has their own house (their own house their castle) and limitless offers of employment.

Mrs Mitsui, Henry's mother, keeps track of paradise by ordering *The Times* once a week, on Mondays. Any news not to her taste she attributes to the famously dark British sense of humour, which she'd have learnt to appreciate more thoroughly if only she'd been allowed more time.

'I should have killed myself there and then,' she says.

Henry Mitsui is eighteen years old and it's not the first time he's heard his mother say this. Britain is perfect and once upon a time, a long long time ago, she was engaged to be married to a perfect Briton, to the Duke of Wellington or William Rathbone or Lord George Gordon.

'It was definitely going to happen,' she says defensively. 'It was published in Forthcoming Marriages.'

'But it didn't happen, did it?' Henry says. 'So why keep on about it?'

A date had been set and it was all arranged. Then, without any warning at all, her perfect Briton was suddenly taken by a dreadful and unlikely disease, by pneumonia or sclerosis or smallpox. And after that everything had been different. Nothing was ever quite the same again.

'But you never actually saw him dead, did you?' Henry says meanly. 'You never saw a body or went to a funeral.'

'It would have been too much for me to bear. Besides, there were visa complications.'

Henry would like to confide in his mother that he's just broken up from his latest girlfriend, who wants to spend more time in Asaka with the self-defence force. His mother, however, has already moved on to the part where if only she'd stayed in Britain, she'd have been sure to live happily ever after. Her lost life is a busy one, involving daily lunches at Royal Ascot or livery dinners at the Saddlers' Hall or gala concerts at the Equinox, Leicester Square.

'I won't be seeing her again,' Henry says, breaking the rules. He's supposed to keep quiet and sympathise in silence.

His mother shoots him an angry look until he concedes, as so often before, that her single definitive regret should be allowed to back up vastly against the smallness of now. It overshadows everything: Henry's break-up from his girl-friend, the dryness of the roses in a vase on the table, the violence of the headlines from today's precious *Times: Massacre* and *Hatreds* and *Killing. Local Education authorities should be axed, says report.* Henry would say he loves his mother, but he doesn't want to end up like this. He doesn't want to live a life stifled by the strength of a single remembered event. He instinctively knows that people should have more than one memory which travels with them, defining who they are. It has to be more healthy to share the influence out over many. That's what being balanced means.

'I didn't know how to keep her,' Henry says, again defying the silence. From his mother, he wants the reassurance of a mother's unconditional love, and then he wants her pity. He's asking for proof that his life touches her life, and that there are other people as well as himself who are truly alive. Otherwise other people have a tendency to fade. It becomes difficult to place them, which can make him wonder why they matter.

'Did you love her?'

'Who?'

'This girl of yours. The one who's gone back to Asaka.'

'I don't know.'

'How do you feel?'

'I wish I cared more for her.'

'Do you feel like killing yourself?'

205

'Mum.'

'If you don't, then it can't be love.'

'How can you say that? How does anyone ever know?'

'You just know. I knew. And when the time comes you'll know too. It's destiny. It's not something you can avoid.'

'You did.'

'I was cruelly handled by fate.'

'You married Dad.'

'His was the best offer, after I felt sane again.'

'But it wasn't love, was it?'

'No-one can mope about forever.'

'You could have gone back to Britain,' Henry says. 'You could still go back, instead of idealising what might have been.'

'I don't idealise. And anyway it's not the same now.'

'Of course it is.'

'It all disappears. It's just another part of Europe now. That's what it says in the paper. And anyway, who said I didn't love your father?'

'You did, you say it all the time. You say you'd rather have died.'

'Oh, Henry. Put a smile on your face. You don't want to believe everything I say.'

'So what should I believe then?'

'Believe what you want to be true. That way everybody's happy.'

———

'Go home, Hazel, I would.'

Talking to yourself was the first sign of madness, or maybe the second. Not knowing which sign it was was the next sign and then you were mad.

After the quiet of the garden, Hazel had been surprised by the busyness of the street, and how close the daily lives of other people came to Spencer's front door. The contrast, and a meaningless gust of wind which blew straight through her, made her feel suddenly displaced and vulnerable, with no idea of what she was made for or how she fitted in. She saw a workman leant on a spade reading a newspaper, but the newspaper was no way to find out what was going on. It couldn't even begin to tell you, for example, why a nice girl like Hazel was all dressed up for a big night out at half-past-one on a dull Monday afternoon. She felt watched, and blamed the dress. She should go home, forget about Spencer who'd never make up his mind, forget about Henry Mitsui who'd soon be gone.

Carrying only her purse and wearing no coat, she'd crossed her arms and stepped into the road. There were plenty of people around, but strangely no cars, so nothing to stop a quick escape. As soon as she got home, she was going to change out of her dress. Then she was going to search for her old brochures about medical training and bar school, because if it wasn't to be Spencer then a change of profession could be just the turnaround she was looking for.

207

'Go home, Hazel, there's a good girl. There's no reason you have to decide everything today.'

Was that her mother's voice?

Playing with her car keys, delaying her return to the car, Hazel hoped that what she was doing was the right thing to do. Teaching at a distance had taught her the names of the plants in William's garden and the correct order of all the Kings and Queens, but not whether she should go home and give up on Spencer. She looked in at the window of the charity shop with its arbitrary display. A brown cloak had been donated, and a long cardigan, and an ashtray made from half a coconut. There was an ornamental duck, a paisley shawl, an embroidered cushion, a Sharp radio, and a six-piece set of period cutlery with a matching initialled napkin ring. Hazel stared at all these things, hoping any one of them might mean something. She wanted a sign telling her to stay, and it could come from the objects in the window, from the workman and his newspaper, from any passer-by. She didn't really care. She just wanted a sign.

The workman whistled, and Hazel walked quickly to her car. She locked the door behind her and then checked the passenger door. There was always this same problem with the present moment. It was never laid out as placidly as the past, with its neat consecutive events, and you never knew quite as clearly where you stood. She started the engine and pulled out into the still deserted road.

She and Spencer were failing to make it through the day. He obviously wasn't ready to move on, and Hazel was nothing more than an awkward intrusion. She found it difficult now to remember her earlier optimism, and could only smile unhappily at whatever sudden enthusiasm had made her give Spencer's address to the school secretary. It wasn't that she'd been expecting him to invite her to stay, but she knew it was always a possibility. Making it public, even in a small way, had been like making a bet on it and trying to make it happen. It hadn't worked, but it was his loss, and he'd always remember this as the day he avoided his one significant opportunity to change things for the better.

And anyway, he still had the perfect Jessica to console him. She wondered if all men did this, and then tried to piece together a perfect man. What would he be good for? Everything, she supposed, which would leave her redundant, and still imperfect. She couldn't change the person she was, and neither could Spencer. Basically, he was never going to make up his mind, and just because he never decided anything he thought that everything was still possible. He was wrong. The two of them, like everybody else, had a dozen or so important events in the past which anchored them to who they were. It was too late to change that now, even if Spencer treasured the vain dream of some kind of redirection sponsored by the gods. He'd just have to accept that their incompatibility was more permanent than that. It wasn't like a temporary case of memory loss, easy to cure with a sudden shock.

At the top of the street, where Hazel should have filtered out into tomorrow and the rest of the world, she found her way blocked by a ribbon of plastic police-barrier, flipping in the breeze. She pulled in at the bus stop, between two lime trees. A crowd had gathered, but she decided to wait it out. There would be no sign now, and nothing encouraged Hazel to turn back. Briefly, it did occur to her that Henry Mitsui might be bluffing. He knew where she lived. He therefore wasn't on his way to Spencer's to miss her for lunch, because in fact he was waiting for her at home, a blister on his thumb from ringing her bell. Nobody would take much notice, not until next month sometime when they read in the paper that children had stumbled across a woman's body abandoned near playing fields.

That was definitely her mother's voice.

The crowd on the library steps began to cheer. Hazel leant forward over the steering wheel for a better view, and saw a flurry of white wedding dress make a hesitant start to an abseil down the front of the library. It made her smile. The woman in the wedding dress descended more vigorously, and this, surely, had to be a sign. The road was closed for Miss Havisham, who'd broken her solitary vigil to abseil in a wedding dress down the face of a library.

Before she could change her mind Hazel turned the car round, reversing close to the lime trees and the black muck made by bacteria on the greenfly waste. Life was everywhere, she thought, and this too could be taken as an omen, and a good one. As she drove back towards the house, she reassured herself that everything she could see was only real life, and there was no reason to be frightened. Whatever she might imagine there was only this, there was what she could see, and she wouldn't see anything else because only a certain number of things turn out to be true. She remembered the flying skirts of Miss Havisham and laughed. This was what there was, every day until she died, and it would have to be enough.

Hazel backed her car into the same space she'd just left. She wanted to believe that coincidence was fate and that luck had meaning, and therefore she wasn't all alone. She wanted there to be a right and a wrong way to proceed. Otherwise there could never be a Damascus but only closed roads (for security reasons), and an insignificant Miss Havisham, and nothing but random events like these to determine what happened for the rest of the day. Or any day for that matter, when day after day became, eventually, a life.

She climbed out of the car, and was thoughtfully locking the door when a long-fingered hand reached for her elbow, begging her attention.

9

No-one wears patterned sweaters in 1993.

THE TIMES 11/1/93

11/1/93 MONDAY 13:24

'I'm so glad you came back,' Spencer said. 'You wouldn't believe how happy it makes me.'

He wrapped his arms round her waist as she reached up into the top cupboard for teabags, the high-heels of her shoes lifting off the kitchen floor. With his nose, he nudged her hair to one side and kissed her several times behind the ear, which was much more fun than what he'd just been doing at the table, pushing birthday cake candles into Jaffa cakes.

'Not now, Spencer.'

'I thought now was always as good a time as any?'

'It was. But it isn't any more.'

'You frightened me,' Spencer said, holding her more tightly and closing his eyes. 'I thought you weren't coming back.'

'For God's sake, Spencer,' Hazel said, shrugging him off. 'He's in the *hall*!'

Spencer took a step back. He pierced a seventh Jaffa cake with a slim candle while Hazel noisily prepared a pot of tea and two mugs. *Celtic Football Club – Forever*, and *Cromer, My Kind of Town*. Spencer tried again, stepping up behind her and splaying his hands across her lower back.

'Your timing's terrible,' she said.

'It's not timing. It's desire.'

'I'm surprised you recognise it.'

She didn't once turn towards him, or move her body back into his hands.

'I looked out of the window for a sign,' Spencer said, his lips moving across her neck. 'I thought I saw a ray of sunshine.'

'Rubbish. Leave me alone.'

'Is he a boyfriend?'

'He has a funny *tooth*. He *looks* at me all the time.'

'Well it was you who invited him in.'

'He still has the labels attached to his sweater.'

Spencer let her go. He considered disappearing to the office for a computer-assisted sulk, but instead he pointedly speared the last of the ten Jaffa cakes.

'Marks and Spencer labels.'

'So why invite him into the house? And why have you left him in the hall?'

Because he might be a mad killer nutcase, why else? He was a foreigner with a funny tooth and a relentless stare and labels hanging off a brand new horribly-patterned jumper. He was a stranger come to murder them all, which was almost certainly untrue. Hazel knew that not everyone unknown was a murderer. To think like that was the beginning of a kind of madness, her mother's kind.

'He's a student of mine who's about to leave the country,' Hazel said. 'I've never met him before and probably never will again.'

'So what are you going to do with him?'

'I'm making him some tea.'

'I can see that. He could be a madman, anything.'

'But probably he isn't. Most people aren't.'

And tea was always useful because it had a beginning and an end, and when it came to an end she could ask him to leave.

Falling in love with Miss Burns was easy. Even finding her in London now seemed straightforward enough, a mixture of patience and destiny. Henry was therefore surprised to discover, now that he was actually here, that he had no idea of what to say to her. She was so young, and so blonde, and there was no sign at all of a friendly black cat. He'd expected her to be older and more like a teacher, but she still had the same unflappable voice and he couldn't say he was disappointed. His love, transcending purely physical considerations, remained intact. It was a pleasure to watch her closely, re-learning her from life. At last this was the real Miss Burns, for two years his distanced teacher at the Central London Institute of Learning, his one true love.

She carried two chairs through into the hall. He took one of them, trying to help, and she made it clear he should sit on it exactly where he was. Only after he sat down did she position her own chair, facing his but far enough away to make them have to project their voices, like actors.

She then remembered the tea, which Henry took as a good sign. It meant she wanted him to stay, and while she poured, he allowed himself the luxury of imagining her as a child, as a series of smiling photographs. She was in vivid colour and very beautiful, usually on holiday, lighting up the sea-shores of Britain. It was a shame she'd put her chair so far away.

'Miss Burns,' Henry said, clearing his throat. 'Miss Burns, I was hoping we might enjoy some lunch together, outside.'

'I'm very busy,' Hazel said. 'I have a lot of work to do.'

A man came in. He was also carrying a chair, which he put down close to Miss Burns. He was wearing a suit which flapped open and a brown shirt with no tie. His hair needed something doing to it. He brought Henry his mug of tea and shook his hand.

'Hello,' he said. 'Spencer Kelly, I live here. Pleased to meet you.'

He was Spencer Kelly, a marine broker at Lloyds (his suit). No, not even close. He was Spencer Kelly, an inter-viewer for the British Forces Broadcasting Service (his voice), or a lifelong train buff and leading opponent of the

216

government's plans to privatise British Rail (his refusal to make small talk). But none of these harmless lives seemed to fit him. He was Spencer Kelly, Hazel's lover. That couldn't be right. He was Spencer Kelly, who fell horribly while climbing near Mochnant, who made Henry nervous and when Henry was nervous he put his hands in his pockets. He slipped his fingers across the consoling plastic envelope of powder, wishing he knew what to do with it, and how it could help him.

In the meantime he tried to break the ice (with Spencer Kelly, tragic victim of a Syrian-backed terrorist attack), with some man-talk. He asked whether anybody knew the price of a professional footballer these days? No response. Had they heard about the Chinese women runners who drank a potion brewed by their coach, Ma Junren, which turned them overnight (in one fell swoop) into world-beaters? They had.

'In the 3,000 metres.'

'And the 10,000 metres,' Spencer said.

'And the marathon, I think. I read it in the paper.'

'I think we all did.'

Other people. If everything wasn't just right it was always their fault. Them and their long intricate lives which refused to make way for his.

———

It is the first of November 1993 and somewhere in Britain, in Lowestoft or Thurrock or Kinloss or Solihull, in Llanharan or Nottingham or Mangotsfield or Dewsbury, Spencer Kelly is a convicted criminal. Paying his debt to society he is working unpaid as a steward at a qualifying gala for the BT-BSAD national paralympic swimming championships. There is a single area of banked seating half-full of spectators, many of them children, but Spencer chooses a seat next to a blonde girl with light brown eyes who seems to be alone. He guesses she's about nineteen, the same as him.

For a while, exercising caution, he just sits there. He lets her get used to his presence while opposite them a huge timing clock by Seiko or Brietling or Heuer times the swimmers. It has no numbers and when the single hand smoothly passes its highest point, at the top where the twelve and the sixty should be, it's as if time just starts up again without anything meaningful like a minute or an hour having passed.

Spencer clears his throat, and then nudges the girl with his elbow.

'Haven't we met somewhere before?'

She leans away and looks at him down her nose.

'Absolutely not,' she says, very well-spoken.

'Sure?'

'Sure.'

'Sorry,' Spencer says. 'I thought we had.'

Spencer blames Hazel for this general discomfort he feels around other women, who all suffer by comparison. Over the phone she is so perfectly disembodied that he can easily imagine her embodying perfection. Unfortunately, it doesn't seem to work both ways, and she keeps phoning him up and telling him how dreadful it is to sleep with arts students or course professors or the younger brother of her next-door neighbour. Spencer then suffers melancholic visions of her brown hair splayed across a pillow and her glistening violated eye. Such thoughts do him no good at all, and he's decided that the best remedy is to seek out proper contacts of his own, girls with bodies. This one, the blonde one, suddenly turns and asks him if he makes a habit of talking to strangers.

'Definitely not,' Spencer says.

'Me neither.'

She looks longingly down at the pool. 'Did you ever want to be a swimmer?'

Spencer shakes his head. The girl frowns. Spencer nods his head emphatically, meaning my mistake of course I wanted to be a swimmer. She purses her lips. Spencer sits on his hands, and wishes she was Russian. She is now watching a well-built, casually-dressed young man by the poolside. He can't be much older than Spencer, but he acts a lot more grown-up.

'I'm doing community service,' Spencer says. 'That's why I'm here.'

'Rob a bank?'

'Poisoned someone who made fun of me,' Spencer says, and that makes her look. 'Only took a few nights in the library.'

As it happens. Reference section. He found out how to make a dangerous poison called ricin with castor-oil seeds, mixed up a non-fatal dose and attached it as a pellet to the end of an umbrella. Then he stabbed his enemy in the Menswear section of Marks & Spencer. Or it might have been Simpson's or British Home Stores. He forgets.

'It can't be true then. You'd remember it if it was true.'

'I was very excited at the time.'

'How were you caught?'

'I turned myself in. The police said they'd be lenient because I wasn't a gang.'

'I was once in trouble with the police,' the girl says. 'At college once.'

'Is that your boyfriend?'

She is still peering down at the big blond grown-up by the side of the pool, who is helping a competitor from the water. It's the girl who's just won the 100-metres breast-stroke or the 200-metres backstroke, or possibly both. She doesn't have the use of her legs, which makes her swimming and winning quite phenomenal.

'He belongs to the swimmer,' Spencer's brown-eyed sad sexy neighbour says. 'Do you have a girlfriend?'

'Sometimes,' Spencer says, and because there's no race immediately scheduled and no urgent stewarding to be done, he and the girl find themselves testing each other out with some basic questions, because nobody wants to be stuck with a psycho. They start with what's your name?

'Why?' she says.

'Well,' Spencer says, 'it's generally considered standard

220

practice. When two people meet they swap names. For future reference.'

'I see,' she says. 'But the name itself doesn't really matter?'

'I don't suppose it does, no.'

'My name could be Emma, for example.'

'If you wanted. It would have to stay the same though, or it doesn't work.'

'Or Grace. Or Anita. Any preferences?'

'I don't know.'

'I'll be Emma then. You be River.'

'Fine, whatever you say.'

She's definitely good-looking, in an alluring blonde sort of way, and Spencer now knows from this name conversation that she's also a bit of a nutcase. It's always best to find out early on. He tries her out on her age and whether her parents are married and who's her favourite famous person. And does she think that life is more about the pursuit of pleasure or the evasion of pain?

Putting that one aside for a moment, Emma answers the other questions almost normally. Her parents are still married, she says, unlikely though it seems these days, and because she's obviously telling the truth Spencer resists making up a story about his adoption. He was going to hint that his real father was a roguish actor from the black and white era, Rock Hudson or Marcello Mastroianni or Ronald Coleman. But instead he surprises himself by telling her the truth. He hasn't seen his mother since she remarried to a twenty-eight-year-old homosexual Kurd who would other-

221

wise have been deported to Turkey. They met at the airport. Spencer's Dad went completely berserk. He was at work, carrying several boxes of furniture belonging to Dirk Bogarde. He smashed them all up into little pieces and became the second member of his family to experience non-voluntary community service.

'He must really have loved her,' Emma says.

'Sorry?'

'Well he must have, otherwise he wouldn't have minded.'

The idea that his father might actually love his mother comes as something of a shock to Spencer. He finds it embar-rassing, as if on Christmas afternoon in the middle of a Disney video they'd come across a wide-eyed, softly-spoken *fuck*.

'Brothers?' Emma asks. 'Sisters?'

And why not? Spencer suddenly goes sad, or pretends to be sad. He hardly knows the difference any more, and this Emma hasn't known him long enough to tell. He once had a sister. He sees in great detail the hatched white lacing on his trainers. His sister died in a car crash. It still sounds like a chat-up line.

'If I think about her today,' Spencer says, 'then somehow she's still alive, today while I'm thinking about her. Do you think that's right?'

'I don't know. Maybe.'

'Except whenever I remember her she's always doing the same things. Playing football. Running. Boring for her really. I'm going to be an actor,' Spencer adds, and the girl looks at him sharply.

'You're an actor?'

'Not yet. I will be. I want to be.'

'You're at college?'

'I work in a warehouse.'

'I know someone who works in a warehouse.'

They both look at each other, but no, Spencer's never going to get anywhere until he learns to put Hazel out of mind. 'Lots of people work in warehouses,' he says, and Emma nods her head vigorously (yes, yes they do) and then smiles, making Spencer think things are really swinging along now. 'I'm only there until I've saved enough money to go to London. Then I'm going to be an actor.'

Emma laughs, which isn't kind of her. 'Let me guess,' she says. 'You go to London, audition, get discovered, become famous.'

'Well yes,' Spencer says, 'and I might go to College in the evenings.'

'Boys,' she laughs. 'You're all the same. Every one an overnight sensation, tomorrow night.'

'Well pardon me,' Spencer says, thinking he shouldn't have said that about College. It seems unlikely that Tom Cruise or River Phoenix or Keanu Reeves ever went to a City Tech, even though it's just a way of passing the time until he's singled out for something special. It's to keep him occupied while he waits for the Act of God which is owed to him, but this isn't the easiest of things to explain to a stranger in a swimming pool. What started out as a good idea, making friends with the nice-looking blonde girl, is quickly turning into another humiliation Spencer may never forget. He tries to change the subject:

'So what plans have you got for your life then?'
'I'm going to be a lawyer or a doctor.'

11/1/93 MONDAY 13:48

Henry was almost the exact opposite of Spencer. He looked
at her all the time, as if hoping to see something extra which
required great concentration. Hazel stood up and went to the
telephone table where she'd left *The Woman in a Car with
Glasses and a Gun*. His eyes followed her, without blinking.
And again (unlike Spencer) she could tell that Henry was
always thinking about tomorrow.

He smiled at her, showing off his brown tooth. He asked
her what the book was about.

'There's a lady in it,' Hazel said.

Looking at his tooth was only centimetres away from
looking at his lips, wondering what it was like to kiss him.
She looked at the tooth. 'The lady has a car,' Hazel said.
'She wears glasses. She carries a gun.'

'You are very beautiful,' Henry said, and Hazel glanced
across at Spencer, who managed a frown and not much else.
No, that wasn't fair. He also crossed his arms, and then his
legs. Hazel went to put the book back on the table, then
found she wasn't happy with the idea of Henry looking at
her from behind. She turned round again, facing him.

'More beautiful than I expected,' he said. 'I hadn't expected
you to be so young.' He smiled again. 'Or so blonde.'

'Spencer was just the same,' Hazel said, and with his frown wavering at about sixty percent compression Spencer told Henry how much he must be looking forward to his flight back to Japan. Henry's gaze never once left Hazel, and she was increasingly keen to escape. She wasn't frightened, and she didn't want to label Henry as something he wasn't, but she'd also quite like a few moments on her own without being stared at. She surprised herself by saying she was going to make some soup. She surprised everybody.

'I'll help you,' Henry said.

'No, you stay here. You can have a chat with Spencer.' The two men both looked at her. 'You can talk some more about sport,' she suggested, and before either of them could think of dissuading her, she'd already left them to it.

Back in the kitchen, Hazel felt an enormous sense of relief. She avoided examining this feeling too closely by keeping herself busy, unnecessarily so, and it wasn't long before she found herself reading the nutritional information on the backs of packets of various brands of soup. Although it was probably useful to know that they all contained less chicken than salt, she'd been hoping for more practical types of information, like how should she deal with a dangerous maniac and was feeding him this soup recommended by the manufacturer? She already knew the answer: not everyone was a maniac. Life would be unliveable if she thought like that.

There was no need to be frightened. He was most likely and most of the time a decent and honourable human being, like everyone else. She wasn't going to condemn him just because he had limited small talk and a funny tooth. He was certainly very polite. And if she really thought there was something wrong with him she wouldn't be making him lunch. She didn't think. So then why was she hoping Spencer would do something spontaneous and male and perhaps even violent, securing their instant rescue from any danger? Only these days she wasn't allowed to think like that, not if she ever wanted an invitation to the Woman of the Year lunch.

She had to make up her mind. Henry wasn't dangerous or even unpleasant; he was a minor inconvenience in the middle of their day. All the same, he *might* be dangerous. He had the fixed gaze and the funny tooth. He had the patterned sweater. He'd tracked her first to her house and now here, although admittedly without any obvious axe. Hazel wished there was some kind of infallible test for murderous psychopaths, but in the absence of such a useful invention she was still convinced it was best not to be frightened. This wasn't a conviction ever likely to be supported by newspapers, or television. Instead, with everything which so palpably *could* go wrong in life (brought daily to everyone's attention), it was more an act of faith, in God or in good luck or in her observation that for most people things turn out bearably in the end.

All the same, she and Spencer would have been safer staying in bed.

Miss Burns, who knew everything, had deliberately left him alone but with someone else in an unfurnished entrance hall, having offered him no encouragement except for a *Cromer, My Kind of Town* mug of cooling tea. An uneasy thought occurred to him: she knew all along that as soon as he had his diploma he'd have to leave the country. She didn't want him and she would never love him and that's why she'd left him alone with Spencer Kelly, a manual worker shot to death after he attacked his employer with a knife. What kind of involved madness was that? Why did the lives of other people complicate themselves so thoroughly? Still nervous, Henry had one hand in his pocket. He pressed and moulded the packet of powder between his fingers, wondering who to poison first.

Ridiculous. Preposterous. Drink the famous British tea. Think like the people you have chosen to live among. Or failing that, remember the difference between thinking a thing and doing it, and behave like everyone else. He didn't, anyway, want to poison anyone. Except perhaps himself, because if Miss Burns didn't love him then it wasn't worth living.

It was all getting out of hand again. Of course she could be persuaded to love him. It was destined. The very fact that he was here was proof of it, and Henry excluded any other possibility by narrowing everything down to the present moment. It was something he could always be sure of. He had a cup of tea. It was in a mug which said *Cromer, My Kind of Town*. The present moment, he thought, sifting through his collection of idiomatic phrases, is my cup of tea. And the wall which is painted a cream colour. And arriving with a big smile, carrying in both arms a fruit bowl full of water, a small girl-child, life undecided.

'Hello,' she said. 'This is my new fish. Try and guess his name.'

She was followed in by an old man, and both Henry and Spencer stood up. Spencer introduced them all and then made it clear he was leaving.

'This is Henry Mitsui,' he said. 'He has lots of interesting things to say about long-distance running.'

Henry watched him leave, stared between his shoulder-blades knowing he was going to join Miss Burns. The treacherous Spencer Kelly, deservedly fed a lethal speedball of drugs in a nightclub toilet, left to convulse and die on a pavement somewhere, like America. The old man was asking him a question.

'Have you come to look at the house?'

'I've come to see Miss Burns.'

William Welsby looked a bit like the film director Federico Fellini. Fellini had been in the news and Welsby was dressed in black. William Welsby, Fellini's bereaved and forgotten cousin. As for the little girl, she could be anyone because she was still young enough to be capable of anything. One day she'd grow up to be a member of both the MCC and the Surrey County Cricket Club.

'Are you sure you haven't come to look at the house?'

Henry wished they'd both go away. They were just more people between him and Miss Burns, and he didn't have enough powder to poison them all.

'You look a bit pale,' William said. 'What you need is some fresh air.'

———————

It is the first of November 1993 and somewhere in Britain, in Macclesfield or Dorking or Gainsborough or Harwich, in Hawick or Keynsham or Milford Haven or Norwich, Hazel is wondering what's a nice girl like me doing in a place like this. She expects her very own River Phoenix to ask her exactly this question any second now. It's his class of line. He is medium-build, black hair. He is nineteen years old and a Scorpio like she is, and he claims to be a criminal. If her accent has dropped slightly during their conversation it's only in search of the authentic, and she quickly discovers how much fun it is to talk to a stranger she knows she'll never see again.

They've moved from the swimming pool to the bar, partly because Hazel is disgusted by the way Olive gets handed towels by Sam Carter, but also because a new set of races needs to be stewarded and River Phoenix is hiding from his supervisor.

'I thought you wanted to be a swimmer?' he says.

They sit right in the corner of the bar, beneath a speaker playing selections from Mozart or Bartok or Rachmaninov by the London Symphony Orchestra or the Vienna Philharmonic or the Ungarica. The bar manager has ambitions for a sideways move to the Arts Centre. Perhaps by way of compensation the television screen shows highlights from

the British Lions against New Zealand, or Bath against Leicester, or England against Australia.

'People change,' Hazel says. 'That's what people do.'

'But a lawyer? A doctor? That's quite a change.'

Hazel recognises this from University. It's the syndrome
of the ruffled boy trying to get his own back, which in this
case he ought to do quickly before he's lured away from his
community service by Quentin Tarantino. She's not com-
plaining, but she wonders why her body has yet to learn a
language which tells men she isn't interested. Dying her hair
brown or black might just work, but in the meantime her
college experiences, not to mention the cautionary example
of her own parents, have made her properly careful of men's
friendship.

Her father, as it turns out, is having the affair her mother
always suspected. With his new secretary *and* an airline
hostess *and* an exotic swan-necked foreigner who doesn't
speak English. It all counts. He has taken full advantage of
Virgin Freeway or Continental OnePass or SAS Eurobonus to
collect air miles for his lovers to travel free to foreign sales
conventions, where he hands over more accumulated air miles
in exchange for hotel reservations. This explains why his bank
statements have never betrayed him. Hazel asks her mother
why they stay married, and not under the influence of drugs
she says that marriage is like an identity card. It reveals who
you are, both to other people and yourself.

'Why would someone like you want to be a lawyer or a
doctor?'

'To be happy,' Hazel says, which is such an unsatisfactory

answer it annoys her. She also sees that River Phoenix isn't going to let her get away with it. He says:

'Happy in what way exactly? You mean your parents' idea of happiness?'

'My mother thinks happiness is Nembutal. Yours?'

'God. For Mum, happiness is God. And hanging on to the right memories.'

'I forget things all the time,' Hazel says, remembering Sam Carter drying Olive's long brown hair. She'll soon forget it, she hopes, hoping that the things you forget don't matter any more.

'It's hardly very ambitious, is it?'

'What?'

'Doctors. Lawyers.'

'Twenty-five percent of candidates fail the bar exams.'

'What are you frightened of?'

'I'm not frightened.'

'You're young,' he says. 'You're gorgeous. Don't you ever dream of a life more exciting than that?'

Hazel remembers, just in time, that she's allowed to retaliate. She mentions that she used to like River Phoenix, until she grew out of him. 'You know you're dead?'

'I read it in the paper.'

'Sad.'

'Tragic.'

'At your age.'

They both think of River Phoenix fixed in time, captured on film, never getting any older. No more tomorrows for River, which in fact is often how Hazel feels. She doesn't

231

actually register time passing. She believes she's going to live forever, and that forever will always look very like today, which she knows is wrong. Time passes and people grow old and accidents happen. That's why she has to be a lawyer or a doctor. That's why she has to be responsible and act her age.

'You have to live in the real world,' she tells her own private River Phoenix, who's doing community service. He must have committed a crime and she bets he didn't go to a private school, which still sounds to her like a more real world than her own. He's now telling her to imagine a parallel universe where there are always several options and everything is always possible. She can be anywhere she wants to be and do anything she wants to do.

'No I can't. There is such a thing as reality, you know.'

'I bet you learnt that from your mother.'

Hazel is almost too angry to reply. There *is* such a thing as reality, whether they like it or not. It exists and you can see it, smell it, sense it, touch it, remember it, even take bits of it home with you in a box. There is the unique moment in which life is real, and that moment is always now. Here they are at the pool, in the bar, music, television, and there's only so far they can bend it to suit themselves. Real life keeps insisting on its own shape, and a million ifs or buts or eithers or ors don't make a blind bit of difference. This is what there is and we have to stand up and get on with it and grow old in it. It won't let us go anywhere we like or do anything we want, quite the opposite, which is why it makes sense to be a lawyer or a doctor, and fully insured

by General Accident or the CIS or Commercial Union.
Things will go wrong. That's how you know that they're
real.

'You can still dream though, surely?'

'Of course you can.'

'Or is that something else your mother made you afraid
of?'

'It has nothing to do with my mother. And anyway, I
don't *have* to become a lawyer or a doctor.'

'I bet you will though.'

He leant back with his arms crossed, certain of victory.
Hazel hated him.

'All girls are the same,' he said.

'*What?*'

'Eventually you'll *become* your mother.'

'You know absolutely nothing.'

'You're sure we haven't met before?'

'Only in your dreams.'

———————

11/1/93 MONDAY 14:12

'Fresh air never hurt anyone,' William said, and Henry
couldn't disagree because he was already feeling better than
he had inside. He and William Welsby, who shared his
cousin Federico's fascination with the burlesque, were standing on the terrace, leaning on a balustrade which overlooked

a semi-circular lawn. It was still overcast, but the cloud was lighter in patches with flushes of sunlight just failing to break through. Grace had carefully put the bowl with the fish in it on top of the balustrade. She tugged at Henry's sweater.

'Guess again,' she said.

'Mr Confusion,' Henry guessed. 'Drum Taps, Very Dicey, Flashfeet.'

'No. Guess again.'

'You said he had a name like a horse.'

'He does.'

This was a very good example of why children made Henry feel nervous. They could always remind him of the many questions it was usually impossible to answer.

'I once had a horse,' he said. 'His name was Benjamin.'

The idea that Miss Burns knew he'd have to leave the country worried away at him. She knew everything else, so why not that? He couldn't make it fit into his idea of their destiny together, and he wanted someone to blame, and to punish, but just then a bird started singing and William held up his hands, as if everything else had to stop.

'Georgi Markov,' William said. 'I don't suppose you've ever heard one of him before. He's a Siberian robin.'

Facts. In times of stress Henry knew he could always calm himself with facts.

'Actually it's not,' he said. 'It's a red-flanked bluetail.'

'Are you *sure*?' William strained to listen more closely.

'*Tarsiger cyanurus*,' Henry said. 'Georgi Markov's a funny name to give a bird.'

'It seemed like a good idea at the time,' William said,

distracted, hoping for another snatch of birdsong. 'It was the Siberian connection.'

'Georgi Markov was Bulgarian.'

Did these facts succeed in calming him? Not really. They didn't seem to make William Welsby very happy either.

'I knew that,' he said. 'Obviously.'

While William stared accusingly in the direction of the mulberry bush, Henry made an effort to speak to the child. Miss Burns might be watching from an upstairs window, and attention to children was known to impress.

'Are you having a good birthday?'

'The best. I've got a brilliant fish and Uncle Spencer's making me a special birthday cake.'

'Is anyone else coming?'

'I asked Granny, but she had a fancy lunch to go to. Are you going to stay for cake? Uncle Spencer won't mind. He never minds anything.'

Henry didn't know what to say. It was all Spencer this and Spencer that. Spencer Kelly, incurable victim of Parkinson's or meningitis or cancer of the colon, died in surgery. Henry looked down at the wet lawn beneath the balustrade, and then beyond at the path winding through small copses, bisecting a mulberry tree and a clump of hornbeams. How could he compete with all of this? What did he have to offer? Hazel knew about wild flowers and British painters and birdcalls and the names in order of every King and Queen, so *of course* she knew he'd have to leave. She knew everything. She probably even knew how to make the poison called ricin, just like he did. Thanks to Dr Osawa, Henry had learnt how to give life to people. It was probably just as easy to take it away. Spencer Kelly, nothing. He would kill them all, leaving Miss Burns a simple choice of one.

What he really needed was that automatic weapon, especially at this time of year. Hallowe'en was yesterday and only a few days to go until November 5. People on the other side of the wall would assume the gunfire was fireworks, and he'd get away with it. Passers-by would pass-on-by as if they'd heard nothing, knowing it was none of their business to intrude on the embarrassing emotional instability of others, even if it led to gunfire, mayhem, bloody death. Easier to believe it was fireworks, and walk right past.

'You're looking a bit shaky again,' William said.

'It's nothing. I'm fine.'

He was only thinking these bad things. He wasn't actually doing anyone any harm. 'It's nothing. Just a little panic attack.'

'Oh, I know all about those,' William said. 'You just have to block some things out.'

'I have to see Miss Burns.'

'Good idea,' William said. 'It worked for me.'

'I'm not quite sure what you expect me to do,' Spencer said. 'He's your friend. You invited him in. I intend to be civil and wait until he goes away again. Unless you have a better idea.'

'You can take over the soup.'

Hazel threw several packets over the kitchen table to

where Spencer was arranging his ten candle-pierced Jaffa cakes in the shape of a happy face. After forgetting to buy Grace a present, this was his improvised attempt at a birthday cake. He was hoping Grace would like the idea of ten cakes instead of one, even if they were really biscuits. It had been a busy morning, and maintaining the illusion that this was Grace's special day was now Spencer's main priority. Just for the moment then, Hazel's student was Hazel's problem.

Unasked, uninvited, her Henry Mitsui had found his way to the kitchen. He stood in the doorway and said he had to speak to her, calling her Miss Burns. He meant somewhere else, alone. It was something very important, yes, and he didn't want Spencer to hear it, no, and because Hazel didn't believe in being frightened she crumpled up Spencer's apron (*If you don't like it write to the Queen*) and took Henry through to the dining room, mostly because she knew where it was. She deftly managed to get the huge table between her and him before saying anything.

'We've met each other now,' Hazel said. 'Which is what you wanted.'

'It wasn't just to meet you.'

'I was your distance-learning teacher. Nothing else. Just a voice on a telephone.'

'You know everything.'

'I know nothing.'

'You know the names of all the Kings and Queens. You know flowers and birds.'

'I know how to look up facts in reference books. All these things are easy to learn. They're only hard to remember.'

'I have money,' Henry said. 'I don't have a house like this but I can play the piano. I've travelled. I want to make you happy.'

'Listen to me, Henry. Listen carefully. The whole point of being a distance-learning teacher is not to get too close to the students. I want to do the work without having the human contact. Basically, I'd prefer it if you weren't here.'

'But here I am.'

And Miss Burns was here too, in the same room, just the two of them. This, surely, was the right time to try out the magic words, which changed entire lives. I love you. But then why, if destiny and luck were indeed on his side, should he launch their life together so timidly?

'Miss Burns,' he said. 'Will you marry me?'

And unbidden, in the silence which immediately followed, Hazel thought: at last, a man who knows what he wants.

10

To the vast majority of the peoples of
Europe, it has seemed since the war that
practical sanity and orderliness has
vanished.

THE TIMES 11/1/24

As of this morning, for example, every
citizen of the United Kingdom is also a
citizen of the European Union.

THE TIMES 11/1/93

11/1/93 MONDAY 14:24

'Shouldn't we wait for Hazel?'

'The candles are melting onto the biscuits.'

Spencer turned off the lights. In the November afternoon
gloom the white core of each of the ten candle flames was

hard and bright. Speared into the Jaffa cakes, they lit up the sign of a happy face.

'Is everyone ready?'

William said it again: 'What about Hazel?'

'She's with that man,' Grace said, hopping with excitement. The candles were burning closer to the chocolate, which shone and slipped in the flamelight.

'He won't be staying long,' Spencer said. 'He's just a student of hers.'

'He seems very nice,' Grace said. 'Can I blow out the candles now?'

'Quickly then,' Spencer said, 'and all in one go, or it's bad luck.'

Grace lunged forward, strafing the candles several times, left to right and back again. When her breath ran out she extinguished at least one of the flames with a direct hit with spit. Her face went pillar-box red, and eventually with no breath left and one candle still alight, she closed her eyes and started inhaling and coughing at the same time. Spencer deftly blew out the last candle.

'Have you made a wish?' William asked. Grace was recovering quickly, still choking but also laughing and bright-eyed. 'Everyone has to make a wish on their birthday.'

'I wish it was my birthday every day!'

'Except if you say it out loud it never comes true,' William said.

'It might.'

'Well you just wait and see if it's your birthday again tomorrow.'

240

'Alright then, I'll make another wish.'

'And you have to cut the cake,' Spencer said, handing her a table knife.

Grace looked up at him slyly. 'If I say the wish aloud it won't come true?'

'Correct,' William said.

'Then I wish Uncle Spencer never sees Hazel ever again in his whole life.'

'Very clever,' Spencer said. 'Very assertive. You put the knife in one of the cakes and you make a wish. When the knife hits the plate you scream.'

Miss Burns hadn't said yes. There again, she hadn't said no. She opened a door. It was a gym. She opened another door and it was an empty paint-flaked billiard room once touched up by David Jones.

'David Jones was a painter,' she said.

Closing this door, she turned an ankle, grimaced, pulled off her shoes and backtracked more quickly to yet another door. Watching her naked feet, Henry followed close behind her. He'd have been a fool not to. He was in love, an instant convert to the idea of a life lived happily ever after, and he couldn't help himself. All this was his destiny, because nothing else could explain why he'd fallen so hopelessly in love. She turned back towards him, closing the door to a jacuzzi, almost touching him. He thought of obstructing her, holding her, backing her against indifferent doorways and caressing her, but he let it remain a thought. She seemed to be lost.

241

'The kitchen,' Hazel said forcefully. 'We're going back to the kitchen where the others are.'

She was either suppressing her emotions or playing hard to get, both of which were admirable British characteristics. It was exactly how Henry would have expected her to behave.

'Stop following me about,' she said.

'Will you marry me?'

'I think you should leave.'

'I'll look after you. I'll never be unfaithful.'

'That's not really the issue.'

They weren't far now from the hallway where they'd started. There was a weak smell of chicken soup, or a smell of weak chicken soup, and Hazel headed for the kitchen. Henry watched the marvellous switching of her buttocks beneath the clinging grey wool of the dress. He looked at her soft white feet. Henry Mitsui, suddenly but peacefully at home in his 75th year, dearly loved husband of Hazel and father of Virginia, Jonathan and Christopher, beloved grandfather of Jessie, William and Georgia, all consultant paediatricians. *J'ai plus de souvenirs que si j'avais mille ans.* And why not? He wasn't a monster. In fact he had the refined sensibility which came from growing up rich. Poor people always wanted money, but Henry had been free to work out what was worth wanting more than money. He wanted the marriage of Miss Hazel Burns to Mr Henry Mitsui, son of Mr and Mrs Mitsui of Tokyo, Japan, at the beautiful church of St Etheldreda's, Worth Matravers. Obviously, he loved her, but he was also offering her much more

242

than love. He was an accomplished piano player. He was well-educated and widely-travelled and spoke several languages.

'I'm not a monster,' he said, following as close as he could behind her, and he believed what he said to be true. Whatever his thoughts he always resisted monstrous actions. He may have had a pocket-full of poison, but he'd never actually killed anybody. 'I didn't fall in love with you because you were beautiful. I didn't even know what you looked like. Doesn't that say something?'

Behind the kitchen door, Grace screamed.

Grace wished. And she carried on wishing, moving her lips slightly, making sure it was clearly spelt out for whoever took charge of birthday wishes. She wished for a little baby brother called Sholto and one of those footballs on a string which comes back to you after you kick it. She wished for the part of leading lady in the school's Christmas production of *Cinderella*, and that if she was ever followed home by a man like her friend Nadine was followed home by a man, then that he wasn't really following her. She didn't wish her parents were dead, just changed overnight into people like Hazel and Uncle Spencer. She made a wish for William not to get any older, and wished a long life for her favourite German fish, Herr Trigger. She wished for world peace, and for River Phoenix to be allowed into heaven. And lastly she made a big secret wish for herself, wishing she could be just like everyone else, but not like anyone she actually knew. Amen.

All this counted as one single wish, because obviously everything was connected.

———

It is the first of November 1993 and somewhere else, in Naples or Srinagar or Riyadh or Hong Kong, in Geneva or Akrotiri or Istanbul or Los Angeles, Hazel Burns is a long way from home, preparing a violent death. A warm breeze brushes her hair against her neck, and inside a ruined villa she inspects a mosaic floor depicting a broken Roman river scene. An American Vietnam-veteran dentist now limps towards her, stopping as instructed when his left foot covers the fishing nets flying off to the side of a leaning skiff. A gloomy Mafioso wearing a suede suit creeps up on him from behind.

'Trick or treat?' he whispers.

The dentist turns, smiles. 'You must be joking,' he says, and the gangster pulls a gun from his pocket and shoots him. The victim falls, shudders, dies, stands up, brushes himself down, asks if he did okay.

'Great,' the director says, 'most authentic.'

This last comment is slyly intended as praise for Hazel, who is the film's research assistant and therefore responsible for making it life-like. The director then adds to the compliment by summoning her to an important meeting in his customised Cadillac. He and Hazel have already worked together on *Il Balcone* and *Hell of a Ride* and *Clarissa*

244

Explains It All, and at the age of twenty-one, only recently released from University, this all counts as valuable experience. Hazel quickly learns, for example, that every film ever made has to be finished today, and no later.

'Come on in,' the director says. 'Sit down.'

The enlarged space in the back of the Cadillac feels like a small room. They settle themselves on the back seat, which is like a bed, and the director unexpectedly wipes his eyes. His upper body begins to shake. He openly weeps. He mumbles a heartfelt 'Ciao, Federico,' and Hazel's experience of the film industry tells her that the unexpected loss of a great hero like Fellini can be made bearable only by sex with a blonde British research assistant.

'Il Maestro would have wanted it that way.'

And Hazel, not for the first time, remembers that she could have been a doctor or a lawyer. She should have listened to her mother, but she was terrified of making wrong decisions simply because she was frightened. Just in time then, and provoked by a stranger in a swimming pool, she made an effort to retrieve her dreams of glory. Examined closely, these came down to books, films, sport, and love. She quite fancied having well-respected novels published by Viking or Flamingo or Hamish Hamilton. But whenever she thought up plots the stories sounded familiar, and she worried about how qualified she was to claim they were true. It seemed almost dishonest to present the plot of a life as a simple story, when her own life had never felt as simple as that.

Far easier to act out the lives of other people and aspire to glory as an actress in films or the theatre, but then she

245

worried about losing herself in the unnatural quest to be convincing as other people. Better then to express her essential self in sport, in Netball or Hockey or Ironman Triathlon, but here the problems were chronic injury and early death and unfair competition from her sister. She uncovered so many worries she might just as well have been her mother, whose only access to glory was love.

Love: either it was Damascus and you had no choice. Or somewhere the faith could be found to make the step and move on. The director says:

'Fellini was a film-maker with a zest for life.'

In a compromise which made sense at the time (now he slides himself towards her along the seat), Hazel becomes a research assistant for a production company. It involves travel and occasional professional politeness, such as attending functions in blouses not shirts. At company parties she's expected to occupy the director's children by asking them what they want to be when they grow up. But essentially, as a research assistant, she's in the business of making films real.

She mostly researches violence. She learns the trajectories of spent bullet cases or how to torch a locked Cadillac or the best way to conceal offensive weapons. She finds out how it's done in real life, and then hands over the information for a film to be made from it, even though once it's in a film it may not turn out to be true anymore. All Hazel can do is make sure it starts out true at the beginning.

'Like Il Mago, I have the most lavish psychic fantasies.'

Film people. An example: Hazel's mother has been ill.

Whenever Hazel plans a visit she's tired of having to explain that some people live in the provinces all year round, and not just at Christmas. As for her mother, she now takes enough pills to convince herself that she lives life to the full. Marriage is like Jerusalem, she finally decides, two nations one capital city.

'In Jerusalem the two nations stone each other, Mum.'

'A little adjustment is sometimes necessary.'

She's usually curious to know which of the film stars Hazel meets in real life, but Hazel doesn't like to name-drop.

'Self-indulgent was the word of reproof most frequently thrown at Fellini.'

The director's bronzed hand slips to the inside of Hazel's knee, and she wishes her remaining phonecards worked in foreign countries. More than anything, she'd like to talk to Spencer. Nobody else seems to match up, because the people she meets now are old enough to have far more memories than can be fitted into the space of meeting them. She knows where she is with Spencer, as if they indirectly spent their formative years together, and despite the distances between them he is the person who feels most real to her.

'Like Federico, I also have the most outré erotic fantasies.'

Any second now, back here in the real world, Hazel is about to get herself fired. She calmly lifts up the director's hand, holding the wrist disdainfully between her thumb and finger-tips, already seeing herself with her nose in *The Times*, looking for a new job.

'I can give you dollars or francs,' he says, 'whatever you want.'

She drops his hand back into his lap, where she has no doubt it belongs.

'Deutschmarks? Yen?'

This is what comes from sitting back passively and waiting for life to start, as if for a long time nothing at all happens and then by some miracle it all of a sudden starts happening. When in fact it doesn't happen like that at all. It's about time Hazel took her destiny into her own hands, although somehow that doesn't sound quite right. How can you lay hands on destiny? It's supposed to swagger up all by itself (7ft 1 inch tall and 21 stone) and say here I am. This is the way it is, destiny says, so take your filthy hands off me.

———

11/1/93 MONDAY 14:48

'What flavour is it?'

'Chicken.'

'It doesn't smell like chicken.'

William sniffed at the pale surface of his mug of soup. 'And there's no bread,' he said.

Grace offered him another Jaffa cake, candle removed, while Hazel wondered if she could escape Henry Mitsui forever by going out to buy bread and never coming back. They were all sitting round the kitchen table, mostly in silence, like a family. They each had a mug of instant chicken soup and all the mugs were identical, from a matching white set. They felt like blank pieces of paper, waiting for messages. 'I could go and get some bread,' Hazel said. 'We could all go out and get some bread.'

A street full of strangers seemed a more likely defence against Henry than this unknown house with its acres of empty rooms. He never stopped looking at her, and in a way so unapologetic and out of date it was almost criminal. It wasn't a crime, of course, she knew that, but he wasn't eating or drinking he was just relentlessly *looking* at her, and maybe it was already too late. He never blinked. He sometimes smiled. He looked and looked at her, and her skin prickled beneath the wool of the dress.

Her chair screeched horribly as she shoved it away from the table. She'd been doing so well, but now she'd had enough. She was, in fact, a neurotic paranoid just like her mother. This is what her whole life had been leading up to, and it was the hidden truth behind all her behaviour at all times up until now. Henry was going to kidnap her, rape her, kill her. His only reason for living was to do her harm, and life turned out to be full of terror and trouble just like her mother had always promised. For the first time in her life, Hazel insisted on her right to be frightened.

'He asked me to marry him,' she said. She had everyone's attention.

Henry placed his plastic envelope of powder on the table. He was going to give her one last chance.

'Will you marry me?'

'No, I will not.'

And this, surely, was when Spencer was supposed to do something, anything. In the absence of Hazel being swallowed up by the floor (Damascus!) or finding the uniquely correct words to say (Damascus!), Spencer could take the situation heroically in hand and instantly prove himself by throwing Henry Mitsui out on his ear (also Damascus).

Henry said: 'We're destined for each other.'

'And if I still say no, what then? Are you going to shoot me?'

'He doesn't have a gun,' William said. 'Does he?'

'Of course not,' Spencer said, standing up at last.

'So who's going to shoot who then?' Grace said.

'Nobody,' Spencer said, pretending to be calm, hoping his pretence was a calming influence. It was like a surprise audition for the voice of reason, and Spencer was still working out an approach. 'Nobody ever gets shot except in films, and in America.'

'And in Belfast,' Grace said.

'Yes.'

'And maybe in places where they take drugs.'

'Yes, Grace.'

'And anyway,' Hazel said, 'I'm with Spencer.'

Spencer smiled weakly. 'In a manner of speaking.'

Grace fed some birthday Jaffa cake to Trigger, crumbling tiny amounts of sponge biscuit onto the surface of the water. William examined his plate, and then dabbed up some splinters of chocolate with his fingertips. Spencer. Hazel. Henry stood up and held his small packet of powder out in front of him, at the same level as his eyes. They were hard, excited, shining like stones.

'Nobody move,' he said.

Reflected in the overhang curve of the fruit bowl, his face warped and flattened by the water, Spencer remained a failure, unable to decide, act, rescue Hazel the woman he wanted to love, had loved, almost loved, had he really ever loved her? He loved her, he loved her not, he loved her but. Stunned by the sight of Henry Mitsui gone mad, threatening them all quite sincerely with a small plastic packet, Spencer found himself hoping for some kind of interruption. That would be the easiest way out. The Italians would arrive to look at the house, or there'd be a late Hallowe'en trick or treat. Two escorted youngsters in the afternoon daylight, perhaps, forbidden to parade in last night's darkness by paranoid parents. Late but determined, they insist on the door being answered, breaking Henry Mitsui's spell. Or Spencer could do something himself, of course. He himself could be the interruption.

'It's poison,' Henry said. 'It's English name is ricin. I made it myself from castor-oil seeds.'

'We know how it's made,' Hazel said.

'How strong is it?' Grace wanted to know.

'It's very, very strong.'

Hazel said: 'Are you threatening us?'

'How do we know it's real poison?' Grace insisted. 'It could be fake.'

251

'It's poison,' Henry said. 'I made it myself.'

'But you might only be *saying* that.'

Henry tore off a strip at the top of the packet, and held it out defensively in front of him, his arm straight. To Hazel he looked like a small boy with a crucifix, playing at vampires, hoping he'd made himself invincible. Spencer took a step towards him.

'Come along now,' he said. 'I think it's time you were going.'

'It's real poison,' Henry said. 'You better believe me.'

Spencer frowned, raised his eyebrows, pushed his chin forward and tried to look belligerent, all to little effect. None of it stopped Henry from leaning over the table, knocking the packet sharply with his index finger, and showering a tiny amount of powder across the top of the water in the fruit bowl. Trigger angled his body upwards, to where every disturbance meant food. William knocked his chair over as he gathered up the fruit bowl and rushed it to the sink. Grace ran after him.

'What's happening?' she said, trying to look round William's back.

'It's alright,' William said, clumsily trying to tip out the water without losing Trigger. 'Everything's alright.'

'Is he poisoned?'

'He's fine.'

'Well it doesn't work *immediately*,' Henry said.

Hazel started to laugh. In fact the more she thought about it the funnier it seemed. She sat herself down again, leant back in her chair and laughed some more. 'You've done it

252

wrong, haven't you?' she said. 'If you want to threaten people you can't do it with poison, not like that. It's not like it's a gun or anything. You have to keep it a secret. It's supposed to be a secret way of getting to people.'

Henry poured all the powder still in the packet into his untouched mug of soup. He stirred it in with a spoon. 'I know it's not a gun. I don't want a gun.' He picked the mug up by the handle, as if he was about to drink it, and Hazel stopped laughing. He raised the mug most of the way to his lips.

'It really is a poison,' he said. 'And this is a fatal dose. Will you marry me?'

———————

It is the first of November 1993 and somewhere in Britain, in Nuneaton or Newcastle or Eastleigh or Hexham, in Meadowbank or Kendal or Loughborough or Hemel Hempstead, Spencer Kelly is twenty-one years old and despairing of all things provincial he declares himself a Republic. As of today he'll take no more orders from an unelected father whose only claim to authority is by birth. From now on Spencer will do only what he wants to do, beginning with not going to work at the warehouse. He shall then prove how serious he is about becoming an actor by going to London to look for work as a waiter.

His father, coming home early for lunch, finds Spencer packing his sports bag. He talks him down into the lounge, suspecting another false crisis changing nothing and soon forgotten. He points out to Spencer that he doesn't become a republic just by saying so. In this house he has certain obligations, not to mention binding attachments.

'The Republic is declared,' Spencer says. 'And I am it.'

His father tries to appease him by conceding that he might just qualify as a disputed territory. 'It's another phase you're going through,' he says. 'You'll get over it.' He then reminds Spencer of all those Mondays the warehouse let him take off for community service. He'd be crazy to leave now.

'They did the same for you.'

'I've been there forever. You're a young man, Spencer. You have prospects. You should settle down.'

It's all his Dad thinks he's good for. Spencer should get married and breed and with any luck (of the kind which Mr Kelly believes he's due) it's his *grandson* who'll have the spark and the golden sporting gene.

Spencer starts to hum *Born Under a Wandering Star*. Predictably, this infuriates his father, who asks him sharply what exactly it is he thinks he wants? In general terms, Spencer thinks, all that I have not got. He wants what the adverts tell him to want, holidays in Malta or Egypt or the Algarve, and a suit from Armani or Simpson's of Piccadilly, and a mail order embroidered cushion, and privileged entry to the latest minority-interest debates. That's why he has to go to London, and the legendary addresses where such miracles begin, in Bond Street or Portland Square or Brook Street or the King's Road. He'll be expecting to neutralise his accent of course, if he's going to make it as an actor, but it shouldn't be too difficult after all the different places

254

he's lived. As soon as he sounds like he could have come from anywhere, and after a brief but glamorous period of undemanding struggle, he confidently expects to make rapid progress from waiter to actor to a life changed beyond all recognition.

He therefore continues to educate himself, adding the Bible to his reading list of newspapers and English literature. This is partly to please his mother, who's now been invited to the Woman of the Year lunch for her work with political refugees and local churches, an event which Mr Kelly falls on as justification for the divorce. His ex-wife would rather go to the Woman of the Year lunch than stay at home with her family.

'I think that's the point of these things, Dad. You get the invitation because you're the kind of woman who says yes.'

'At the expense of your family?'

It's too tiring to explain, and Spencer sometimes wishes he hadn't read so many improving newspapers. This is another reason he's moved on to the Bible, which he reads like a history book to discover whether in other centuries they had the same impatience for miracles, and single moments which changed everything. Occasionally, late at night, it occurs to him that in another seven years he'll find out for himself, without even having to read anything.

'Stop that and listen!'

Spencer stops humming. His father has pushed up very close, and Spencer wants to retreat but he's already backed up against the bunched curtains. His father is losing control of his voice, from trying so hard to be reasonable.

'You read too many newspapers,' he says. 'It's about time you got a grip on reality. You can't leave now, where would you go?'

'I'm twenty-one years old. A man's gotta do.'

'What about me? Why do you think I've always worked so hard?'

'So I could play football for Tottenham Hotspur.'

'Or Manchester United or Southampton or QPR.'

'Let's face it, Dad. I'm not even going to play for Wimbledon.'

'Do you have any idea how much *money* I've spent? The *sacrifices* I've made? What about all those cheap-rate holidays in November?'

'I'm sorry, Dad. I'm not going to make it as a great sportsman.'

'In the prime of your life, look at you. I should be living next to a golf course by now, putting my feet up.'

'I'm going to try something else instead. And I don't mean a warehouseman.'

Spencer isn't just thinking of London and its lists of cinema hits. He's also thinking about Hazel and running out of coins and their shorter conversations now that neither of them steals any more. When he meets her, preferably as an international star, he imagines they'll fall straight into bed. It's the natural next step, because they've already done all the talking.

'Time moves on, Dad,' he says. 'I want to make something of myself before it's too late.'

Mr Kelly holds up his hands, palms outward and fingers

splayed as if he's heard enough. Then he suddenly straight-
ens his arms and pushes Spencer in the chest, clattering him
back into the curtains. He says,

'This is the fourth dimension, son. There is no time. To
me you'll always be a snotty ten-year-old in a replica
football shirt falling on your arse in the mud. You useless
beggar.'

He pushes Spencer again, and as a newly-declared free
and independent Republic Spencer ought not to be standing
for this. Using only the tips of his fingers he pushes his
father back in the chest, but it doesn't move him anywhere.

'What would Rachel think?' Mr Kelly says. 'What would
your sister Rachel think if she were alive today and she
could see you now?'

Mr Kelly hits Spencer with a clean uppercut to the jaw,
jarring his teeth together and jerking his head backwards.
Before Spencer can react he is hit again, twice, two left
hooks to the face before he can get his arms up covering
his head and his elbows sticking out to protect himself. Mr
Kelly starts punching and slapping at Spencer's arms, and
behind his elbows Spencer takes quick shallow breaths and
tries to recover. His father is leaning his face forward to see
where best to hit him next, to finish it, and Spencer instinctively makes a fist and punches him, hard and straight on
the nose.

His father, his Dad, Mr Kelly, looking amazed, astounded
even, and then he falls over backwards to the carpet. Oh my
god, Spencer thinks. He helps his Dad up onto the sofa,
where they both try to rub at his face, getting their hands

257

all mixed up. Spencer's Dad shakes his head. He seems dazed.

'It's alright, Dad. It's fine.'

'I don't believe it,' his Dad says. 'Boxing.'

'It could have gone either way. Really.'

'Super middle-weight,' he mumbles, 'a spot of running makes you a light-weight, even super bantam-weight. Spencer, my boy.'

The fight has probably lasted no more than ninety seconds, but both Spencer and his Dad register that something fundamental has changed. At last, Spencer the Republican thinks, I may have lived to see the moment it all began.

11/1/93 MONDAY 15:12

With the exception of the magnificent Miss Burns, today had confirmed Henry Mitsui in his long-held belief that other people were mostly banal. Spencer and William Welsby, both grown men, had failed to intervene and save Miss Burns until it was too late. Now they seemed shocked by his threatened suicide, and he wondered if either of them had any idea of what was meant by commitment. Henry couldn't live without Miss Burns. He meant it.

'You can't poison yourself,' Spencer said. 'There are people coming to look at the house. Italians.'

Spencer could have added that there was a child in the

room and he still had his library books to take back, but he didn't. He'd moved towards Henry once, planning to force the mug from his hand. Henry raised it closer to his lips. Spencer backed away. On a points-scoring system Henry judged that this skirmish, in the mind of Miss Burns, could plausibly be scored as a victory in his favour. This being the case, he couldn't understand why she should shake her head, pick up her own untouched mug of soup, and leave the room.

'Where's Trigger?'

'He's in the water in the bowl,' William said, blocking Grace's view with his body. She was insistent, trying to squirm a view round either side of his back. 'He's in the bowl, I said.'

'You're lying. He's been poisoned.'

William grabbed a tea towel and covered the top of the bowl. 'Alright,' he said. He turned with it, lifting it higher than Grace's reach, his fingers spread out over the base. 'He's been poisoned. But he's not dead. He's just feeling a bit poorly.'

'Let me see him.'

'He needs to be kept in the dark, like an ill person. He's resting.'

'Really?'

Trigger the goldfish was dead. In fact he wasn't even in the bowl any more. William had managed to pull him out without Grace seeing anything, and Trigger the fish was now stiffening up in William's trouser pocket. This sudden emergency had inspired William. It was like a revelation, and he knew instinctively what to do next. The most important thing in the entire world, outside not excluded, was to fetch one of the other goldfish from the shed and get it into the bowl before Grace suspected the truth. Otherwise, from here on in, she'd live the rest of her life thinking that the world was a terrifying place where psycho nutcases could stroll off the street into all her best birthdays to kill her favourite presents.

'What he needs is some fresh air,' William said.

'I saw him on his back.'

'He was relaxing. He was doing backstroke. Let's go outside.'

Still carrying the fruit bowl, full of water and now covered in a tea towel explaining the rules of cricket, William fumbled his way out through the double-doors in the dining room. At least it wasn't raining. Grace followed close behind him. He put the bowl down at the base of the balustrade, and checked it was completely covered. He told Grace sternly that Trigger was not to be disturbed for any reason while he went to fetch some fish-medicine from the shed. He'd be back as soon as he could but she had to promise not to look. If she lifted the tea towel, even just a little bit, that might be all it took to kill him.

'What if that man comes back?'

'Run away.'

The man was completely mad. He was standing at the top of the steps which led down into the shallow end of the

260

empty swimming pool. Hazel was already in there, sitting in a corner behind the billiard table with her mug in both hands, knees up to her chin.

'You let me into the house,' Henry said, climbing backwards down the steps. 'You wanted me to be here.'

Spencer looked into the swimming pool, wishing he could stop Henry from doing this. Why hadn't he already stopped him? He'd never have believed things could change so quickly, but today he kept on being taken by surprise. He wished he'd acted differently, more positively, and suddenly realised how much he didn't want to grow old regretting all the things he'd never done. There was no point waiting for outside intervention. This wasn't even a case where the police (Damascus!) could be expected to intervene, because Spencer wouldn't know how to explain about being held hostage by a man armed with a lethal chicken cup-a-soup. No, officer, he's not trying to force anyone to drink it.

Spencer had to provide his own intervention. He had to take responsibility. He ought to be devising ingenious ways to lure Henry into a fight, or at least make him put down the mug, but Spencer had no secret Damascan skills. He wasn't a covert MI6 agent or an itchy ex-serviceman equipped to turn everything around, like in a different type of story. He had to think of something else, because heroism was all about *doing* something. Otherwise this could go on indefinitely, not knowing what he thought or who he loved or what was worth defending.

Hazel stood up and kept the billiard table between herself and Henry Mitsui. She looked angry as well as frightened

261

but Spencer feared the worst for her, for them, seeing for the first time with absolute clarity that his mother was wrong. Rachel his sister didn't live on each time he remembered her. Rachel was dead, and memory did nothing to revive her. She was stuck forever in the same remembered episodes, jamming exactly where she was each time he tried to make her come forward. He couldn't help her, she couldn't help him, and she receded a little with each day and every week that passed. And the same thing could happen without warning to anybody, wherever. Spencer realised it was imperative that at least once in his life, and he was thinking of now, he should concentrate on the present tense. The vivid green cloth of the billiard table. The dark blue tiles, the dry white floor. Hazel, her dress, her pale bare feet and her angry eyes. Henry Mitsui, his sweater and his unpatterned mug.

Now is now, he told himself, looking from Hazel to Henry and back again. He absolutely mustn't let anyone die, because when you die you're dead.

William would have to hurry. Here was his chance to be a hero. He'd have to run. He'd left Grace on the terrace where it was cold and probably boring for a ten-year-old, and if he didn't get a move on she was going to find out for herself that the fruit bowl was empty. He shambled forwards across the grass, clenched his fists and started to run. After five uneven paces he was already telling himself he had to keep going, appealing to his legs and lungs to remember the movement called running because running was necessary for this heroic act, in which he would defy the odds to make the world seem a better place. That was what heroism was all about.

By the time he reached the path he was breathing hoarsely and his head was giddy with rushing blood, feeding his brain, nourishing strange connections. His brain wanted some of Ma Junren's magic potion (half a marathon in sixty minutes was truly a miracle). Or it cast William back to Prince's Park, or Leazes Park or the People's Park, living destitute and free. By the boat-house he had his own statue, the running man, erected in honour of this heroic moment. He stood face to face with it, to check he was still himself, and these hallucinations were either too much oxygen rushing the brain or his life flashing before his eyes before cardio-respiratory failure and a stroke. He kept on running, past the mulberry tree and a brief nod in the direction of Georgi Markov, the rare Bulgarian Siberian blue-tailed red-flanked robin, or whatever he was. He was William's *friend*. Through the rustling chestnut trees past the lemon hornbeams and at last he was there, at the door to the shed. He could stop running now.

Inside the shed he grabbed a lavender-coloured sandcastle mould to scoop both unsuspecting fish from the top yellow bucket. He then used up time but also recovered some breath by pouring one of them back, before gritting his teeth for the return journey. Did he really have to run all the way back as well? No sign told him he had to. He thought of mountain rescue, unpaid medics in war zones, the marriage of school-leavers, recruiting to the UDR, and many other heroisms he'd never attempted because there was never a sign telling him it was the right thing to do. He shouldn't have been so frightened.

Holding the sandcastle-mould with the fish in it well out in front of him, he left the shed and lumbered into a jog.

He felt sick, but tried to forget this and his straining, shrinking lungs by pretending it was him who was the fish, with a thankfully short memory of only three seconds. It worked, several times. After the trees he left the path and cut across the wet lawn wondering how long, in between each three seconds, the fish allowed themselves for the act of forgetting. How long did it take to forget something? The house and the raised terrace were in sight now, and William wasn't a fish and he felt terrible and he couldn't suddenly forget it. He wanted to stop, he had no choice, he had to stop. He stopped running and slowed to a fast walk, bending almost double to keep himself moving. His ankles hurt and he needed more air. He slowed to a slow walk. He started limping.

Why was it always so difficult to do good things?

11

Is it to be evil and violence or dialogue
and peace?

THE TIMES 11/1/93

11/1/93 MONDAY 15:24

'It doesn't matter what the game is,' Hazel said. 'The whole
point of destiny is that it takes care of the details.'

'It's not fair,' Henry said. 'I've never played before.'

'If we're destined to be together, then it doesn't matter.'

Henry had managed to follow Hazel on a complete tour
of the gradients of the swimming pool, always looking at
her, never once spilling any of his lethal soup.

'Maybe you don't believe I'll actually drink it?'

'Don't worry,' Hazel said. 'Spencer can't play either. It's
in the hands of the gods now.'

Hazel had made a decision, and now life would have to

follow on from it. This was how any decent decision worked. She told Spencer to stop prowling round the edge and to climb down into the pool, which he did. Then she put the red billiard ball on its spot at one end of the table, and a white ball behind the line at the other end. Because neither of the men knew how to play billiards Hazel had devised the simplest of contests. Whoever potted the red first would be the winner. If Spencer won, Henry had to leave. If Henry won, well then, Hazel would marry him.

Spencer's jaw dropped. Then he pushed his lips together until they went very thin.

'What's the matter?' she asked. 'Don't you believe me?'

'No.'

'We haven't had much luck trying to decide rationally, have we? Instead of deciding anything useful you just build up defences, scared of what a decision might mean. It's already a kind of miracle, after so long, that we're here together at all, so maybe the answer is to trust in miracles. If you and me is the right thing to happen, Spencer, to the right people at the right time, then you'll win.'

'What about him?'

'The same principle applies. He believes he's destined to marry me. Perhaps he is. If destiny's on his side, there'll be a sign. He'll win.'

'There's no such thing as destiny,' Spencer said, but Hazel only had to look at him to see that neither of them really believed this, not really, not somewhere deep inside themselves untouched by the twentieth century.

Hazel snapped a cue from its clip beneath the table and

offered it to Henry Mitsui. He refused to let go of his mug. His hands were sweating, and he held the mug in both hands. Spencer stepped forward and took the billiard cue. This would be the sign he'd been waiting for. He lined up the white with the red and closed one eye, telling himself that this was no time to panic. He pushed the cue forward, making good contact with the white. The white ball rolled down the table and hit the red. The red deflected neatly towards the bottom left-hand pocket, but then inexplicably missed it by some distance.

William still wasn't back from the shed, so Grace decided to take a peek under the tea towel. She hunkered down next to the bowl and took a corner of the cloth between her fingers. She didn't believe she could kill Trigger just by looking at him. It didn't sound like something that was true. But then earlier on today she'd have sworn it was impossible for a complete stranger to invade her birthday party and poison her best present. Come to think of it, she'd also have offered to fight anybody who called River Phoenix a drug addict.

Maybe her parents were right, and it always made sense to be careful. She let go of the cloth. A telephone started ringing inside the house but she was too frightened to go inside and find it, even though it was cold outside. She stood up and flapped her arms and stamped her feet. Then she ran up and down the terrace, mostly to get warm but also to practise her running away. She ran on the spot next to the fruit bowl. Why would anybody want to poison a fish who'd done nothing wrong? People shouldn't be made that way.

She wanted to go to the bathroom, but the man with the funny sweater might be waiting inside to poison her. She crossed one leg over the other and spun herself round like a dancer. If Trigger died, she wondered if something else could happen just as suddenly which would make everything alright again. Or if he did die, there had to be a reason, making it an important sign of something important. If so, she should be able to learn something from it, and now she was ten she was old enough to learn the truth.

She decided to take a peek under the tea towel.

William made it to the bottom of the stone staircase leading up to the terrace, bent double, his tongue hanging out, the lavender-coloured sandcastle-mould inches off the ground.

Nobody would poison an animal, or even a fish, for no reason.

He dragged at the stone railing with his free hand, pulling himself up towards the terrace, one step, and then another step.

She touched the edge of the cloth, and started to lift it.

William rounded the corner of the terrace on his knees. He saw Grace about to look inside the bowl, but was too busy breathing to be able to speak. He watched her lift away the cloth.

There was no fish at all in the bowl. So what lesson was *that* supposed to teach her?

William put down the sandcastle-mould, suddenly unable to focus. He had the impression that Grace was coming

268

towards him. He stood up, waved her away, and vomited his kippers over the balustrade.

Henry had the billiard cue in one hand and his mug in the other.

'You're going to have to let go of the mug,' Hazel said. 'You're not going to pot the red and win the game one-handed. Unless God overdoes it, of course.'

Henry wasn't sure. He didn't know. Would he place a bet on it? Only to make it happen. Obviously he believed that he and Hazel were destined to be together, or he'd never have punched his father or found his way to the house or felt so jealous about Hazel and Spencer Kelly (in a coma, brain-damaged, stretched across a railway track). It was therefore only logical to conclude that if he hit the red ball with the white ball, the red ball would fall into a pocket. It would be cowardice to think otherwise, and offend his sense of destiny. It also demeaned him to consider acting any less courageously than his rival. Spencer had already tried and missed, but still Henry was reluctant to loosen his grip on the poisoned soup. He said:

'How do I know you'll do what you said?'

'You love me, Henry. You couldn't fall in love with some-one who didn't tell you the truth. Give me the mug.'

'And if I hit the red into the pocket you'll marry me?'

'Yes, I will, if the red goes into the pocket.'

Henry couldn't afford not to believe her. He had an idea that theirs wasn't a conventional British courtship, but then

269

Hazel Burns the woman he loved and intended to marry (quietly, in Barbourne, Worcester) was no ordinary woman.

'How can I be sure?'

'Sure of what?'

'That you'll marry me.'

'Because we'll have had a sign. Look, Henry. Nobody knows how to play billiards so it's all in the hands of the gods.'

'But why billiards?' Spencer asked, still trying to work out how he could have missed. And what if Henry Mitsui was secretly the Japanese champion? 'Billiards has nothing to do with anything.'

'Nothing has got anything to do with anything,' Hazel said. 'Or everything with everything. Depends how you look at it.'

'And how are you looking at it?'

'Everything with everything. Even billiards. It's Henry's turn.'

'And you promise to marry him?'

'I'll have no choice.'

'You promise you promise?' Henry said.

'Look,' Hazel said, 'if you pot the red and then I don't, then whenever I'm unhappy later in life I'll automatically think it was because of that. I'll regret not taking the sign seriously for what it was. I'm taking it seriously. I've decided to believe that we connect with something bigger than ourselves, and that sometimes we're offered signs for guidance. If you pot this red and I marry you, then when things are difficult I can always be consoled by the thought that we were given a sign. I'll think it's worth persevering.'

'And you really believe?'

'Don't you?'

'I love you. I believe we're destined to be together.'

'Then give me the mug. Take the shot.'

It is the first of November 1993 and somewhere in London, in Tower Hamlets or Shepherd's Bush or Hampstead or Battersea, in Camden or Kensington or Chiswick or Knightsbridge, Spencer has an unexpected and horrifying insight into what rich people must think: life is fair. He's twenty-three years old and wondering what he's ever done not to deserve this.

He has a Shark's Fin Soup Special with Commanderia wine to deliver to a table of men or women or both who are still hungry after the East Lancs Annual ATC dinner or The Woman of the Year Lunch or the annual get-together of the Naval 8/208 Squadron Association. He body-swerves between tightly-packed tables, leaving them standing, bamboozled even, reminding himself of Rachel. He finds a big smile for the group at the table, and although he desires every woman he sees, he feels much purer for wanting to marry them all. This is London, however, and he's already discovered that it's mostly the not nice girls who do, who are, not nice.

He flounces his empty tray between occupied tables as he swerves stylishly back to the kitchen, because this is not a restaurant or a café or a wine bar, it's a *brasserie*. And when it's full of important and influential people, as it is today, it doesn't seem so foolish to rely on the possibility of sharp divisions between today and tomorrow. Anybody could come in. Anything could happen.

Spencer is beckoned to a corner table by Lord O'Brien Welsby, who invests in films and sits alone.

'Sit down,' Welsby says, indicating the empty seat opposite.

'I can't. I'm working.'

'Be a good boy and sit down. If the manager comes back I'll vouch for you.'

Spencer sits down. Welsby pushes some spare cutlery to one side and leans forward across the table, making a square dam of his hands by interlocking his fingers.

'I have a proposition to make,' he says.

As an actor, Spencer naturally feels superior to all businessmen, whether they're the director general of Ofgas or Sega Europe's financial director or the Governor of the Bank of England. Lord O'Brien Welsby has made his fortune speculating in property, predicting gilt yields, and rescuing businesses which manufacture leisure products. More importantly, he invests in films, and Spencer has been waiting for this moment ever since he arrived in London. It is now more welcome than ever because he urgently needs to restructure his banking arrangements, meaning he's desperately short of money. Originally he'd phoned to share a garden flat in Wimbledon Village for £85 a week, but he was rejected in favour of a female professional. He now lives instead in a studio in Marble Arch or Wandsworth or Lambeth, paying £110 a week and far too much for his waiter's wages.

Because despite countless auditions where he places himself deliberately in the aim of the gods, Spencer has failed to land the role of tonight's overnight sensation. He hasn't been offered a part in any number of films which signal the re-emergence of the British film industry. He is not in *Howard's End* or *The Remains of the Day* or *Raining Stones* or *Truly Madly Deeply*. Television treats him with equal indifference, and he is yet to feature even in the background of *Cracker* or *Casualty* or *House of Cards*. Even children's TV seems beyond him, and he isn't hiding away making a perfectly decent living on *Wizadora* or *Star Pets* or *Bodger and Badger*. In fact, it looks increasingly unlikely that he'll ever return to every place he's ever lived, rich and famous and therefore beyond reproach.

He is therefore more than ready to listen to any proposition made by Lord O'Brien Welsby, who invests in films.

'I have a property which is standing empty,' he says. 'I want somebody to look after it for a while.'

One of Spencer's colleagues, also absent from adult television but once famously fired for artistic differences from *Bodger and Badger*, stares at him angrily. Spencer raises an eyebrow, as if to say: 'It's only a full-length feature film.'

'It's not in a film, is it?' he asks.

'No.'

'It's not really what I'm looking for,' Spencer says.

'I've been watching you,' Welsby says. 'You strike me as someone who'd appreciate a bit of peace and quiet.'

Spencer toys with a fork, thinking this is exactly what he has to resist. He doesn't want peace and quiet. He wants a tomorrow full of everything he wants today which he still hasn't got, because it's always tomorrow that it turns out fine because otherwise all those adverts would be wrong. Every day, in some form or other, he's promised that tomorrow is a Peugeot 405 or a Simpson suit or an original artwork, no problem, leaving him like everyone else stranded in a today which repeats this habitual ritual state of never enough.

'You wouldn't have to pay rent,' O'Brien Welsby says. 'You'd have to look in on my brother, but only until I find a buyer.'

Welsby is offering him the chance to want less, wanting only what is necessary and possible like food, a roof, a library card, until eventually the world begins to diminish. It shrinks to the size of a small hard disc (circles not spheres) of fulfilled desire, just perfect. Small. But perfect. But small.

'You could still do auditions.'

'Why me?'

'Why not you?'

'You don't think I'm going to make it as an actor, do you?'

'It's up to you, Spencer.'

'You don't even think I'm making it as a waiter.'

After children's TV, as a very last resort, Spencer auditions for the theatre. He gets it wrong for *The Mandrake Theatre Company* or *Chicken Shed* or the *RSC*, even though his voice is now almost perfectly neutral, betraying nothing of his past.

'I'll have to think about it,' Spencer says.

'I'd like your answer today, if at all possible.'

In a region of his mind barricaded against common sense, Spencer thinks he could maybe ask his Dad for some money. But then he remembers his Dad has been told by the warehouse that he has to be adaptable, which means he's about to be sacked. As for his Mum, Spencer knows as a fact that she splits her maintenance payments between the St Oswald's orphan fund and the Princess of Wales, to show support for all the selfless work Diana manages over lunch at the London Hilton or Chequers or Kensington Palace.

'I need to make a phone call,' Spencer says, and pushes himself away from the table. He ignores customers who try to flag him down and heads for the pay-phone on the counter at the bar, wondering if his lucky break is ever going to come. He wears a pointed metal hat beneath trees during storms and lightning refuses to strike. He shakes his fist at God and gets nothing in return, not even the common courtesy of retaliation.

'We're not being very calm about this, are we?' Hazel says.

'What should I do?'

She could suggest they meet up, fall in love, instantly erase his other failures in the triumphs of requited passion. If it works like that.

Silence from Hazel.

'You never feel like this? You never feel like all the paths you can take lead in the wrong direction?'

'Sometimes,' Hazel says. 'Sometimes I sit in bed in the middle of the day with my coat on. I mean when it's not even very cold.'

'Why would you want to do that?'

'If I'm feeling a bit mad and depressed.'

'And then what?'

'Then I get up again and take my coat off.'

'Why?'

'Because sooner or later I have to get up and get on with it.'

'With what?'

'Real life.'

Spencer's money runs out, and O'Brien Welsby is leaning back in his chair, arms folded, waiting. He isn't going to offer Spencer a part in tomorrow's consolidation of the British film industry, and it suddenly seems a little foolish ever to have hoped that tomorrow could be all that different from today.

———

11/1/93 MONDAY 15:48

The second goldfish was now in the fruit bowl, full of fresh water, and it had pride of place in the centre of the dining room table. The water curved elegant shapes from the var-

276

nished table-top, and also from the lavender plastic of the sandcastle-mould. Grace had put her face close to the bowl so that Trigger II had something to look at. He flicked from one side of the bowl to the other, living a brand new now every three seconds, every discovery both dramatic and familiar. William had tidied himself up, though his white shirt was splashed with water. His hair was wet and plastered flat on his head, and he sat opposite Grace, the bowl and the fish between them. He looked deathly serious, and not very well.

'You knew Trigger was dead, didn't you?' he said.

'Fish don't backstroke.'

'Perhaps the first fish wasn't Trigger at all. This fish is Trigger. The other fish was Trigger's evil twin.'

'I don't need cheering up,' Grace said. 'I understand that Trigger's dead. We can't turn the clock back and pretend it never happened.'

'I wasn't trying to trick you,' William said. 'I just didn't want you to think the world was that kind of place.'

'What kind of place?'

'I didn't want you to be frightened. I wanted everything to be alright, especially on your birthday.'

'I know,' Grace said. 'But it's not as though fish are the same as people, is it? Fish live forever, and then they die. No, that's not right. Fish live forever *before* they die.'

The telephone rang, and William let it ring until it stopped. Nothing could be important enough to make him stand up again so soon.

277

'But if the first Trigger is dead,' Grace said, 'it means that Chinese man has real poison in his soup.'

'It does indeed,' William said.

Grace looked solemnly across the top of the fruit bowl. 'What should we do?'

'Nothing,' William said.

'We should do something, shouldn't we?'

'We'll leave them alone long enough to make fools of themselves.'

'But someone might get hurt. Someone might get poisoned.'

'I doubt it,' William said. 'And remember he only wanted to kill himself.'

'But we don't want anyone to die, do we? Not even him?'

'Of course we don't, and no-one will. They're all having a moment of madness. It's only love. It doesn't last forever.'

'I still think we should do something,' Grace said, so William, over the head of the new goldfish, tried to explain why nothing they could do would make any difference.

All of them, Spencer and Hazel and the foreign man, they were all desperate to believe in the one moment which changed everything, the instant Damascus in which dreamers set such store. Nothing anybody else did could change this, because they'd all grown dependent on the Damascus-type promises made indiscriminately for love, or religion, or drugs, or art. Or just as often it was for something less grand but more urgent, like a cash windfall or a quick divorce or access to the latest craze, and there were as many different versions of Damascus as there were people. It could be getting the CSA off your back or selection for Wales or the first day of the school holidays so that then, and only then, is everything made better, instantly.

Grace blinked at him, impressed and a little confused. 'So we're not going to do anything?'

'They all know what they want. We shouldn't interfere, just in case they get it.'

'Get what?'

'What everybody wants. One moment which changes everything.'

Grace thought about this. 'It's not everybody,' she said. 'I'm not like that.'

'That's because you're too young. Everything you do *is* amazing and it *does* change you forever, because it's always the first time you've done it.'

'What about you? Are you like that?'

'It's different for me,' William said. 'I'm old enough to know that time sorts things out.'

Henry had no choice. If he was a believer he had to bite the bullet, as they liked to say. He handed Hazel the cold mug. For a moment, before he let go, they were joined by it. She had the mug now and she didn't betray him. She didn't pour the soup over his shoes, bragging victory. She put it calmly in the corner with her own mug of soup, also untouched. She replaced the red billiard ball on its spot, and then the white. Henry took the cue and lined up his shot, just like Spencer had. He fired the white ball at the red. It made good contact, and the red rolled diagonally towards the pocket. It missed.

Spencer's shot. Hazel picked up the red ball, wiped it on her dress like an apple, and replaced it. Spencer lined up the white and cursed himself for not paying more attention to his father. Those first missed steps towards £60,000 a tournament seemed a long time ago, and no matter how hard he tried to remember them, they weren't among the moments which stayed with him as clearly as if they'd happened today. The only way the red ball was going to fall into a pocket was through an outrageous stroke of luck. Or, as Hazel would have it, if it was destined to go in, as a sign in itself that they were meant for each other.

He slapped the cue down onto the table.

'This is ridiculous,' he said.

'It's your shot, Spencer.'

The mugs of soup were behind Hazel in the corner. They didn't have to do this anymore because Henry had given up the poison. They could tip it down the drain and throw him out. Forget the gods. This was Spencer's chance to make a change in things, and one of the memories always available to him was the left-right side-step perfected by Rachel. To reach the mugs, all he had to do was dodge round Hazel, so stopping this stupid game before somebody won and somebody lost, because love wasn't a sport. It wasn't about winning and losing. And then, after seeing off Henry Mitsui, he and Hazel could return to the more familiar torment of godless indecision.

Hazel wouldn't let him pass. He tried the side-step, and

she easily moved in front of him, blocking his path to the mugs.

'But it's stupid,' Spencer said, appealing for her agreement. 'It *is* stupid.'

'It won't be stupid if you win.'

There was no changing her mind. It was the gods or nothing. Spencer went back to the table and took his shot. He missed.

Is it raining or is it not? Make up your mind. It was a godforsaken country in which even the weather was indecisive. Mr Mitsui, Vice-President (Design) of the multinational Toyoko corporation, had spent the kind of day from which international promotion was supposed to have made him exempt. He'd walked much further in a strange and reputedly dangerous city than could ever be considered sensible, and the woman at the school had been especially tiresome. Once they'd established that he was genuinely Henry's father ('the pushy oriental with the evil tooth'), she'd made him agree that all men in general but his son in particular were a danger to women. Mr Mitsui sighed and smiled and agreed, and then asked about Miss Burns.

'Poor harassed woman.'

'I'm an old man,' Mr Mitsui said. 'I mean her no harm. We have to find my son.'

'I couldn't agree more,' the secretary said, and because she was confident she knew everything of importance about the school, its distance-learning side-line, and almost everything else, she was able to tell Mr Mitsui where to find Miss Burns.

He pushed at the doorbell again, almost relieved that nobody was home. If the house was empty then there was nobody for Henry to hurt. Unless he'd already done it. It started raining more persistently, and Mr Mitsui turned up the collar of his blazer, at last conceding that he'd failed as a parent. He must have done, or he wouldn't be here, doing this. He'd failed to prepare Henry for the world as it was without the allowances of childhood, where he couldn't have everything he wanted, and not everything was possible. Real life wasn't about constant gratification or great adventures or strong-willed triumphs against the odds. It was this street now, where Mr Mitsui could see any number of people who by the end of the day wouldn't be elected mayor of New York or Salesperson of the Year, who wouldn't be engaged or married or announcing the birth of a child. Real life was all these people not blown up or shot, not exhausted from international contest, not murdered or mugged or with meningitis. Real life was all the accidents that never happened. It was all the people daily unreported. And, it should now be added, all the doors unopened.

He heard the latch turn from the inside.

———————

It is the first of November 1993 and somewhere in Britain, in Omagh or Haverhill or Lancaster or Runcorn, in New-

bridge or Exmouth or Hereford or Darlington, Hazel Burns
is sitting cross-legged in the bed of her rented studio, wearing
her coat, surrounded by a mess of exploded newspapers. She
answers her portable phone. She says,

'Dublin is not in the United Kingdom, no. Yes, Belfast
is. It's a long story.'

Or she says, 'Yes, there are women priests in the Church of
England, and no, the Maastricht Treaty won't change that.'

Or she says, 'Punjabi, Gujarati, Bengali, Hindi, Urdu, and
Welsh.'

She has developed a particular voice to use on the telephone in her professional capacity as a distance-learning
teacher. She tries to project an image of herself as older,
spectacle-wearing, with perhaps her only vanity some long
greying hair gathered in a bun. Not wanting to seem over-
bearing, she tries to add to her voice a kind of cat-owning
warmth, hoping to sound something like an old-fashioned
librarian or an earnest female egghead, with the endearingly-
shaped head of an egg. It also occurs to her, now that she
spends so much time on the phone, that she might be trying
to recapture the satisfaction of the long conversations she
once enjoyed with Spencer. Back in the good old days, she
means, in the permanent golden age of younger than now.
At 23 she is suddenly old enough for nostalgia, and she
can remember or regret certain events as clearly as if they
happened today. Almost all her memories, at her age, include
her parents.

Her father, despite being elected Salesperson of the Year
'93, and in something of an embarrassment for the Institute

of Sales and Marketing Managers, is being investigated for fraud. It's alleged that he pays bribes to the Italian government or exports aphrodisiacs or sells instant soups labelled chicken which contain more salt than meat. He claims innocence, protesting that none of these things are uncommon, even though Hazel and many thousands of others think he's rather missing the point. Her mother, at last, has decided that marriage isn't like a sports team or a place safe for diversity or two nations one capital. Nor is it even very much like an identity card. Without question, it's a hell on earth.

At times like these, Hazel often finds herself nostalgic for the car crash, and how brilliant her mother was. She wishes she'd been old enough to appreciate it at the time, and now that she *is* older she *does* appreciate it more, and from now on always will do whenever she remembers it.

The phone rings, and someone else is about to learn something at a safe distance.

'The meadow pipit is brown. It's the red-flanked bluetail which is red.'

Or, 'Yes, that's right. Only talking can end 800 years of violence.'

Or, 'It's extracted from castor-oil seeds and was widely used by the Bulgarian secret service.'

But if someone were to ask her, thinking it a simpler question, whether her own real life had started, she wouldn't know how to answer. Avoiding the troublesome contact of life she is rewarded with a portable telephone, the mobility to live wherever she wants, and enough money to pay for reference books and her own correspondence courses for a

Master of Arts or a Bachelor of Science or a PhD, in English Literature or Marine Biology or Psychology.

Using her experience as a movie researcher she spends most of her time travelling round the country gathering information, wanting to believe that the more facts she collects about life the less inexpert she'll become at living. Every day she reads *The Times* and the *Telegraph* and the *Sun* and the *Mirror*. She also skims magazines like *Foreign Affairs* or *Private Eye* or *Strand Magazine* or *Country Life*. With time on her hands, she often attempts to catch the mood abroad by reading *an-Nahar* or the *Corriere della Sera* or the world's most sinister newspaper, the *Neue Zürcher Zeitung*. It makes her feel as if she's somehow exploring all the variety of the real world, as it is now. She snatches at it, trying to catch it on the way past, and even as it slips through her fingers she can't help wondering if this is what it means to live life to the full.

She's hoping that the more she learns the less likely she is to be frightened, and like her mother. But then how much does she need to know before she finds out what's truly frightening? She learns facts about birds and trees and flowers and kings and queens, hoping to subdue the world with knowledge. But it isn't subdued, or never stays that way for long. Or she forgets what she learns, and is no better off than before.

Her students are rarely rewarding. She has aspiring professional sportsmen from Asia or Africa or Australasia, who only enrol for their resident's permit. Or she has the bored children of the international rich. Some of them take it far too seriously, but it doesn't really matter. There's no risk involved because in the distanced world of telephones and computers no-one is anywhere. Or everyone is everywhere. Or nowhere. Wherever.

To maintain a meaningful connection with the real world, Hazel likes to call Spencer. Nostalgically, she always uses card-phones, although she now only has five phonecards left from her original and mostly stolen collection. She asks Spencer what she should do.

'When?'

'When my phonecards run out.'

'Steal some more.'

'Stealing is wrong.'

'Then come to London,' he says. 'The streets are paved with gold.'

'Do you want to meet up?'

'This is London,' he says, making Hazel think he hasn't heard her properly. 'Anything can happen.'

And maybe it can. Maybe not all Londoners are like the ones she met at the film company, and it's possible to live in London without becoming an idiot. Perhaps relationships can begin to mean more than her transitory affairs with men for whom she holds out so little hope she even supplies the condoms. But London seems very close, and because distance-learning is like an open admission that things happen elsewhere, Hazel is increasingly tempted by travel for its own sake. She imagines herself abroad, in poor and dangerous places, expecting to learn something from the distress of others. Or she imagines herself anywhere she wants to be in Europe, now that we're all Europeans and all of it's supposed to be home. Eventually, however, she manages to resist the old lie that life abroad is more real. It's just that the stories there are less familiar, and therefore harder to ignore.

She sits up in bed in the middle of the afternoon with her coat on, even though it isn't very cold. She spreads her last five phonecards over the red tartan blanket. Her mobile phone rings, and she decides it's time to take her coat off.

11/1/93 MONDAY 16:12

What's the point of living if you can't have what you want?

It was Henry's shot, and this had been going on for some time now, so that Henry had the impression he'd taken more shots than he could count. How difficult could it be? Both men felt that by the law of averages the red ball should have fallen into the pocket by now, so the only sign Hazel's God had given them was that he wasn't going to give them a sign. And what kind of a sign was that?

Since his last visit to the table Henry had made a shocking discovery. Whether the red ball fell into the pocket or not was genuinely beyond his control. This wasn't a sport, because neither he nor Spencer had any skill. Hazel was therefore right. If his love for her was destined as he believed, then this game of billiards could provide as convincing a sign as any other. If their marriage was inscribed somewhere before the event, then nothing could stop it happening. So why had he missed the first time round? And the next and the next? He wanted his mug of poisoned chicken soup back, because it represented a much more simple equation. If Hazel refused him, then life wasn't worth living.

He left the cue on the table, neatly side-stepped Hazel, and picked up one of the mugs. 'I don't think this is working,' he said. 'I don't want to lose you on a game of chance.'

'It's not a game of chance,' Hazel said. She pushed him aside and picked up the other mug.

'Say you'll come with me,' Henry said. 'He's missed as often as I have.'

'It's your shot.'

'Or I'll drink the soup. It doesn't frighten me.'

Hazel faced him squarely, and it was as if the two of them had been photographed auditioning for a gun-fight. Someone later, an advertiser perhaps, had replaced the guns in their hands with plain white mugs, full of chicken soup.

'You better take your shot, Henry,' Hazel said. 'Or it'll be me who drinks it.'

Henry Mitsui looked puzzled. Somewhere behind him, Spencer looked much worse. He'd worked out just before Henry what Hazel was about to say:

'Well how do you know which mug has the poison in it?'

Oh Jesus Christ Mary and Micah, Mr Mitsui thought (remembering the phrase from his time in New Jersey),

288

another fine mess. A stand-off involving mugs of soup. A man called William Welsby, leading him through the house, had tried to explain about the poison while the little girl joined in with something about a goldfish. They'd forgotten to mention there was someone else involved, a tall miserable black-haired chap in a suit.

'Henry,' Mr Mitsui called down to him. 'Come out of that swimming pool at once.'

Henry looked up, and the shine in his eyes was familiar to his father – it meant no. It also meant he wanted Mr Mitsui to sort everything out, maybe pay somebody some money so that Henry could have exactly what he wanted. Not this time, son. Pay attention to the young lady. She's talking to you.

'Well go on then,' Hazel said. 'Drink up. I will if you will.'

Henry looked at his soup. There was a thickening white skin across the surface, hiding any powder which might have stayed on top. Nor was there any obvious residue sticking to the sides of the mug. There was therefore no way of telling if this was the poisoned soup, or if Hazel had it. Well there was another way. He could drink it.

'You take the first sip,' Hazel said, 'and then I'll match you all the way down, swallow for swallow.'

'But yours might be the poisoned one,' Henry said.

'So then I'll be poisoned. But how can I poison myself to death if we're destined to live happily ever after?'

'Bad things happen,' Henry said.

'Exactly. That's my point exactly. So how dare you force

your way into this house and tell me you know what's good for me, or for you, and what destiny has revealed to you?'

'That's what I think.'

'Then drink up.'

'Don't drink it,' Mr Mitsui called down. 'Come up here, Henry. We'll leave these good people alone. We ought to make a start for the airport.'

'Drink it,' Hazel said. 'Because if you refuse to take your turn at the billiard table, we aren't going to get married. And if we aren't going to get married you said your life wasn't worth living.'

For the first time in two years, Henry stumbled over his English words. 'I don't want to drink it,' he said. 'I want you to marry me.'

'Stop it, Henry,' his father said. 'Stop it right now. You're putting the fear of God into these people. You're putting the fear of God into *me*.'

Henry couldn't do it. He thought he could do it, but there turned out still to be a difference between thinking and doing, and he didn't really want to kill himself. More importantly, Hazel might have the poisoned soup and he definitely didn't want to see her poisoned. That was never one of the lives he'd imagined for the woman he loved.

Taking very small steps, he made his way down into the deep end, his body slanted backwards against the slope. He left his mug against the far wall, and walked back up to the billiard table.

'What else could I have done?' he asked Hazel. 'What did I have to do to convince you I was serious?'

'Take your shot, Henry.'

He took the cue from the table and hit the white ball towards the red. The red skewed off towards the pocket. It missed.

Henry and Mr Mitsui stood in a gap between parked cars waiting for a taxi. It had stopped raining but the daylight was fading, which made it feel like rain again. To anyone else, perhaps, it was just another anonymous late autumn weekday mid-afternoon, soft and grey and after-rain. But even that wasn't certain. People turned out to be more surprising than the lives Henry had stolen to describe them, just as the world was more complicated than the facts supposed to explain it.

Henry looked at nothing and the tarmac. He understood exactly what Hazel had been trying to tell him with the soup. She wanted him to doubt himself, and it had worked. He couldn't risk her drinking the poison, because he'd made the ricin himself and she would have died within the hour. If, however, they were genuinely destined to be together, he would have been certain it couldn't have happened. He wouldn't have been frightened of her dying. And if they were going to live happily ever after, as he liked to imagine, he should also have been confident of winning the game of billiards. But he'd been scared of losing, and suddenly nothing seemed so certain any more. Accidents happen, she'd reminded him, and if not now in an empty swimming pool from a soup full of poison then tomorrow or the next day murdered by terrorists or falling from a cliff edge or crashing a car. She could be a victim of any of the familiar disasters suffered daily by someone, somewhere, and this possibility was a long way from the certain bliss Henry had once imagined. She'd shown him that uncertainty was everywhere in life, and therefore it was an important part of being in love. (He wiped a tear away from his eye and onto his sweater.) If he couldn't abide this uncertainty, then it could never have been love.

'It's alright,' his father said, putting an arm round Henry's shoulders. 'Life has a habit of adding day to day. Memories fade. Life moves on.'

Back in the pool Spencer and Hazel looked up at the glass panels in the roof. Then across at each other, the width of the billiard table between them. They'd both seen it. The daylight was fading away.

Spencer said: 'It's time for Grace's bus.'

'I'll take her,' William said. He and Grace were holding hands by the shallow end steps. 'We'll go together.'

'No you won't,' Spencer said. 'You know what you're like.'

'William will take her, Spencer,' Hazel said.

'William won't get anywhere near the bus stop. You've seen how he is. He's a sick man.'

'He's better now. This is more important.'

'Grace is my niece.'

Spencer looked up for some support, but hand-in-hand

292

Grace and William were already leaving, had already left.

Hazel said: 'Well?'

'Let's go back to bed.'

'We haven't finished the game.'

Spencer squeezed his head between his hands, and then shook out his hair. 'There are people coming to look at the house.'

'They won't come now. It's late, Spencer. It's nearly dark.' She took the white ball from where Henry Mitsui's shot had left it and put it back behind the line at the other end of the table from the red. Spencer still didn't pick up the cue. He said:

'You can't force God to intervene.'

'Can't you?'

'We have to make the decision ourselves.'

'And how long do you think it would take you to decide, left to yourself and your dreams of the perfect woman? It's your shot, Spencer.'

'You can't force God to intervene.'

'Maybe courage is knowing that.'

She held out the cue to him and he took it. He placed the white right in the middle of the table and fired it at the red as hard as he could. The red missed the first pocket and rebounded to the opposite corner where it missed again. It lost energy as it travelled the middle of the table before dropping sweetly into the centre of the centre pocket, like an apple.

'At last,' Hazel said. 'God or the gods intervene.'

She came up behind Spencer and hugged him, her hands

crossing over his chest, her cheek pressed against the hollow between his shoulder-blades.

'Now,' she said. 'Now let's go back to bed.'

12

"I checked with the clergy and they
checked with God, and She said the
weather's going to be fine on Tuesday.

THE TIMES 11/1/93

11/1/93 MONDAY 16:24

It is the first of November 1993, and all over London dusk
is falling. Grace has her European Space Mission rucksack
on her back and in one hand she holds the Union Jack
carrier-bag, heavy with water and Trigger II. In the other
hand she has a Jaffa cake with a hole in the middle. She is
waiting for William to close the door behind them, while
William wonders what kind of madness could possibly have
made him offer to take her to the bus stop. Perhaps he wants
a second chance at being a hero, or just to believe that Hazel
might be right when she says he's better now. Could she

295

really have made that much difference, in a single day?

'It won't be as much fun at my house,' Grace says, still waiting for William to close the door. William agrees that it probably won't be as exciting. 'There again,' she says. 'You never know.'

She puts the Jaffa cake whole into her mouth and offers William her hand and he takes it. It is slightly sticky.

He pulls the door closed and the two of them, holding hands, step into the centre of the pavement and turn right, towards the library and the bus stop. William holds his free arm straight out, as if expecting problems with balance, but otherwise tries to remember everything Hazel has taught him. As they walk away from the house he is aware, with a vagueness he cultivates, of a hundred and one different individual sources of information. He blocks them out and puts one foot in front of the other. He watches the pavement, glances at the lime trees, squints at the parked cars. He puts one foot in front of the other, and grasps tightly Grace's small hand inside his own.

'Look,' Grace says, 'a clown.'

A man is juggling kiwi fruit in front of the music shop (JEPSONS!). He is collecting money for National Library Week. All around the country . . . William stops it before it can go any further. He watches the juggler, telling himself that this is the wonderful world. If it wasn't so wonderful, there wouldn't be any need to be frightened. If there was nothing worth defending, then the prospect of sudden disaster would carry no threat. Is that right? It sounds about right.

He asks Grace if before today she was ever frightened of

something terrible and sudden happening to her. She swallows the last of the Jaffa cake while she's answering.

'I'm only just ten. But I'd say that if a disaster's coming your way you're going to get it anyway, whether you're frightened or not.'

A National Express coach overtakes them and wheezes in at the bus stop, neatly framing itself between two lime trees bleeding some kind of black muck. About the coach, William resists thinking and observing many things. Coach Fares Cut to a Third of Rail. A Diadora bag jammed against the emergency exit. Several of the passengers being single men, anonymous, and a stone-chip in a side window, stop it right now.

When they're beside the coach, Grace pulls on William's hand until he bends down so that his face is level with hers. She kisses him on the cheek.

'Thanks for a really nice birthday,' she says. 'And thanks for a brilliant present.'

'I'm sorry about, you know what.'

'It wasn't anybody's fault.'

'Yes it was.'

'Say goodbye to Hazel and Uncle Spencer for me.'

'I'll do that. You feel better about going home now? You've decided your parents aren't so bad after all?'

'They're my Mum and Dad. It's where I live. What about you?'

'Don't worry about me,' William said. 'We're an island people. We stay afloat.'

'You're sure you'll be alright? You won't go all funny?'

'Of course not. I'll just block some things out, like Hazel said.'

Grace kisses him again, and William hands her up onto the coach. Almost immediately the doors swing closed, and Grace weaves her way down to the back. She waves several times, although without looking outside. She is holding the plastic bag very carefully, trying not to jog the fish. The coach pulls out and away, leaving the street, London, and heading for the darkening countryside of Britain. William watches it go and puts his hands in his pockets and it takes a little while for the fingertips of his right hand to register the unfamiliar coldness pressing against them. He pulls his hand away, but he doesn't panic. He blocks out the fact that there is a dead goldfish in his right-hand trouser pocket. He thinks, blocking out this and blocking out that, that he might continue this small miracle of excluding information in the lounge bar of the Rising Sun. Before setting off in the correct direction, one foot in front of the other, he looks around himself with narrow eyes and wonders what, exactly, he can allow himself to appreciate without flinching.

He is outside. It is the end of the first day of November 1993 in Britain and Europe. To the west of the street, over the roofs of the buildings, the clouds striplight an autumn sunset, and it starts softly to rain.

It doesn't matter what day it is and Spencer could be anywhere.

He is fast becoming such an expert in the art of the minimum that divisions of time and place seem meaningless. He doesn't work at the brasserie any more, which anyway was only a café-restaurant financed by city types, and he has no auditions scheduled for today or any other day. He moves calmly from room to room in Welsby's big silent house, living less than the dolce vita he'd imagined for himself, but doing nobody any harm.

He should phone Hazel. He jumps two at a time up some stairs. He really should. This is a thought which recurs more frequently than any other, but he puts it off because phoning now would be like saying that today is different from other days, and to differentiate each day from the next suddenly seems immature, vain, and plain tiring.

He has a hundred and one things to do as it is. He has to clear up William's breakfast, probably while learning the difficult evolution of the tomento or discussing today's version of Jessica. At some stage there are Italians coming to look at the house, and he still has his room to decorate. Then there are the long hours to spend at the computer like a working person, where he regularly comes first second and third at *TOCA Shoot-out Touring Cars* or the *PGA European Tour*. He'll probably make a brief visit to the street, where he doesn't so much buy food as lay up supplies. He might take his library books back or check what time his niece is arriving or see if there's any racing on the telly. He ought also reserve a moment for some inconclusive introspection, notably about why he shied away from the Hallowe'en fancy dress party at the Rising Sun, even after hiring an astronaut costume. But first he should phone Hazel.

Time stretches out flatly into the future, and somewhere out there he can always phone her. No need to rush. In the meantime he makes a major discovery thanks to the grand empty town house of Lord O'Brien Welsby. It's not love or work or travel or rebellion which reveals us to ourselves, but solitude. He has the space and the leisure to wrestle with impossible questions he previously dismissed as impossible. Like would he have been a different person if he'd been born into a different family?

Is there a specific death, horrible or otherwise, out there waiting for him?

Is it sensible to be frightened?

Is he only confused because he wasn't born intelligent enough to understand?

That wouldn't be very fair, but then he is still haunted by the horrific possibility that everything is fair and he has the life he deserves. So what was it about him, before now, which led to this? Could he really have gone any other way instead? And could he still be influenced by those other mislaid lives, misled, unlived? With a private education he could perhaps have formulated more and better unanswerable questions not to answer. After Oxford or Cambridge he might even have been able to answer them, but now he'd never know.

He'll phone her tomorrow, from a phone-box, for old times' sake. He's too old now to steal (one of the lessons learnt from solitude). That chapter of his life is over, and so becomes a complete memory, finite but repackaged in each remembering. He'll phone her tomorrow, but feels no great sense of urgency now that he accepts his life is unlikely to turn itself round in a single instant. You're born and you're on your way. You've had the beginning and now it's straight ahead to the end, and nobody ever turns round and comes back. Individual events make only slight adjustments to the inevitable, and this knowledge is somehow reassuring. It allows Spencer to gradually estrange himself from the actuality of the world, and its basic nowness. Time, in any meaningful sense, will cease to exist for him. Where he is and how old he is and what he eats and buys and wears, and all the information which would normally place him in the world will no longer signify. If he ever wavers, he'll remember his sister Rachel and remind himself that he's lucky to be living, as an excuse for not doing all sorts of things.

It makes him feel young again, because doing nothing everything remains possible, and he can be comforted not by what he's achieved but by what he still dreams of achiev- ing. He can still play Rugby League for Great Britain or seduce Emma Thompson or govern the Bank of England or triumph on the stage of the Shaftesbury, because he's never distanced himself from any one of these ambitions by moving in any other direction.

In brief: it is the first of November 1993 and Spencer is not elsewhere in Britain, he is not in Pontypridd or Dorchester or Ryedale or Eton, in Northfleet or Telford or Droitwich or

301

Halifax. He doesn't have his own Peugeot or Ford or Vaux-hall, nor a steady job nor a loving wife nor a son with an extraordinary aptitude for professional ball games. Instead he has all these lives stretching out before him as possibilities, and doing nothing he is never disappointed.

It does occur to him, though only rarely, that there might be better ways of coping with failure, but waiting for miracles isn't one of them.

The phone rings. It's very late and it's dark and it takes Spencer some time to reach the hall and answer it. It's Hazel, and just like in the old days she leaves off the beginning of the conversation.

'You remember the game?' she asks, 'Right Now?'

'Of course I do.'

'What are you doing, Right Now?'

'Talking to you on the phone.'

'Let's meet up,' she says.

'When?'

'Now.'

'What? Now?'

'Right now,' Hazel says.

'You mean *now* right now?'

'Now today now. It's about bloody time.'

It is dusk. The curved amber cover on the street-light outside the bedroom window is pale, unilluminated, and beyond the roofs opposite the day bleeds itself to death. Spencer is lying on the mattress. He's wearing no clothes and he covers himself with the blanket. Hazel moves between the mattress and the window, pulling the sweater-dress up and over her head. She shivers, covers her breasts with her hands, then folds herself under the blanket next to Spencer. They press up close to each other for the feel of warming skin, and both of them sense that at last their lives are almost up to date.

They wonder why they haven't done this, or tried this, before now. Not the going back to bed, but why they waited until now to spend a day together. Perhaps at some significant stage in their growing up they both missed a crucial sign telling them that this is what they should do and what they should become and how they should cope. But then if a sign had existed just for them, they wouldn't have missed it. More importantly, here is where they are now, and even in each other's arms, wearing no clothes, there is no insistent revelation that this is the right place to be, with the right person, doing the right thing.

Spencer pulls himself away slightly.

'Would you really have married him if he'd potted that red?'

303

'I think I would.'

Spencer thinks he believes her. It frightens and ex-hilarates him. 'He could have been a champion billiards player.'

'But he wasn't, was he?'

'You'd really have married him for something like that?'

'Maybe,' Hazel says, 'but also because he was rich and I quite liked his sweater.'

Spencer grabs her and somewhere in among the wriggling he manages a pinch and gets a punch straight back, first day of the month.

'Anyway,' Spencer says. 'It was me who potted the red. Sweet as a nut.'

'You had one more turn than him.'

'Home advantage.'

Hazel reaches up and touches her index finger to the index finger pointing down at her from the red-and-white glove pinned above the bed.

'The glove of love,' she says, staring up at it. 'The love-glove.'

Spencer strokes her arm from elbow to shoulder, amazed at his certainty that this moment has an obvious and immediate significance, as if he's already remembering it. He thinks that if the event or the decision which changes a life could be traced to one single moment, then for him that moment is probably now. He asks Hazel what she's thinking, and she lets her arm drop, pressing closer to him under the covers.

It is the first of November 1993, and Hazel says you can kiss me if you like.

––––––––––

It is the first of November 1993 and everywhere, all over the country without rhyme or reason, in Bishop Auckland or Sheffield or Clydebank or Cwmbran, in Portadown or Whitley Bay or Cornish Hall End or Stoke-on-Trent, Hazel is twenty-three, thirty-four, forty-five, sixty, seventy-five, eighty, ninety-nine years old, aged and nearly dead and left with no-one a long way from everywhere. Her life has spread, distorted, accelerated, lost all recognisable shape.

Concentrate on now. She is walking fast along streets in the black after-midnight morning, wearing a tight grey dress for going out in, in which she has not been out until now. It is London. There has been rain, and the tyres of a passing bus roll fat lines along the wet road. She finds a public phone-box, and claws at the handle to swing the door firmly shut behind her. Dead raindrops lace the glass sides of the box, and when Hazel shakes out her hair specks of old rain spin to the concrete floor. She fumbles inside her purse until she finds a phonecard. It is the last of her original collection, and an unusual greyish colour. It shows Charlie Chaplin's eyes. She feeds it in and picks up the receiver and is about to punch in the numbers when she hesitates. She looks at her fingers, which are trembling or turning blue, or both.

She pushes the return button and the card slides out again.

305

She feels calmer. Her fingers redden slightly. She turns the card in her hand and cradles the telephone between her cheek and the damp wool of her dress. She listens to the dialling tone, which sounds like flies swarming on something sweet, undisturbed, confident that nothing is coming to disperse them.

'Hello, Spencer,' she practises, and the flies drone back, indifferent. 'Let's meet up. Yes, now, I know it's late.' It's late and she may see things differently in daylight, but so what? The early hours of the morning are as honest a time to have feelings as any other.

'Hello, Spencer. Yes, today. It's as good a day as any, no? What could possibly go wrong?'

Hazel puts the receiver back on its cradle. Today *is* as good a day as any. In fact today is a better day than any other precisely because it's today. She blows into her hands. She forces herself to think of the alternative, and her imagined life as an ageing unloved spinster, old and alone like one in three of all people, with nothing much left to do but sit around and drink tea, read the paper and wait out the day. She snatches up the receiver.

'Hey, Spencer, listen to me,' she says. She puts the phonecard on top of the phone and combs her fingers through her hair. She wonders if she should have brought condoms, even though she made a conscious decision to leave them behind. Yes, no, it was the right thing to do. She's fed up with the safety of sex, and this time it has to be the real thing, or nothing.

'Hey, Spencer, I just wanted to say.'

It was always you who made each day distinct, every time I phoned you. You gave my life a difference which made me proud. Talking to you, I never felt like I was going to turn into my mother. I was never frightened, and I'm not frightened now, even though I often think about Mum. She was right to say that marriage is a sports team or a place safe for diversity or Jerusalem or an identity card or a hell on earth. It's probably all these things at some stage, but it's also one of the few chances we get at a happy ending.

Spencer, it has to be you.

It's too late for Hazel to learn the people she meets now, where they've been and what they've done and why. They carry in themselves too much information from elsewhere, which takes too long to absorb and understand. Spencer's past, however, she knows almost as well as her own, and she wants each of them to work a miracle on the other. She wants change and lightning and revelation, even though it's easy to doubt such things exist when they're not actually happening. Life flattens itself out retrospectively, to make itself understood. Memory takes any thunderbolts and cools them and lays them down in a flat observable sequence, as if surprise itself was never worth remembering. But Hazel refuses to grow any older unmiracled, and her life is going to start right now because she's determined to make it start.

'It has to be now!' she says, and then takes several quick breaths, rounding out her cheeks as if stepping up for a swimming race. She does it again, and pushes the phonecard into the phone. She dials Spencer's number and while she's waiting for an answer, time draws itself out, making an

307

exception, almost miraculous, from the more common divisions of seconds minutes hours.

What it is: it's when you look up and around, wherever you are, and suddenly ask yourself how the hell did I get here. But then that becomes insignificant against the fact that here is where you are, and now what are you going to do about it?

Spencer picks up.

It is Hazel's last phonecard, and also her first. It is the greyish one with Charlie Chaplin's eyes, and for each one sold a contribution is or was made to the Royal National Institute for the Blind. A unit disappears, sinking into silence. It is nearly the end, and after so many other phone calls there's nothing much left to say if not goodbye. Nothing much to say if not I love you.

'Hold on to your hat, Spencer,' she says. 'I'm coming on over.'

11/1/93 MONDAY 17:12

'That was amazing.'

'Unbelievably amazing.'

'Completely utterly amazing yes.'

They lie sprawled across the mattress, only outlines now that outside it's almost dark. The street-light turns itself on, and an amber glow filters their skin between the darker shadows trailing from limb to limb.

'Rapid,' Hazel says. 'But still amazing.'

She pulls at the blanket until it covers them both.

'What a day,' Spencer says.

'What a day.'

'Tomorrow we'll do something different.'

'Something a lot calmer, maybe.'

Tomorrow, yet again, anything is possible. They could take a trip in Hazel's car or by train or by bus, to the country or the seaside or the nearest swimming pool. They could search Oxfam or Help the Aged or Mencap shops for animal ornaments or detective novels or mugs with funny messages on. They could check the travel agents for bargain flights to Malta or Egypt or the Algarve, or laze about the house with nothing planned but the return of Spencer's library books. They could visit Hazel's parents or her sister, or Spencer's Mum or his Dad or his brother. They could read the papers or watch videos or play computer games. They could work or not work, see William or not see William, stay in or go out.

'No more either ors,' Hazel says. 'Let's just make up our minds.'

'Okay then,' Spencer says. 'We'll make up our minds.'

'A fresh start.'

'Like any other day.'

'So what's it to be then?'

'Easy. Let's spend the whole day together in bed.'

'Excellent plan, Spencer,' Hazel laughs. 'Impeccable.'

They grow quiet, remembering and re-arranging the events

of the day. Already the details vary, multiply, or disappear altogether. But the feelings are clear, and what actually happened, and today is already being added to their catalogue of formative events. Like everybody else, Hazel and Spencer carry their past with them into the present. Their most intense memories, even as they revise and clarify them, remain the clue to who they are now.

Just getting things straight, Hazel asks Spencer what he'd have said to the Italians who cancelled their visit to look at the house.

'I usually tell people it's unsafe,' Spencer says. 'I try to discourage them from buying the place, seeing as it's where I live, and where William lives. I say it's a very old house with very old ceilings which have been known to collapse. I warn them about the flight paths from Heathrow, and the danger of debris from passing aircraft crashing through the roof of the swimming pool, tumbling lethal daggers of glass down towards the pale unformed bodies of their naked children splashing innocently below. Easy, scary stories, anything like that.'

And just for a moment, both Hazel and Spencer imagine a hundred and one unlikely but possible catastrophes, of the kind routinely reported in newspapers. Hazel holds Spencer tight, and he closes his eyes in the curve of her neck. Whatever it says in the papers, it's not going to happen today. Or at least not to them.

Acknowledgement

All except twelve of the nouns in *Damascus*
can also be found in *The Times* (London)
of November 1 1993